"MY WIFE WILL BE YOUNG. SHE'LL DO AS SHE'S TOLD. SHE'LL NOT CHANGE MY LIFE IN THE SLIGHTEST!"

So said the cynical young Earl of Meridan as he went to marry a girl he had never met.

But she was not the ladylike blonde he had bargained for. Lucinda was dark, tousled, and outrageously frank—for a well-bred young miss she knew a shocking lot about the world of men. And she had curious, obstinate notions about love!

Only when she became the best-dressed woman in London—only when she delighted the Prince of Wales himself—only when the very qualities that infuriated Meridan had endeared her to all his friends and enemies did he realize he had finally met his match. . . .

Also in Pyramid Books

by

BARBARA CARTLAND

THE
UNPREDICTABLE
BRIDE

Barbara Cartland

PYRAMID BOOKS ▲ NEW YORK

THE UNPREDICTABLE BRIDE

A PYRAMID BOOK

Copyright © 1964 by Barbara Cartland

Pyramid edition published December 1969
   Eighth printing, May 1976

Printed in the United States of America

_____

Pyramid Books are published by Pyramid Publications (Harcourt Brace Jovanovich). Its trademarks, consisting of the
word "Pyramid" and the portrayal of a pyramid, are regis-
tered in the United States Patent Office.

PYRAMID PUBLICATIONS
(Harcourt Brace Jovanovich)
757 Third Avenue, New York, N.Y. 10017

"I will not marry him—I will not!"

Hester's voice rose into a passionate crescendo and the tears started to well into her pale blue eyes and run down her pink and white cheeks.

The early sun coming through the windows of the breakfast room at that moment haloed her fair curls and shone like tiny rainbows from the tears hanging from her long dark lashes.

She looked so incredibly lovely that her father, looking up from the letter in his hand, stared at her as if he had never seen her before.

"I will not marry him, Papa—I will not!" Hester cried again. "You know I am affianced to Colin and we are only waiting until he is twenty-one and that horrible guardian of his gives permission for us to announce our betrothal. And now this man—this beast—dares to suggest . . . !"

Hester's voice faltered into silence by the tempest of her tears and she groped blindly with her hand inside the crisp muslin fichu which encircled her white shoulders.

"Give your sister a handkerchief, Lucinda," Lady Belvil said sharply. "And stop making such a noise, Hester!"

She turned her lined aristocratic face towards her husband.

"What is all this about, my dear?"

"Have you not been listening?" Sir Edward enquired, with a note of justifiable irritation in his voice.

"Start from the beginning, my love," Lady Belvil said, realizing as she spoke that Lucinda had not been able to obey her because she, too, had no handkerchief.

"Here, take mine," she said impatiently to her younger daughter.

She passed the small square of cambric edged with lace across the table. Taking it, Lucinda rose and went to Hester's side, trying to mop the tears from her cheeks.

Hester took the handkerchief from her, made an effort to wipe her eyes and then said through lips which quivered pathetically:

"You will not make me marry him, Papa?"

Sir Edward cleared his throat and looked down again at the letter.

"Please . . . please, dear Papa," Hester pleaded. "You know that my heart is already given."

She was using the tone which her mother and sister knew full well was one her father usually found irresistible.

Defiance he could sometimes counter with authority, but when Hester was in her pleading mood he was usually prepared to give her anything she asked.

"Please, Papa . . ."

Sir Edward walked agitatedly across the Persian rug towards the mantelpiece and back again.

"This is a very serious matter," he said pompously.

"Do stop fidgeting about, Edward," Lady Belvil interrupted. "Sit down and start at the beginning."

"I have already tried to tell you what happened," Sir Edward said.

"You have done nothing of the sort!" his wife retorted. "And if you did, I was not listening. Now tell me exactly what occurred."

"Very well," Sir Edward said in a resigned tone. He seated himself in his armchair and, avoiding the beseeching eyes of his elder daughter, said to his wife:

"You must not feel, Margaret, m'dear, that I have been deceiving you in any way. I meant to inform you what occurred last week when I was in London, but to tell the truth I have been so worried and distraught that I could not find words in which to break the news of such a disaster to you."

"Edward, you have been gambling again!" Lady Belvil exclaimed, clasping her hands together.

"I have tried to tell you of this ever since I returned home," Sir Edward said.

Lady Belvil sighed.

"I thought it was your liver," she said. "You are usually out of sorts and dyspeptic when you return from a visit to London. Is it more serious?"

"Very much more serious," Sir Edward answered.

"How much?"

Lady Belvil spoke the two words almost inaudibly, yet both her daughters knew what a poignant and important question it was.

For a moment there was silence and then almost soundlessly Sir Edward made his reply:

"Thirty-five thousand pounds."

"Edward!"

Lady Belvil could hardly breathe his name. Then putting her hand against her chest, as if she feared she might have a heart attack, she said faintly:

"Can you . . . can we . . . pay it?"

"Only—if everything goes," Sir Edward replied brokenly. "That is why I did not dare to tell you."

"Oh Edward, how could you? The girls . . . Hester's marriage and Lucinda's Season . . ."

"I know, I know," Sir Edward muttered. "I was a fool —no, crazed, if you like—but Meridan got under my skin. I felt that he was taunting me, jibing at me, looking down at me as an oafish country squire. I wanted to prove a match for him."

"Meridan?" Lady Belvil exclaimed, catching the name. "Do you mean the Earl of Meridan—that man?"

Sir Edward nodded.

"But . . . your letter?" she enquired. "Did not you say . . . ?"

"Yes, m'dear, this letter is from him."

"Then . . . then . . . I do not understand," Lady Belvil said, looking from her husband to her daughter in a bewildered manner.

"Perhaps I had best continue with the story," Sir Edward suggested.

"Yes . . . of course," Lady Belvil said.

"Do go on, Papa. What were you playing?" Lucinda interposed.

Her mother gave her a glance of disapproval, as if she thought that such an interruption was unnecessary.

7

Sir Edward, as if determined to make a clean breast of the matter, gave her the answer she required.

"Faro."

"Oh, Papa, it must have been exciting—even if you lost!"

"Be quiet, Lucinda, and let your father tell us this story in his own way," Lady Belvil commanded.

Lucinda sat back in her chair and in the momentary pause before Sir Edward spoke Hester gave a deep tearful sigh which seemed to come from the very depths of her being.

"We played at Brooks's," Sir Edward said hastily, as if he could hardly bear to face Hester's distress. "When I realized the game was finished and what I had lost I felt too dazed to do or say anything. Until that moment I had not thought of the consequences. And then as Meridan rose from his seat it flashed through my mind that I might be unable to meet my debt of honour."

"You did not tell him so, Papa?" Lucinda asked irrepressibly.

"No—no, of course not," Sir Edward said. "I behaved, I hope, like a gentleman. But when he said: 'Come, Belvil. Let us cross the road and drop into Almack's,' I felt too bemused to refuse him."

"I quite understand that," Lucinda said reflectively. "Joe was telling me he feels stupid and in a cloud when he has had a punch on the head in a mill ..."

"Lucinda!'" Lady Belvil interrupted. "I have told you until I am tired of telling you that I will not have you discussing such matters with the stable-boys. Next time ..."

Lady Belvil stopped suddenly and turned her face piteously towards her husband.

". . . next time there will not be any stable-boys, will there, Edward?"

Sir Edward passed a hand over his forehead. Although the morning was cool, there were beads of perspiration on his brow.

"Let me go on, Margaret," he continued. "Meridan and I walked a few yards from Brooks's to Almack's. There was no point in calling a carriage. As we reached the steps, a coach drew up with the Prince of Wales. He got out and said to Meridan in a somewhat peevish tone, "I was expecting you at Clarence House." "Forgive me, Sire,"

Meridan answered, "but I was kept from such an honour by what appeared to me to be rather important business." One of the Prince's entourage chuckled. "Plucking another chicken, eh, my Lord?" he asked. You can imagine what I felt."

"Oh, poor Papa!" Lucinda exclaimed. "It was certainly a blow below the belt to be spoken of like that after you had lost so much."

Lady Belvil gave her younger daughter an angry look. But Lucinda, with her elbows on the table and her small face cupped in both hands, was gazing rapturously at her father.

"Go on, Edward," Lady Belvil said tersely.

"We all went into Almack's," Sir Edward said.

"Almack's?" Lucinda queried. "It is a club, is it not?"

"No—an assembly," Sir Edward corrected, "and the most important social gathering conceivable. A Committee of Lady Patronesses control Almack's. Only those of whom they approve can enter the rooms, or Society, for that matter."

"Do not bother your father with such inconsequential questions, Lucinda," Lady Belvil said. "Pray continue, Edward, such unimportant details can be explained later."

"Unfortunately they are not unimportant," Sir Edward replied unhappily. "But to continue. Naturally the Prince and his companions went first and Meridan and I fell in behind them. When we reached the vestibule one of the attendants came up and said, "If your Lordship will wait a moment the Countess of Jersey wishes to speak to you." Meridan raised his eyebrows. He had to wait while the man hurried away apparently in search of Lady Jersey, so I waited too."

"Had you said anything to him all this time, since you left the club?" Lucinda asked.

"I do not think I had," Sir Edward answered simply. "But to tell the truth I cannot remember."

"And what did you say to him then, while you were waiting?"

"We said nothing," Sir Edward said. "The delay had obviously put Meridan in a bad temper. He stood beside one of the marble tables, leaning against it nonchalantly, engaged with choosing a pinch of snuff from a diamond-studded box which he drew from his vest pocket. If I had not been so preoccupied with my own affairs I might have thought he looked a trifle apprehensive."

"Apprehensive?" Lady Belvil echoed. "But why, Edward?"

"That is what we were about to learn," her husband answered her. "Lady Jersey arrived a few minutes later. She was ablaze with diamonds, with an aigrette on her head which must have been worth a King's ransom. She is a damn' good-looking woman, and it is not surprising that the Prince . . ."

"Edward!" Lady Belvil said sharply, with a glance towards the end of the table. "Not in front of the girls!"

"Sorry, m'dear," Sir Edward said.

He drew a deep breath and continued the story. Because he was himself deeply moved he described the scene so vividly that his wife and daughters sat as if spellbound, unable to take their eyes from his face for fear of missing anything.

He told how Lady Jersey, looking at Meridan with big, dark eyes, had said—in a voice which seemed to echo round the vestibule:

" 'I wonder, Lord Meridan, you have the effrontery to come here!'

"Lord Meridan raised his eyebrows and looked at her quizzically with the faint smile at the corners of his lips with which he had taunted me earlier in the evening.

" 'Have I offended your Ladyship?' he enquired.

" 'Offended is hardly the right word, Lord Meridan,' she replied. 'Your behaviour has been outrageous, and if it were not for the personal intervention of His Royal Highness the Committee of Almack's would dismiss you immediately from the list of members and you would never be allowed to enter this club again.'

" 'Now, come,' Meridan replied, 'my crime is not so heinous as to deserve such punishment. It was a wager and your Ladyship knows as well as I do that it is impossible to refuse a wager . . .'

" 'When it is outrageous enough to offend all decency,' Lady Jersey said icily, 'then it can neither be considered sporting nor amusing.'

" 'Strap me,' Meridan exclaimed. ''Twas not as bad as all

that. I was wagered a thousand guineas, if you wish to know, that I would not bring into the club someone of whom your Ladyship and your friends would not approve, but who would be accepted on her face value . . .'

"'Face value, nothing!' Lady Jersey snapped. 'You pretended that this woman—this play-actress—was a Princess of Liechtenstein, paying a visit to this country. You even went so far as to assure us that she was staying with you as your guest.'

"A smile creased Lord Meridan's face.

"'She was, as it happens,' he said softly.

"Lady Jersey stamped her foot.

"'You are incorrigible and unrepentant!' she said. 'But this time you have gone too far. As I have already said, it was our original intention to bar you from Almack's for life.'

"'You couldn't be so cruel!' Meridan protested. 'Besides, think how dull you would find it without me to find fault with, and to disapprove of, three hundred and sixty-four days out of three hundred and sixty-five.'

"There was a silence for a moment, and then in a very different voice Lord Meridan said:

"'You will miss me, you know.'

"For a moment it seemed that Lady Jersey was softening towards him. Then, as if she forced her voice to an unaccustomed hardness, she said:

"'We have made our decision. Almack's is barred to you, my Lord, until you are introduced by a lady of whom we can approve—your wife.'

"'My wife? Good Lord! But I haven't got one!' Meridan exclaimed.

"'Exactly,' Lady Jersey said. 'And until you find one your Lordship must remain among those who vainly seek admittance, only to be refused.'

"'Tare an' hounds!—you cannot mean this!' Meridan expostulated.

"'I assure you that I have never been more serious,' Lady Jersey answered. 'It is the ruling of the Committee. We are unanimous for once.'

"'This is nonsensical,' Meridan said. 'You know I am always with the Prince, you know that he likes to drop in here two or three evenings a week . . .'

11

" 'The Prince has agreed that you need a lesson,' Lady Jersey said.

"Lord Meridan's face darkened.

" 'This is your doing,' he said.

"Lady Jersey shook her head.

" 'No, indeed,' she said. 'If it had not been for me you would have been barred for ever.'

" 'But—good God! Where can I get a wife?' Meridan asked. 'I do not know any girls. As you well know, I never could stand the species.'

" 'Then you had better start cultivating one,' Lady Jersey said coldly."

Sir Edward paused dramatically. He drew out a handkerchief and blew his nose. The three women around the table did not move or speak. They were waiting breathlessly for him to continue.

"As Lady Jersey turned to leave," Sir Edward went on, "she saw me, as if for the first time. I suppose I had been standing there gaping, rather like a foolish yokel. I was certainly feeling like one.

" 'Ah, Sir Edward,' she exclaimed, 'how nice to see you! Perhaps you will escort me back to the ballroom.'

"Then, as if a sudden thought struck her, she turned again to Meridan.

" 'Sir Edward has a very beautiful daughter, my Lord,' she said to him. 'We all remarked last year when she was in London what a charming girl she was. Perhaps Sir Edward will introduce you. Why not? I am sure it would be a very suitable match.'

"She laid the tips of her fingers on my arm, and there was nothing I could do but lead her to the ballroom, leaving Meridan behind."

"What did he do?" Lucinda asked eagerly.

"I have not the remotest conception," Sir Edward replied. "But when I left a few minutes later the vestibule was empty and he had gone."

"And you did not see him again?" Lady Belvil asked.

"No—and I had no desire to do so," Sir Edward replied.

"But . . . but . . . the debts?"

"I have over a week in which to find the money," Sir Edward answered. "As we rose from the gaming table after Meridan had counted up my IOUs, he said, 'The usual seven days will suit you, Belvil?' And I replied, 'I suppose so, my Lord.' He gave me a sharp glance, as if he knew I was hard-pressed, and said, 'Well, fourteen days, then.' "

"How mean!" Lucinda exclaimed. "He might have given you more time."

"It would not have helped if he had," Sir Edward told her. "He is noted as being a stickler for convention besides being unwilling to concede a kindness or mercy to any man."

"This is the Earl of Meridan of whom I have heard . . . certain things?" Lady Belvil asked tentatively.

"Of course you have heard of him," Sir Edward answered. "He is an intimate of the Prince of Wales, a man . . ."

He hesitated as if lost for words.

"I mean is he the man who was involved with . . . ?" Lady Belvil asked, dropping her voice so that their daughters could not hear the name.

Sir Edward nodded.

"Oh!" Lady Belvil cried. "Then he is indeed a monster . . . a man I would not tolerate to enter my house. The impropriety of that story shocked me to the core!"

"It was a scandal, I grant you," Sir Edward said wearily. "But Meridan is accepted in the very best Society; and, besides, he is one of the richest men in England."

"If he is so rich why does he want your money?" Lucinda asked, then gave a little laugh and answered her own question. "But how stupid of me—of course I know that gaming losses are debts of honour and must be paid before anything else, before even those poor tradespeople who are kept waiting year after year."

"He sounds terrible . . . I will not marry him!" Hester said tearfully.

They all stared at her for a moment as if they hardly realized what she was talking about.

Then hastily Sir Edward picked up the letter which lay in front of him.

"I was trying to tell you, m'dear," he said to his wife, "what had occurred, to break the news to you that I had lost such a vast sum—and then this letter arrives."

13

"Yes, of course . . . the letter," Lady Belvil said. "When did it come?"

"A groom brought it," Lucinda said before her father could speak. "And he had ridden from London in under four hours! I told him it was almost a record."

"Lucinda, I have told you not to gossip with strange servants!" Lady Belvil said in an exasperated voice.

"But, Mama, there was no one to answer the front door. Durham had gone down to the stables and I saw this man come up the drive wearing the smartest livery I have ever seen—claret with gold buttons and white breeches. And you should have seen his boots—I swear they must have been cleaned in champagne like the dandies use for theirs!"

"Will you be quiet, Lucinda!" Lady Belvil stormed.

She laid her hand on her husband's arm.

"Read the letter, Edward dear. We must know the worst."

Hester gave a little sob, but her father ignored it and read aloud in a voice which trembled slightly.

> *"Meridan House,*
> *Berkeley Square,*
> *London.*
> *Thursday, April 3rd, 1803*

"My Lord,

"I have the Honour to request the Hand of your Daughter in Marriage. This should in itself Settle the differences which Exist between us after our Play the other night. My Solicitors will call on yours to Facilitate the drawing up of a Marriage Settlement. I cannot at the moment leave London for a visit to the Country, but it would be most Convenient to me if the Marriage could be Arranged to take Place at the end of April, preferably after the Newmarket Races.

> *I have the honour to remain, Sir,*
> *Your most obedient servant,*
> *Meridan"*

Sir Edward ceased and for a moment three pairs of eyes stared at him in incredulous astonishment.

Then Hester gave a little choking sound and slid slowly from her chair on to the floor.

"Good God!" Sir Edward ejaculated, jumping to his feet.

"It is all right," Lady Belvil said. "The child has only fainted. Lucinda, fetch some water and a feather we can burn under her nose."

"She will be all right, Mama," Lucinda answered, already kneeling on the floor beside her sister.

Hester's faint was certainly not a deep one. The colour had not left her cheeks and her breast was still moving agitatedly beneath her muslin gown.

Lucinda helped her back to the chair and taking one of her small white hands in hers stroked it gently.

"It will be all right, dearest," she said in affectionate tones. "Papa will not make you marry this man. You would be utterly miserable."

"I am going to marry Colin," Hester murmured, her lips trembling, her eyes filling again with tears.

"Yes, of course you are," Lucinda said.

"But, damn it all, do you know what this means?" Sir Edward enquired. "It means we have got to sell the house —the estate—everything we own. The horses will have to go. And we will have to live in one of the cottages down by the stream—if they do not have to be sold as well. Think, Hester, what it will mean to have everything you have ever wanted—a house in London, a great ancestral place in Sussex. You would have the entrée into Society— the Prince would dote on you. . . ."

Sir Edward suddenly ceased speaking as he saw the expression on Hester's face. She had always been his favourite. He had made no bones about it. And now the agony in her expression was more than he could bear.

He felt as if he had struck her, or was trying to destroy something small, soft and vulnerable. With a muttered oath he crunched up the letter in his hand and chucked it on the floor.

"Damn Meridan!" he exclaimed. "He can go to the devil!"

"I will marry him, Papa."

For a moment Sir Edward hardly realized who spoke.

But then both he and his wife stared in amazement at Lucinda.

"What did you say?" Sir Edward asked.

"I said I would marry him," Lucinda replied.

She stood facing them beside Hester, her chin raised, her eyes as steady and resolute as her voice.

"But it is impossible!" Lady Belvil exclaimed.

"Why, Mama?" Lucinda enquired. "I was seventeen a month ago. You promised to talk to Papa when he came from London about my making my début this year. It is only because you have been so worried about money that it has not been arranged before."

"Seventeen? Good Lord, I had no idea!" Sir Edward said.

"There have been so many expenses," Lady Belvil began apologetically. "And it was not as if . . ."

She stopped suddenly as Lucinda supplied the words she had been unwilling to utter.

". . . it was not as if I was beautiful, like Hester," she said. "It did not seem to matter if I did not go to London for the Season."

She spoke without rancour or jealousy.

"And of course we want all the money that is available," she said with a smile, "for Hester's trousseau when she marries Colin."

Her elder sister reached out her hand and caught her eagerly.

"I am going to marry Colin, Lucinda, am I not? You always promised me it would be all right. You saw it in the cards, do you remember?"

"Yes, yes. I am sure it will be all right," Lucinda said soothingly.

"I have told you not to read the cards," Lady Belvil said angrily. "All that nonsense you learned from the gypsies! It is unhealthy superstition and I will not have Hester mixed up in it."

"But Lucinda is clairvoyant . . ." Hester protested, only to be silenced by a squeeze of her fingers.

Sir Edward rose to his feet and picked up the letter where he had thrown it on the floor, smoothed out the crumpled paper and read:

16

"Lord Meridan writes, . . . *the Hand of your Daughter in Marriage* . . ."

"There you are, you see," Lucinda said triumphantly. "He does not say which daughter—he just says . . . *your Daughter* . . ."

"But Lady Jersey," Sir Edward began.

"Lady Jersey was not to know that Hester was already engaged—and the only daughter available was the one who was not already bespoken," Lucinda said.

"But it would be cheating," Lady Belvil said.

"I really cannot see why," Lucinda answered. "He asked Papa for the hand of his daughter in marriage. And one of his daughters is ready to marry him. I do not see why he should complain—especially as he cannot spare the time to come down and ask her himself."

"That I agree is insulting," Sir Edward said. "He takes it for granted we will accept."

"I expect he found out how hard-up you are," Lucinda said practically.

"Nevertheless, it is intolerable," Lady Belvil said. "He is treating it all as if he were making a bargain with a tradesman—'give me your daughter, I will cancel your debts!' If you ask me, Edward, the man is no gentleman!"

"In a way, I wish I could say he is not," Sir Edward said almost miserably. "I dislike him, but he is well bred. And although he has got into a large number of scandals and escapades, this is really the first time he has incurred the wrath of the leaders of Society."

"I would like to write back and tell him what I think of him," Lady Belvil said.

"So would I," Sir Edward agreed. "But can we afford to?"

"The whole thing is utterly ridiculous!" Lady Belvil said. "Lucinda is far too young—and how could she cope with such a man? Why, she would be running home within twenty-four hours of being married to him."

"Do you really think that Hester would be able to manage him better?" Lucinda asked smilingly.

Lady Belvil looked at the lovely face of her elder daughter and looked away again.

Nobody had ever pretended that Hester, beautiful though she was, had any brains. She was sweet and gentle, kind and childish. Everyone loved her just as they might love a pretty child whose entrancing ways captivated their hearts.

"I shall write to Meridan and tell him we must wait at least a year," Sir Edward said ponderously.

Lucinda laughed.

"Really, Papa, cannot you see the whole point of marrying me is so that he should be allowed back into Almack's? He likes going there with the Prince. I can well see how inconvenient it would be if, every time the Prince elects to spend an evening there, Lord Meridan has to sit outside on the doorstep! A wife is his ticket of admission—and a wife he is going to have. If you do not accept this proposition it is quite obvious he will find someone else."

"A very good thing, too, if you ask me," Lady Belvil said.

"It will not be so good for Papa to have to find thirty-five thousand pounds, will it?" Lucinda enquired.

Lady Belvil shivered.

"Oh, Edward . . . how could you . . . ?" she wailed.

"I know, my love, I know. I have told you I was crazed that night. But this does seem to be a way out."

Lady Belvil looked doubtfully again at her younger daughter. It was obvious that Lord Meridan was going to get the worst of the deal if he was expecting anyone as beautiful as Hester.

It was impossible to imagine that two sisters could be so different.

Hester, with her fair curls, blue eyes and pink and white complexion, was the very embodiment of what an English girl should look like.

And, as if in direct contrast, Lucinda had dark hair, dark eyes and no colour. Her skin was slightly sallow in contrast to the rather untidy white fichu she wore round her shoulders. Her hands were brown against the faced pink muslin skirts of her gown, which had once belonged to Hester.

Just for a moment there flickered a thought in Lady Belvil's mind that it served Lord Meridan right if he got Lucinda instead of Hester. Then she pushed the thought from her mind. After all, difficult though she was, the child was her daughter.

"I think," Sir Edward said, "that we must explain to Lord Meridan that Hester is engaged and that if he wishes . . ."

"Oh, really, Papa!" Lucinda interposed. "Has he treated you so well that you owe him anything? He has won your money—we presume fairly—but you say yourself that he egged you on, goaded you into risking far more than you could afford. And then he insults you by sending what is really an ultimatum."

She paused, then realizing that she had her father's attention, continued:

"I would not mind betting that his Lordship knows to a sixpence how pushed you will be to find the money—if you can find it at all. And as it suits him to get hold of the only girl he has ever heard of, he is prepared to come to terms. I don't suppose he would show you much mercy if you did not have a daughter to bargain with!"

"That is true enough," Sir Edward murmured. "Meridan is a hard man, nobody would deny it."

"Very well, then," Lucinda said. "Sit down and write to him and say that you accept with pleasure the idea of having him as a son-in-law."

"God damn it! I am not going to say that!" Sir Edward exclaimed.

"Well, put it how you like," Lucinda said. "But make it quite clear that the debts are cancelled and that you will accept a good fat marriage settlement."

"Do you mean to say that you are prepared to accept this proposition as it stands?" Sir Edward asked.

"Of course I am," Lucinda answered. "Tell him that the wedding is fixed here for the twenty-eighth of April and that all arrangements will be made. And as the house is very small and will be full of relations, you expect that he would prefer to drive down just in time for the ceremony."

"Good heavens, he will not agree to that!" Sir Edward said.

"I bet you a monkey he does!" Lucinda challenged.

"Lucinda!" Her mother exclaimed.

"Sorry, Mama," Lucinda smiled. "But, like Papa, I'm a gamester."

Lady Belvil closed her eyes as if to shut out the horror of it all.

19

"How can you expect to go into Society behaving in such a manner?" she asked faintly.

"If I am to be the Countess of Meridan," Lucinda said, "I dare say people will tolerate my eccentricities."

Sir Edward stared at her for a moment and then he guffawed.

"By George!" he said. "If anyone could be a match for Meridan I believe it might be you, Lucinda. You always have been a little hell-cat!"

"I think in the brief time that we have before the wedding," Lady Belvil said, apparently accepting the inevitable, "Lucinda had best try and learn how to behave like a lady. I have done my best with her all these years, but failed."

"Nonsense, Mama!" Lucinda said. "You have been far too busy trying to catch an important husband for Hester to worry about me. Now Hester is to be married to a country squire, and I shall find myself amongst the *haut ton* of St. James's."

"It is not right," Lady Belvil wailed. "The whole thing is wrong and I disapprove. I would wash my hands of it were it not for these terrible debts of yours, Edward."

"I quite agree, m'dear. 'Tis all my fault," Sir Edward said miserably. "But who knows—it may all turn out for the best."

"Think, Papa, you might never have found a husband willing to take me on," Lucinda said. "You must write the letter quickly before Lord Meridan changes his mind."

Sir Edward looked at her, and she added:

"The groom is waiting, you know."

"Good heavens, did not the man give us time even to consider the matter?" Lady Belvil asked.

"Why should he?" Lucinda asked impishly. "After all, he was quite, quite certain we were going to accept."

2

Lucinda walked slowly through the garden to the stables. It was a warm April day and the sun glistened on the small water lily pool. When she was a child Lucinda had tried to catch the goldfish as they swam in and out beneath the flat green leaves.

Now there were no fish, and she noticed as if for the first time that there were weeds and moss round the stone basin and that the whole garden had an air of neglect and desolation.

She looked at the apple trees badly in need of pruning, at the greenhouses where many panes of glass were broken and had not been replaced, at the thistles cluttering the paths, and knew that poor old Jarvis, the head gardener, was long past his work and had never enough men under him to keep the place tidy.

It had always been the same trouble, Lucinda thought—money, or rather the lack of it!

She could hear, like an echo from the past, her father exclaiming not once but a dozen times a year:

"Blood-suckers! All they want from me is money—and I'm damned if they shall get it!"

"Some of them have been very patient, dear," her mother would say gently, looking at the names on the bill-heads and recognizing them immediately because they had been presented so often.

"They can't get blood from a stone!" Sir Edward would ejaculate, and as often as not would pick up the bills, crumple them in his hands and chuck them into the fire.

It was not because he was a spendthrift that he was always in debt. Lucinda knew that on the whole he was very careful with what money he had and spent it wisely; it was not that he often indulged in bouts of gambling. The truth was that he could not afford to live at the Hall as her father's father and his grandfather before him had done.

Sir Edward, however, could not imagine life without the traditional number of servants—a butler and two footmen to keep the silver shining on the table and to wait on the local gentry, who dropped in continually, sure of their welcome and certain that the hospitality they would receive would ensure that they were comfortable, well fed and well wined.

It was inconceivable, Lady Belvil told him, to manage in the kitchen without a cook, two kitchen-maids and a scullery-maid, while three housemaids were the minimum requirement of such a large house.

Then there were the horses—expensive animals not only for the carriages and phaeton which Sir Edward drove so dashingly, but horses to join the Hunt, to ride in the neighbouring point-to-points and even occasionally to take part in the local race meetings.

It was inevitable that some things could not be afforded, and Lucinda found that the items neglected were the gardens, repairs to the roof and the staff quarters of the great house—and herself.

She wondered now how long it was since she had had a new dress and not merely had one of Hester's altered for her.

She made a little grimace at the thought of how she had hated the bony fingers of the village seamstress pinning the cotton bodice tighter around her small breasts, altering the length of the skirt and striving to make a muslin fichu which had long since lost its crispness sit properly on her shoulders.

Clothes did not worry her much; nevertheless, as she had grown older she had become only too well aware of the surprise in other people's eyes when they learned that she was Hester's sister.

They did not exactly say that she was too plain and unattractive to be related to the pink and gold vision that Hester presented to the world. But she could see the criticism and the astonishment in their faces and hear it in the way they said almost incredulously, "Hester's sister?"

It would be absurd and untruthful to say that these things did not hurt. She tried not to think about it, to shrug it off as something which was inevitable and unimportant, but at times it had been difficult.

She was not jealous of Hester, she loved her sister. But if she had dared to face the truth, even to herself, she would have said that she found Hester a bore. They had so little in common, and Lucinda thought now that she would have found her loneliness almost unbearable—if it had not been for Nat.

It was Nat she was going to see at this moment, as she had gone a thousand times since she had grown old enough to realize that she could talk to him as she could talk to no one else in her narrow, secluded life.

The gardens ended with an Elizabethan brick wall and Lucinda passed through a rusty iron gate which was swinging on its hinges and saw in front of her the stables.

They too were dilapidated, but the horses with their heads out of the loose-boxes looked fit and well and their coats were shining.

Lucinda looked in through the stable door and saw Joe polishing the bridles which were adorned with her father's silver crest.

He was whistling between his teeth. As his big hands moved deftly with the cloth, his muscles rippled beneath the sleeveless woollen vest which was all he wore above the waist. It was easy to see that he had the build of a powerful fighter and to understand why the local squires put their money on him whenever Sir Edward entered him for a fight.

"'Mornin', Miss Lucinda," Joe grinned, showing as he smiled that his two front teeth were missing, and that his bottom lip, which had been split three weeks ago, had not yet healed.

"Where's Nat?" Lucinda asked.

"I think he's a-groomin' Seagull," Joe replied.

Lucinda nodded as if she had expected that was where Nat would be. Seagull was Nat's favourite mare and he had always believed that one day she would win a race which would enable them to buy a number of other animals to fill the few empty boxes in the stables.

She walked over the cobbles and found Nat, as Joe had said, brushing Seagull until her coat shone almost blindingly.

He was a wizened little man, nearly sixty years old.

"'Mornin', Miss Lucinda!"

Nat touched his forehead respectfully with his forefinger, then reached out for Seagull's cloth which was lying over the edge of the stable partition.

"Whoa, my beauty, whoa!" he said as she pranced a little, just to show, Lucinda thought, that she had some spirit in her.

"Seagull's looking well," Lucinda said, knowing it was expected of her.

"An' if she don' win the cup fer yer father next month, at least she'll be the best-looking mare in the race!"

It flashed through Lucinda's mind how awful it would have been to have to tell Nat that he was dismissed and that Seagull was to be sold. Could he have borne it? she wondered, and knew that if that had to happen she could never face the agony in his eyes and the knowledge that his whole world had fallen apart.

"I have got something to show you, Nat," Lucinda said, almost shyly.

She took her hand from where she had been hiding it in the fulness of her muslin skirts and held something out to him. Her fingers were brown from riding without gloves—something which had been forbidden over and over again by Lady Belvil. But they were long, thin and beautifully shaped—in fact it was a pretty hand, although no one would have noticed it at this moment.

Nat stared and gave an exclamation beneath his breath. His shrewd, bird-like eyes were fascinated by the huge ring which Lucinda wore on her third finger.

The diamond in the centre, round which a number of other diamonds clustered, seemed almost to light up the darkness of the stable.

"It came yesterday," Lucinda said. "And there was some other jewellery with it, family jewels I believe they are—a necklace, a bracelet and a pair of ear-rings. Mama says I am too young to sport the ear-rings."

"It mus' be worth a powerful lot of money," Nat said, still looking at the ring. "Oi reckon we could afford a rare piece of horse-flesh with that!"

Lucinda laughed.

"I cannot very well wear a horse on my finger!" she said. "It is an engagement ring, Nat. I told you I was going to marry the Earl of Meridan, and the announcement appeared in the *London Gazette* yesterday."

"Did it, indeed?" Nat said almost sourly. "Well, Oi hope ye'll be happy, Miss Lucinda. We'll certainly miss ye here."

"And I shall miss you, Nat," Lucinda answered.

She followed him into the saddling room, sat down on the edge of a bench and watched him as he put away the brush he had used on Seagull.

"And when be we goin' to see this gentleman?" Nat asked.

Lucinda knew without being told that his voice was gruff because he was worried about her.

"You have seen him, Nat," she said softly.

"Oi 'ave?" Nat asked in astonishment, turning round to face her. "Oi don' remember him ever staying here with yer father."

"No, he has never stayed with my father," Lucinda answered. "I do not suppose he would think we are grand enough, for one thing. But do you remember, Nat, when you took me to the mill at Colney Heath—it must have been eighteen months ago?"

"Ay, Oi remembers," Nat told her. "Ye badgered and badgered me. And when Oi did take you 'twas agin my better judgement. 'Twas lucky we were that her Ladyship was away and no one told her that we'd bin seen there."

"I told you she would never find out," Lucinda said. "I have never met anyone as nervous as you were."

"And rightly so," Nat answered. "Oi shouldn't have done it, and ye know that as well as Oi do."

"Well, we did it," Lucinda said. "And I would not have missed that mill for anything in the world."

"Ay, they were fine fighters," Nat said with satisfaction. "Yer don't often see the like o' two men perfectly matched and fightin' fifteen rounds without either of 'em being knocked down."

"It was very exciting," Lucinda agreed. "But do you remember, Nat, when we arrived there in the old pony-cart, how we got in the way of a curricle painted black and yellow and how the driver cursed us?"

"Ay, Oi remembers him well," Nat said. "A fine flow of language he had. Oi like a man who can swear like a man —but he shouldn't 'ave done it in front of a lady."

"He did not look on me as a lady," Lucinda said. "Don't you remember he said, 'You and that damned child of yours—get to blazes out of here!' "

"That's right, that's what he said," Nat answered. "A fiery sort of chap, he was. But Oi wasn't noticing him so much as his horses—a better pair of chestnuts Oi've seldom set me eyes on."

"I noticed him," Lucinda said. "He was frightening; at the same time in a way he was rather magnificent—the angle at which he wore his hat, his riding coat, the way he held the reins—and the horses did everything he asked of them."

"Ay, Oi admit he were a grand driver," Not said grudgingly.

"He took our place," Lucinda said. "We could see from where we had to move to, but not as well as if we had stayed where we were."

"These gentry—they think they can do what they like with the likes of us," Nat said. "If ye hadn't bin with me, Miss Lucinda, Oi'd have said a great deal more. We were within our rights to have stayed where we were."

"We moved because we had to," Lucinda said. "Well, Nat, the man who moved us was . . . the Earl of Meridan."

"The bloke ye be goin' to wed?" Nat exclaimed in astonishment.

Lucinda nodded.

"Well, Oi be damned!" Nat exclaimed again, and coughed, as if to cover the oath that he should not have uttered in front of her.

"I have often thought, Nat," Lucinda went on quietly, "of what fun we had that day at the mill."

"Never ought to have gone!" Nat said sharply.

There was silence between them as Nat started to take down a saddle which he wanted to repair.

Lucinda watched him and knew he was digesting the

news she had given him. She wondered what really was going on in his head behind those shrewd pale blue eyes which seemed to her to see so much more than other people.

She was conscious of the smell of leather, of hay and of horseflesh. It was a smell which she knew would always be an indivisible part of her childhood.

It was here in this saddle room she had come with all her worries, with all her problems and with her unhappiness.

She had come when her mother had been cross with her —which was frequently. She had come when she had been punished and when Hester, looking smugly beautiful, had made life seem almost unbearable.

And she had come when she was happy and when she wanted to learn something, because Nat seemed to her to hold all the wisdom of the ages in his bullet-shaped head, to know far more of life than anything her father, her mother or her governess could teach her.

"Nat," she said now, "tell me something. When you went into a fight with someone bigger than yourself were you afraid?"

"Oi were usually in a fight with someone bigger than Oi," Nat replied. "Oi were a fly-weight—and a small fly-weight at that—but nevertheless Oi nearly always won. 'Tis tactics, Miss Lucinda, that counts—tactics and using yer brains. They might be bigger than me, but they didn't reason out that because Oi were smaller Oi could move quicker. Oi could close in suddenly and sting 'em like a gnat and be gone ag'in before they could catch Oi."

"Is that why they called you Nat?" Lucinda asked. "I never thought of that."

Nat shook his head.

"No," he answered. "Oi were christened Nathaniel—and a horrid, tongue-twisting name that turned out to be. So Nat they called me when Oi came here as a stable-boy, and Nat Oi've been ever since."

"You have not answered my question," Lucinda said, bending forward to raise her elbow on the table and cupping her chin with her hand, the diamond winking wickedly in the light as she did so.

"About being afraid?" Nat enquired. "Well, Miss Lu-

27

cinda, every man who tells the truth is feared as he steps into the ring for a fight—he'd be a liar if he told ye that he wasn't. Yet he'd lie all the same because he wouldn't want to admit his weakness. But it's fear mixed with something else—excitement, if ye like—a sort of funny feeling in yer stomach and a kind of breathlessness in yer throat. At the same time yer heart is beating fast—and ye know that somehow, with a touch o' luck, ye be a-goin' to win."

"You are sure of it?" Lucinda asked.

"As sure as yer stomach will let ye be," Nat answered. "That is, if yer happen to be the right sort of fighter."

He glanced at her across the stable room and saw that her eyes were fixed on his almost beseechingly.

"And what is the right sort of fighter?" Lucinda asked.

"Them as has courage," Nat answered. "Ye can teach a boy to fight, ye can get him as fit as a fiddle, ye can put him between the ropes with another who is not even in his class—but he'll lose if he hasn't got courage. 'Tis courage that counts. 'Tis the sort of courage that has a bit o' optimism and a bit o' faith and perhaps a bit o' superstition all mixed up in it as well."

Lucinda gave a little sigh.

"I suppose you always had that, Nat."

"Ay," he said simply. "Oi've always kept me chin and me pecker up and Oi knew that somehow Oi would win through. It wasn't often Oi was beat."

"And Joe has got it, too," Lucinda said. "He is not your son for nothing."

"Oi think all the people that's worth while in this world has courage," Nat said. "And that's something ye have always had, Miss Lucinda. Not that at times it's not come out in sheer mischievousness or what some might call naughtiness, but it's there all right—even when ye badgered Oi to taking ye to Colney Heath."

"I am glad you said that," Lucinda said a little breathlessly, "because I have a feeling, Nat, that I am going to need courage—a great deal of it."

She rose as she spoke and turned and went from the saddle room without saying another word.

Nat watched her walking across the yard, her muslin skirts blowing a little in the breeze.

"Damn him!" he said softly between his broken teeth.

"Damn him—if he ain't kind to her, Oi swear Oi'll kill him with me own hands!"

The Earl of Meridan, having no idea he was incurring such bloodthirsty sentiments, was having breakfast in his house in Berkeley Square when the butler announced that Colonel Holstead would be grateful for a moment of his time.

Lord Meridan looked up from the lamb chop he was tackling.

"Show the Colonel in," he said briefly, and a few seconds later Colonel Holstead, who was a fair-complexioned young man of not quite thirty, came into the room resplendent in the uniform of His Majesty's Life Guards.

"Good God, Charles!" Lord Meridan exclaimed. "Why the fancy dress at this hour of the morning?"

"I'm on duty in half an hour." the Colonel answered, "and because I wanted to see you I thought I would drop in on my way to the barracks."

"You jingle and creak like a damn' clarion," Lord Meridan complained. "Sit down and drink a glass of brandy. Or do you prefer coffee?"

"Brandy will do me," the Colonel replied, and the butler poured him out a glass and placed the decanter in front of him.

"Anything to eat?" his host enquired.

The Colonel shuddered slightly.

"The very idea makes me sick," he answered. "I got to bed at four o'clock. The Prince insisted on going on to Almack's and from there we went to the White House and a couple of other bawdy houses before His Royal Highness had enough."

Lord Meridan said nothing, and after a moment the Colonel continued:

"Damn it all, Meridan, I quite envy you this morning! I suppose you went to Brooks's?"

"I gambled until about one o'clock," Lord Meridan answered, "and because no one else seemed keen to play with me I came home."

"Early to bed!" the Colonel ejaculated. "That is what makes you so hearty this morning. It makes me feel quite unwell to see you munching away at that lamb chop."

"I am delighted to think it annoys you," Lord Meridan retorted, and signalled for the butler to bring him another.

"Honestly, Meridan, you missed nothing," Colonel Holstead said hesitantly.

"You wouldn't believe those blasted women really meant it!" Lord Meridan exclaimed.

"The Hen Committee at Almack's?" Colonel Holstead enquired. "Oh, they mean it all right—they are getting more and more dictatorial. It's like having half a dozen female Bonapartes ordering one about!"

"I cannot think why anyone ever goes there," Lord Meridan said sourly.

"The respectability of it is nauseating, I agree," Colonel Holstead said. "But as long as H.R.H. insists on dropping in to see her Ladyship there is nothing we can do about it. But it was fun later on at the White House. The old Abbess produced some really pretty girls—God knows where she got them from! One of them was Persian, or something of the sort. Anyway, they livened up the evening a good deal. You might have joined us there."

"If you think I am going to kick my heels about half the night until the Prince gets fed up with Society and condescends to go on to a brothel you are much mistaken," Lord Meridan said, pushing his plate away with a clatter. "The whole thing is nonsensical and humiliating in the extreme. If anyone had any sense they would stick a keg of gunpowder under Almack's and set the place on fire!"

"You are hipped, my dear fellow—that's what is wrong with you," Charles Holstead said.

His host gave him a look which caused the words to die on his lips.

"No, I don't mean that," he said quickly. "It was damn' bad luck and we are all sorry for you. I saw the notice in the *Gazette* yesterday. So you have taken Lady Jersey's advice? You won't go far wrong—everyone's saying that she is a damn' pretty girl and will look jolly fine in the Meridan diamonds. Has she got anything to say for herself?"

"I have not the slightest idea," Lord Meridan replied in a bored voice. "I have not met her."

"You have not—what?" Charles Holstead's jaw dropped

open. "You mean—you proposed to the girl without seeing her?"

Lord Meridan yawned.

"I sent a letter to her father asking for her hand in the proper manner," he replied. "He accepted—he could not do anything else, as he owed me thirty-five thousand pounds."

"Thirty-five thousand pounds!" Charles Holstead exclaimed. "She's costing you a bit!"

"That is not really important," Lord Meridan said. "As you say, she will look well in the family diamonds, and doubtless in due course produce an heir. It would be a pity if the estate went to that dissolute cousin of mine."

"Pretty cold-blooded, aren't you?" Charles Holstead asked.

"Nobody had ever accused me of that before," Lord Meridan said, with a little twist of his lips.

Colonel Holstead threw back his head and laughed.

"No, certainly not! By the way, what has happened to Juanita?"

"She had to rest down at Kew for a few days," Lord Meridan replied. "She was not feeling well. She is dancing tonight at Covent Garden—are you coming to see her?"

"But of course," Charles Holstead said, "if that is an invitation. Are we dining here, as usual?"

"As usual," Lord Meridan said. "And I believe Walter is bringing some of the prettiest little love-birds imaginable. He assures me that no one has ever seen better."

"How does Walter do it?" Charles Holstead said in tones of the deepest admiration. "He produces the prettiest girls and the smartest horses from pockets which everyone assures me are to let. By the way, I still owe him for that bay—do you think he is going to press me for the money?"

"I should take one of his love-birds off his hands," Lord Meridan replied.

"I might do that very thing!" Charles Holstead exclaimed. "I am getting bored with the one I have been sponsoring for over a year. She seems to have gone off a bit, and even across the footlights she has not the allure that she used to have."

"Drop her, my dear boy," Lord Meridan said briefly. "I

never believe in keeping women when they have become bores."

"You are right! And I'll have a look tonight at what Walter can produce," Charles said.

"I'm sure he would be extremely grateful," Lord Meridan said, a trifle sarcastically.

Charles Holstead looked at the clock on the mantel-shelf.

"By Gad, I must be going!" he exclaimed. "But that reminds me—I have not told you why I called. I'm having a party at my house at Newmarket at the end of April. If you would like to come I promise you some good cock-fighting and a mill between Joe Blecher and Bill Fielden—both champion heavyweights, as you know. There will be half a dozen of us, and of course the love-birds can come for part of the time if anyone wants them. What about Juanita? Would you like to bring her?"

"What is the date?" Lord Meridan enquired.

"I thought we would forgather on the twenty-eighth," Charles Holstead said. "You could drive me down, if you like. I hate to say it, but your horses are quicker than mine."

"I'm sorry," Lord Meridan said in a bored voice, "but I cannot manage the twenty-eighth. I am being married that day . . ."

"Well, that is disappointing," Charles Holstead began, only to be silenced as Lord Meridan completed his sentence.

". . . but I will join you on the twenty-ninth. I do not want to miss that mill."

The Colonel stared at him for a moment and then threw back his head and was still laughing as he left the house a few moments later.

Lord Meridan walked from the dining room to the library which was situated at the back of the house in Berkeley Square and overlooked a small paved garden.

It was a beautiful room lined with books, with a big leather-topped writing desk on which were laid his letters beside a silver-cornered blotter engraved with his coat of arms.

He looked at his letters disinterestedly and then, without

opening them, turned, walked to the mantelshelf and tugged at the bell-rope.

A footman opened the door almost immediately.

"You rang, m'Lord?"

"My carriage," Lord Meridan said briefly.

"It is waiting, m'Lord."

He moved through the hall, took his beaver hat, stick and gloves from the butler, and walking down the carpet which had been lain over the paving-stones stepped into his coach.

"Twenty-four Half Moon Street," he said to the footman who opened the door, who repeated it to the footman on the box, who repeated it to the coachman.

The horses moved off and the footman out of the corner of his mouth said to the coachman:

"So she's back! His Nibs may be in a better temper now."

"They say she's cost him thousands already," the coachman replied. "Can't say as how she's my fancy—too thin. I likes a woman with a bit of flesh on her."

"You wants a woman ter look like a horse!" the footman said scornfully.

The short journey into Half Moon Street was completed in under five minutes. They drew up at a small, discreet-looking house and the footman got down and rang the bell.

The door was opened by a manservant dressed in a flamboyant uniform, but with a manner which somehow belied his servility.

He took one look at the coach standing outside and opened the door widely. There was an impudent grin on his face.

"She's a-waiting!" he told Lord Meridan's footman pertly.

The footman hurried back towards the coach.

Lord Meridan got out without haste.

"Come back in an hour," he said, and moved slowly into the house.

The footman shut the door and preceded him up the narrow stairs.

He opened the door of the drawing-room with a flourish.

"His Lordship," he said briefly, and there was a little

shriek of delight from the sofa on which a woman had been reclining.

"Me-Lord Sebastian!" she exclaimed in her broken English as she ran towards him. "Nevvaire I thought were you coming to see me! All yesterday afternoon I waited . . . and waited!"

She flung her arms around Lord Meridan's neck and pulled his head down to hers.

He kissed her, almost perfunctorily, and then settled himself in the armchair, his legs crossed.

"Let's have a look at you," he said. "Has the rest done you good?"

"Thank you, I am again in excellent health," Juanita da Riva answered.

She was small and exquisitely made, with a wreath of red hair that owed more to artifice than nature, and huge black eyes which could flash anger and defiance or seem soft and liquid when she was making love.

Born in Madrid, she was a tempestuous creature with full, curved breasts and a sensuous mouth which had captivated a number of men before Lord Meridan had seen her dancing at a theatre at Brighthelmstone and brought her to London.

"You are looking very attractive," he said appraisingly, as he looked her over rather as though she were an animal at a show.

"Why you not come to see me yesterday?" she pouted. "I send my footman to tell you I had returned."

"I was busy," he replied. "I was bidding for some horses at Tattersall's. The sale went on longer than I expected."

"And last night?" she queried.

"I had an appointment at Brooks's," he replied.

Her eyes were suddenly slits and she stared at him ferociously.

"Is there another—woman?"

He shook his head.

"Nothing to make you jealous," he answered. "But I expect that you have already learned that I am to be married."

Juanita gave a little shriek and clasped her hands to her breasts.

34

"To be . . . married?" she echoed. "You . . . you to be married? Is this a joke?"

"No, indeed," Lord Meridan told her. "You knew before you left that I had been barred from Almack's. The only way to remedy this situation is to produce a wife. I have taken steps to do just that."

"But you are mad . . . crazed! What would she be to you? She will interfere with your life—she might even come between us!"

Juanita's voice rose in a high crescendo, but Lord Meridan merely smiled.

"She will do none of these things," he said. "She is young and she will do as she is told. She will not interfere with me in the slightest. She will bear my name and of course will be treated with respect. There must be no scandals, no more flaunting of conventions, no more public appearances in places where my wife would be expected. But otherwise, my dear, our arrangements will go on as before —as I have already said, you are very attractive!"

She stood in front of him and he knew that a conflict was taking place in her mind.

Should she make a scene? Or should she accept what he was willing to give her? She knew him only too well, knew how he disliked anyone to cross him, anyone who did not accept his decision the moment it was made.

Just for a moment her temper almost got the upper hand of her.

And then she remembered that wives were not of the least importance. They stayed at home bearing a man's children, appearing with him occasionally at assemblies and balls where the *haut ton* congregated. But otherwise there was no need to worry about them.

She saw him watching her, saw his handsome sardonic face with its slightly bored expression and his finely chiselled mouth which could sometimes be cruel—and she knew that above all else she wanted to keep him.

She was not in love—Juanita did not know the meaning of the word, but she desired Lord Meridan as she had never desired another man—wholly and completely with her heart as well as her body.

"Me-Lord Sebastian . . ."

She said his name softly in a tone which he found in some way irresistible.

"Yes?"

He waited, knowing himself to be the conqueror, knowing that she dare not defy him.

"I do not mind . . ." she said, still softly with a little catch in her breath, ". . . for you to have twenty wives, just so long as you find me attractive . . . ver-ry attractive."

He held out his hand—the gesture of an Emperor. Then she was in his arms, the softness of her cheek against his, and the strange Eastern perfume which was so much a part of her in his nostrils.

3

Sir Edward was in a good humour. He came into the room rubbing his hands and exclaimed:

"Well, everything is settled. His Lordship's actuary has just returned to London."

Lady Belvil glanced up at him.

"The settlement is generous, then?" she said, knowing the answer by the expression on her husband's face.

"Very generous—very generous indeed."

"You are indeed a fortunate young woman, Lucinda. I hope you will recollect to express your gratitude to his Lordship."

Lucinda turned round from the dressing table where she was seated while a lady's maid fixed a lace veil on her head.

"Has he given me any private money to spend as I please, Papa?" she enquired.

Sir Edward frowned a little, as if he thought the question a trifle gauche.

"I think, Lucinda," he said pompously, "it will be time when you are married for your husband to explain to you the intricacies of finance."

Lucinda got up from the dressing table and walked towards her father.

"I want to know now, Papa," she said. "I want to know exactly how much money I have to spend on myself."

She paused, and realizing that her insistence was being received badly, added tactfully:

"There will be presents I want to give, for one thing,

presents to . . . y . . . you and Mama, and of course Hester."

Lady Belvil also got to her feet, putting down on the bed a small pile of nightgowns which she had been handing to Hester to pack in the deep, round-topped leather portmanteau which stood in the centre of the room.

"I think, Edward," she said in her quiet, unhurried voice, "that it would be wise for Lucinda to know now exactly what sums she can spend. She has never had the handling of money, and to imagine that she can plunge into expenditure without the least consequence might be disastrous."

"Lucinda will find it very hard to spend all that his Lordship has settled on her," Sir Edward answered, "unless, of course, she goes to the gaming tables."

Lady Belvil gave a little cry.

"The idea—as though a daughter of mine would stoop to such things!" She paused and then added: "Despite the example she has had in her own home."

Sir Edward flushed.

He had not expected the conversation to take such a serious turn, and he said quickly:

"Here is a copy of the settlement."

He drew a bulky parchment from his pocket.

Lucinda said hastily:

"Tell me briefly, Papa. You know how difficult legal language is to comprehend."

"Briefly," Sir Edward replied, "your husband has settled on you the sum of fifty thousand pounds, the income being yours to spend as you may wish."

"Fifty thousand pounds!"

Lady Belvil hardly seemed to breathe the words.

Lucinda said nothing, only one small hand crept up to her throat as if to reassure herself that she was still there.

Hester sat back on her heels beside the trunk.

"I am glad, Lucinda, very glad," she cried. "What fun you will have spending it!"

Lady Belvil glanced towards her elder daughter and her expression darkened.

"It is a lot of money," she said. "And who knows when Lord Meridan finds out . . ."

She stopped, her eyes on Hester, who, with her cheeks

flushed with the exertions of packing and her golden hair a little untidy, managed to look incredibly beautiful.

"Hester," Lady Belvil said suddenly, "listen to me—there is still time to change your mind. Lord Meridan has not yet seen Lucinda—it is you that he imagines he is to be wed. Why not do the sensible thing and marry him? You will have money and you will live in London. Everyone will admire you. Your position in Society will be unassailable. Change your mind, Hester! Lucinda will understand."

There was a sudden silence in the room and everyone, including the lady's maid, turned to stare at Hester.

She looked up at them, her red mouth smiling.

"But I am betrothed to Colin."

"Now attend, Hester," Lady Belvil insisted. "Colin is a pleasant young man and we all like him, but he will only have what money his guardian allows him. He may be poor for years."

"We are going to live in that little house by the river," Hester answered dreamily. "We shall be very happy—we will not need much money."

"But think what it would be like in London!" her mother pleaded. "You could have a box at the Opera; you could have the finest carriage in which to drive in the Park. Everyone will wish to be invited to your assemblies. The Queen herself would receive you. Oh, Hester, you would look so beautiful in the Meridan diamonds!"

Lucinda stood watching her sister, saying nothing.

She had not yet put on her bridal gown, but was wearing the silk petticoat which went underneath it and was tightly laced into a pair of new stays which were already cutting her under her small breasts. She had on a voluminous white wrapper; in contrast to the crisp freshness of it, her face seemed dull and colourless as she watched and listened, her whole future hanging in the balance.

"Hester—please, Hester, consider! Think what you are throwing away!" Lady Belvil pleaded.

"You do not understand, Mama," Hester replied. "I love Colin. I do not want to be married to anyone else. I could not marry a man I have never met. Think how brave Lucinda is! I have never been brave."

She shook her head, and her curls danced round her lovely little face.

"Good God! It's too late now to change things!" Sir Edward interposed roughly. "You are being nonsensical, Margaret, as well you know. The settlement has been signed and sealed."

Lady Belvil made an exasperated little sound and walked across the room to a chest of drawers.

Lucinda knew quite well that her mother was hiding the expression on her face. It was one of disappointment and irritation. Disappointment that her favourite child should not shine in Society; irritation that her younger daughter—for whom she had never cared—should have the chance of such a trememdous and exciting future.

But Lady Belvil's pleading had left a tension in the air which was embarrassing.

Sir Edward looked at his watch.

"It is one o'clock," he said. "There is an hour before we need leave for the church. I cannot understand his Lordship wishing to be married so late. Two-fifteen indeed! Maybe it's the fashion in London! We will be uncontrollably hungry before we can sit down to a decent meal."

"I thought you said last night you had a letter to say that Lucinda and her husband would not return here for the wedding breakfast," Lady Belvil said.

"Yes—yes, of course! I had forgotten," Sir Edward agreed hastily. "I have not told you, Lucinda, that your husband, as soon as you are married, wishes to drive straight back to London from the church. An extraordinary manner of behaviour! And he didn't write to me personally. Just a letter from his secretary!"

"Then he is not coming here at all?" Lucinda asked, surprised.

"What about her going-away dress?" Lady Belvil exclaimed. "Is the child to drive straight to London in her wedding gown? Never in my life have I heard of a bride being so mortified!"

"I thought myself that there must be some mistake," Sir Edward agreed. "I will speak to his Lordship when he arrives and say that out of courtesy he must stay for the wedding breakfast. Our relatives and friends will expect to meet him."

"I should think it extremely unlikely his Lordship will agree if he has already made his plans," Lucinda said.

"The fellow must behave with decency!" Sir Edward barked, a frown appearing on his forehead, as was usual when there was any opposition to his plans.

Lucinda smiled.

" 'Twould be best to pack my going-away dress, Mama, or it might be left behind. And the boxes must be brought down into the hall so that they can be loaded into his Lordship's carriage while we are at church."

"But you cannnot drive to London in your wedding gown!" Lady Belvil exclaimed in horror. "No girl of sensibility could endure it! Besides, what will people think?"

"I expect they will think that I am very lucky to get a husband of any sort," Lucinda answered, "let alone anyone as important and rich as the Earl of Meridan!"

"Really, Lucinda! How can you say such ill-bred things?" Lady Belvil snapped. "I have never heard of anything so vulgar. Edward, you will find a cold collation and a glass of wine waiting for you in the dining room. I know how irritable you get if you are hungry. And, as it is so late, Lucinda had best have a bowl of bread and milk, otherwise she will be swooning during the service. Remember, child, that men find vapourish wives a terrible nuisance—especially on their wedding day."

"You need not worry, Mama," Lucinda said. "I am not hungry and I shall not swoon."

"I had no idea it was so late!" Lady Belvil exclaimed. "We must go and dress. Agnes will finish your packing, Lucinda, and you can put in the last few things yourself. And as we do not want your wedding gown to be creased, that must wait until the very last second."

"Yes, Mama," Lucinda said meekly.

Lady Belvil bustled from the room and Sir Edward followed her.

Hester rose slowly to her feet.

"Oh, Lucinda," she smiled. "I do wish it was my wedding day, but I have only got a few months to wait now. Promise you will come to my wedding? I could not bear to have it without you!"

"Of course I will come," Lucinda answered. "And I will give you the loveliest present that anyone has ever had."

41

Hester put her arms around her sister's neck and gave her a little hug.

"Thank you, Lucinda," she said. "I only hope you will be as happy as Colin and I are going to be."

Lucinda did not answer. She went back to the mirror and saw her reflection gazing at her with wide, rather troubled, eyes.

"Agnes," she said to the maid, "do something for me— slip downstairs and send the pantry-boy to fetch Nat. I want to speak to him."

"Nat is in the pantry, Miss Lucinda," Agnes answered. "When I came upstairs he was helping lay the tables. There's such a flutter over the breakfast that everyone's giving a hand."

"Please tell Nat I want him," Lucinda said. "And do not forget to tell him that I am not in my own room."

"Very good, Miss Lucinda, but her Ladyship won't a-like him coming upstairs if she a-sees him."

Lucinda watched the middle-aged woman who had been Lady Belvil's maid for twenty years go heavily from the room, then she turned back again to her own reflection.

She thought for a moment she looked frightened, but realized it was only a trick of the light. There was no fear in her dark eyes and her lips were firm.

She stared at herself critically and pinched her cheeks to bring some colour into them. She thought that the way her hair was arranged was heavy and a little old-fashioned, but Agnes had resisted every suggestion of changing the style.

The lace veil, slightly yellow with age, which had been passed down the Belvil family for generation after generation, hung limply on each side of her face, seeming to curtain her from the world outside.

How long Lucinda waited she did not know. She just sat watching herself until a knock on the door made her start.

"Come in!" she called, and almost apologetically Nat sidled into the room.

He was wearing his best cutaway jacket, and his breeches, although they were old, had been cleaned until they were spotless. His boots shone like twin mirrors, and the stock round his neck was whiter than the satin bridal robe which lay waiting for Lucinda on the bed.

" 'Mornin', Miss Lucinda," he said cheerily.

"Good morning, Nat. You haven't forgotten what I told you?" Lucinda asked.

Nat shook his head.

"No—Joe'll be a-waitin' at th' church and Benjamin—he's but just turned six, but he's got all his wits about him—will be at the turn of the drive. When his Lordship arrives Joe'll wave his 'kerchief, and as soon as Benjamin sees him he will come running up to th' house to tell ye."

"That's right," Lucinda smiled. "And do not worry, Nat, if I do not come at once."

"Ye be a-going to be late, are ye?" Nat asked with a smile on his old lips. "Well, they say 'tis a woman's privilege."

"Yes, I am going to be late," Lucinda repeated almost to herself.

"Oi weren't expecting to find ye in this room," Nat said, looking round the big spare room which was kept on other occasions for the most important visitors.

"It seems that my family do not think that the room I have always occupied is good enough for me now," Lucinda said, a slight note of sarcasm in her voice. "And is it my imagination, Nat, or is everyone more respectful than they used to be?"

"Ye be a-grown now, Miss Lucinda," Nat said. "Ye be a woman and ye be a-going to be married and become a lady of quality—all overnight. so ter speak."

"It is a big step, is it not?" Lucinda said.

"Marriage'll always be that," Nat answered. "It's hopin', Oi am, that ye'll find happiness, Miss Lucinda."

There was a note of sincerity in his voice which touched her; and because she knew, as she had known all her childhood, that he was the one person who loved her more than anyone else, she turned to him now with the question which was uppermost in her mind.

"Tell me, Nat," she said, "tell me truthfully—what is wrong with me? I do not look right, do I? Oh, I don't expect to be beautiful like Hester—you know that—but I could contrive to appear better than I do. Is it the veil? My hair? Or what?"

Nat knew by the tone of her voice how urgent this question was, and slowly, because he seldom rushed his answers, liking to think them out before he spoke, he looked Lucinda over.

He saw her little heart-shaped face; he saw the wide, dark eyes that somehow seemed too big for it; he saw the small, somehow unnoticeable mouth and the tiny upturned nose. He knew exactly what she meant, and yet just as she could not find the answer, he did not know it either.

"Now yer a-givin' Oi some hard questions, Miss Lucinda," he said. "If ye were asking Oi about a horse—well, Oi could tell ye exactly what was wrong with it! And what was right, for that matter! But women—Oi knows precious little about women, except that a wise man keeps a-clear of 'em! But there must be those who can tell ye what ye want to know. If there be 'em as knows about horseflesh, why not 'em as knows about gowns or beauty, for that matter?"

"Nat!" Lucinda's eyes were shining. "You have given me the answer! Thank you, Nat. You have never failed me, have you?"

"Now, see here, Miss Lucinda," Nat said. " 'Tis not going to be easy for ye to be a-leaving home and all the things ye have known all yer life. The world's a big place, and a hard one. No one has it soft! Perhaps the Almighty who made us didn't mean it to be too soft. But if ye are knocked down just get up on yer feet and go on fighting. Don't lie there—don't let 'em defeat ye! That's what Oi always says to th' boys before they goes into the ring—an' Oi reckon 'tis much the same for a woman! Don't let anything get ye down!"

"I won't, Nat," Lucinda promised. "And thank you for being so understanding."

She rose from the dressing table and walked towards him. They were much the same height and she held out both her hands and he took them in his.

"God bless you, Miss Lucinda!" he said.

She stood looking at him for a moment and then she kissed his wrinkled cheek.

"If I am ever in real trouble I shall send for you, Nat," she said. "You will come, won't you?"

He murmured something which she knew was in the affirmative, but he could not speak clearly. And because he

44

was ashamed of showing his emotion he hurried away from the room, shutting the door behind him.

Lucinda walked to the window.

At the far end of the park she could see the square tower of the little Norman church in which she was to be married.

In a short time now the carriages would be driving up to the lich-gate and all their friends from the county would be crowding into the pews—excited and eager, as Lucinda knew, to see the famous Earl of Meridan about whom there had been so much gossip.

Even in the vastness of Hertfordshire people had heard of the style in which he lived, the rakish company he kept and of his close friendship with the Prince of Wales.

Lucinda knew that the news of his engagement had been received at first with incredulity.

"Not Lucinda? There must be some mistake! Hester, perhaps—at least she is beautiful, although bird-witted—but Lucinda—that is impossible!"

She had not been deceived by the crowds of carriages which had come to the house every day since the announcement appeared in the *London Gazette*.

People whom Lady Belvil had not seen for years came to call and ask what would have been impertinent questions if they had not been covered up by gush and compliments and the invariable opening of, "As we are such old friends . . ."

At first Sir Edward and Lady Belvil had been hard put to it to hide the fact that Lucinda had never met her future husband and the whole marriage was one of convenience as far as Lord Meridan was concerned.

And then, of course, the truth began to leak from St. James's and Pall Mall to the country towns and hamlets of Hertfordshire.

They never mentioned it in front of Sir Edward and Lady Belvil, but Lucinda knew that they were aware of the truth by the inflection in their voices, by the expression on their faces and the twist of their lips.

She could imagine them mouthing it over in their own homes . . . "Lady Jersey told him he would not be admitted! The Prince went in without him! They say the porters at Almack's are warned!"

It was easy, too, for Lucinda to envisage their laughter and the inevitable remark, "So that is why he has married her . . . !"

Agnes came hurrying into the room.

"You would hardly credit it, Miss Lucinda," she said, "but that dratted girl nearly left all your handkerchiefs behind. I told her to wash and iron them last night and she had been fool enough to take them up to your old bedchamber. 'Tis lucky I thought of them, or you would have arrived in London without a scrap of lawn in which to blow your nose!"

With the familiarity of an old servant she went on grumbling as she finished packing.

"Time must be getting on," she said at length, not noticing that Lucinda did not answer. "I'd best get you into your gown and then hurry down to the church. I don't want to miss seeing you get married."

"No, of course not, Agnes," Lucinda agreed. "Dress me, then. It doesn't matter if I am ready too early."

"What's more," Agnes continued as if she had not spoken, "her Ladyship will be wanting me in a few moments, and Miss Hester, too, I shouldn't wonder."

She picked up the heavy white satin dress off the bed and helped Lucinda into it. It had been made in St. Albans by a dressmaker who was patronized by many of the country matrons.

The material had looked lovely, Lucinda thought, before it was cut and fashioned to her figure; but now it seemed stiff and she could see that the waist needed tightening and the lace with which the bodice was trimmed was not an exact match with the veil which covered her hair.

"I do not like this gown," she said aloud, speaking to herself rather than to Agnes.

"Miss Lucinda, how can you be so ungrateful!" Agnes exclaimed. "This gown has cost a small fortune! There's not a bride in the length and breadth of the country who has had a finer and more expensive one this last twenty years."

Agnes took an inordinate interest in marriages, and Lucinda was sure she had spoken the truth.

"I am sorry, Agnes," Lucinda said, "but I just know it isn't the right dress for me."

46

"Now, don't you get such ideas into your head," Agnes said tartly. "You look a real bride, Miss Lucinda, and proud we'll all be of you."

There came a heavy knock at the door and before Lucinda could speak, Jarvis, the old gardener, put his head around the door.

"Be ye ready for yer bouquet, Miss Lucinda?"

He brought it into the room as he spoke, a stiff round bouquet of white roses and white carnations, tied with a monster bow of white satin ribbon.

"Looks real fine, don't it?" Jarvis asked eagerly.

"Indeed, it's magnificent," Lucinda answered almost automatically. "Thank you, Jarvis."

"The church be a picture!" Jarvis confided. "We've bin a-workin' there since five o'clock this mornin'. There's lilies on th' altar, and all the other flowers that we could find in th' garden and th' greenhouses around th' pulpit. We had to use daffodils round th' font, Miss Lucinda. It seems a bit shabby, but there b'aint a bloom left in th' hot-houses and th' lilac's barely in bud."

"Yes, I know," Lucinda said, "and I am sure it will all look lovely, Jarvis."

"Wall, I'll be a-getting back to th' church, Miss Lucinda, an' good luck to ye!"

Jarvis touched his forehead and went from the room.

Lucinda carried the large bouquet with its stiff wired flowers and set it down on the bed.

As she did so the door was swept open and Lady Belvil came bustling into the room. Her dress of grey silk was not new, but it looked surprisingly elegant, with a new hat trimmed with green feathers.

"Ah, so you are ready, child!" she exclaimed. "Hester and I are leaving for the church and we will send the carriage back for you and your father. Do not be late, now. We would not want his Lordship to be kept waiting, would we?"

She glanced at Lucinda perfunctorily, as if she hardly saw her.

"I see Jarvis has brought up your bouquet! I told him to leave it in the hall. The stupid old man never seems to hear what I tell him. Well, I must go—do not be late!"

"No, Mama," Lucinda said dutifully.

47

Lady Belvil went down the passage calling for Hester, and Lucinda heard the patter of Hester's feet hurrying after her and then a little while later she heard the wheels of the carriage going down the drive.

She stood staring once again at herself in the mirror and then picking up the skirts of her dress she ran from the room and up the flight of stairs to her room.

Here was her bedroom and Hester's side by side. Opposite was their sitting room which had once been the nursery and where the furniture had not been changed since they were babies.

Lucinda opened the door of Hester's bedroom. Everything was scattered about in confusion and untidiness. There was Hester's dress which she had worn that morning flung on the bed; her slippers were in the centre of the floor; the hat-box out of which she had taken her hat for the wedding was lying on its side, tissue paper spilled out of it on to the worn carpet.

Lucinda noticed none of these things. She crossed the room to the cupboard, pulled it open and began to search the shelves. At last she found what she wanted.

It was a wreath of red roses which Hester had worn with one of the ball dresses she had taken with her to London for the Season. They were small roses, hardly in bud, vividly red, glowing like the heart of a ruby.

Lucinda looked at them for a moment and then going to the mirror she took from her head the small encircling wreath of waxed orange blossom which Agnes had pinned there and placed in its stead the wreath of red roses. She pinned them on, pulling back the veil from her face.

The roses gave her height and they seemed to change the pallor of her face into something more vivid, more alive.

Lucinda stared at herself, then opening another cupboard she revealed Hester's dresses hanging in a row.

At the far end in the corner, because she wore it so seldom, was a ball dress with blue ribbons held up with tiny clusters of roses which matched the wreath which Hester had worn on her head.

Hastily Lucinda dragged one of the small bunches from the dress, breaking the threads which held it to the rib-

hands down the stairs to the room below.

She pinned it in front of her bodice. It looked strange, a vivid patch of colour against the whiteness of the satin and the frills of lace which encircled her shoulders.

And yet she knew that it had swept away the limpness and the overpowering whiteness of her appearance.

She might look strange—who had ever heard of a bride wearing a wreath of red roses and a posy of them at her breast?—but at least she was no longer the crushed, rather insipid figure that she had been when Agnes left her.

She turned towards the bed.

The stiff, ugly bouquet lay waiting her, and instead she picked up her prayer book. It was of dark blue leather. She looked at it somewhat distastefully until she remembered something else.

By her mother's bed there was a prayer book with an ivory cover. It was one Lady Belvil seldom used because it was too elaborate for her taste. It took Lucinda only a few moments to find it, and, holding it in her hand, she sat down composedly at the dressing table until it should be time to go to church.

She heard the clock strike the hour. His Lordship should have arrived by now, but Benjamin had not yet come running with the news, and she had a feeling that it would be like him to keep her waiting, perhaps not intentionally, but he was not as yet particularly concerned with her feelings.

She heard her father shouting for her from below. She paid no attention. She guessed that quite some time would pass before he would make the effort to climb the stairs. In the meantime he shouted that they should be leaving.

Lucinda was right in guessing that Lord Meridan was likely to be late.

He had in fact left London in a flurry of bad temper, curses and recriminations, because he found that one of his horses in the coach which was to take him to his wedding was off colour.

He had ordered the chestnuts deliberately because they were his most spectacular horses and he felt the least he could do was to impress his in-laws with his horseflesh.

Because his servants were in the habit of obeying him the coachman had taken the risk of bringing them round even though he well knew that his Lordship would not travel with a horse which was not completely fit.

So a change had been made at the last moment. The coach was taken back to the stables, the bays were substituted for the chestnuts, all of which put Lord Meridan in an exceedingly bad humour.

As they waited, Colonel Holstead, who was acting as his best man, tried to pacify him.

"There is plenty of time, Sebastian," he said. "Your animals always go a damned sight faster than anyone else's."

"I am not worrying about being late," Lord Meridan snapped at him, "but the fact that that fool coachman of mine could think he could deceive me. You cannot trust anyone, Charles! They are all the same, and if they can will sneak something by under your very nose!"

"You frighten people, that's what's wrong with you," Colonel Holstead said, stretching out his hand for another glass of wine. "If you want to know the truth, I'm deuced sorry for this wretched girl who has promised to marry you."

"She is doing well enough out of it," Lord Meridan retorted.

"You've been generous, have you?" Charles Holstead asked, raising one eyebrow, which was rather an engaging trick of his.

"Of course I have been generous," Lord Meridan said angrily. "Do you imagine I begrudge the future Countess of Meridan a few measly shillings? To put it bluntly, Charles—I have had to buy myself a wife and I might as well pay a good price for one."

"Is that for her benefit, or a salve for your conscience?" Charles Holstead asked.

"Don't ask such cork-brained questions!" Lord Meridan replied sharply.

"Well, it is not the sort of wedding knot that I should look forward to, personally," Charles Holstead said. "I am not romantic, mark you! I don't propose falling into a heart-aching depression and marrying the woman of my dreams, and all that sort of fustian! But I would like to wed someone with whom I could exchange a trifle of conversation occasionally. After all, the girl will be living in the same house!"

"My house is big enough for us never to meet, if necessary," Lord Meridan said. "Or perhaps Miss Belvil has some conversation. How do you know?"

Charles Holstead threw back his head and laughed.

"My dear Sebastian, you sound quite nettled. The point is, you are spoiled. You have always had everything your own way and you think you are going to marry some sort of paragon who will be everything you expect in a wife— just because she is your wife."

"Damme, why shouldn't she be?" Lord Meridan enquired.

"All right—have it your own way," Charles Holstead said. "I am not going to quarrel with you on your wedding day."

"I cannot for the life of me see why it is different from any other day," Lord Meridan answered, "Except that I had to rise at an uncommonly early hour."

"Dash it! You get up far earlier than this when you are going to Newmarket or hunting," Charles Holstead replied. "It is just that you are irritated at the thought of getting spliced! Who should blame you?"

"If it wasn't for Lady Jersey—curse the woman—it would never have happened! I'll get even with her one day!"

"Well, I hear His Royal Highness is bored with her, at any rate," Charles Holstead remarked.

"He has been bored with her for some time now," Lord Meridan answered, "but she will not let him go, she clings to him. My God, Charles! I hope my wife is not going to be the clinging type!"

"Perhaps we had better go and find out," Charles Holstead suggested deliberately.

As though he did not intend to be hurried, Lord Meridan helped himself to another glass of wine.

When that was finished they set off from Berkeley Square, the bays moving at a spanking pace towards the north.

They stopped at a coaching inn about two miles from their final destination.

Lord Meridan was annoyed to find that the wine was of

a poor quality and the bedroom into which he was shown to wash and refresh himself before arriving at the church was badly furnished.

"Good God, Sebastian! What did you expect?" Charles Holstead replied to his grumbles. "You know as well as I do that half the county would have been delighted to throw their doors open to you. I myself saw several invitations inviting you to go and stay the night. You could have had good wine at any number of houses."

"You know I had to be in London last night," Lord Meridan told him.

"Only because Juanita insisted on it," Charles Holstead answered. "I really believe she is jealous of your getting married, Sebastian."

"Jealous? Why should she be jealous?"

"As a matter of fact, she is rather fond of you."

"Fond?" Lord Meridan laughed in a somewhat unpleasant manner. "My dear Charles, creatures like Juanita go to the highest bidder! And respectably brought-up girls are not so very different. They also sell themselves as high as is possible. I have yet to find a woman whose heart did not beat faster when one offered her diamonds, or a mama who did not look archly at me when she had a marriageable daughter in hand."

"You are a cynic," Charles Holstead said accusingly. "I will tell you what will happen to you one day, Sebastian. You will fall in love, mark my words—I will even take a bet on it!"

"Done!" Lord Meridan exclaimed. "What do you fancy? A monkey?"

"I will make it more than that," Charles Holstead said, suddenly serious. "And we will set a time limit on it. I think two years would be about right. Let me see, you are twenty-seven at the moment. Well, Cupid should be getting at you at about this time."

"What the hell are you talking about?" Lord Meridan asked.

"I'll bet," Charles Holstead said, "five thousand pounds that you are in love before April twenty-eighth, eighteen hundred and five."

"Done!" Lord Meridan said. "The only problem, Charles, is—are you going to afford to pay me?"

"I shan't have to," Charles Holstead said cheerily. "Five thousand smackers will be a warm pocketful when I want to set up housekeeping—with a wife."

"You're mad as Bedlam!" Lord Meridan told him. "By the way, don't forget that I am coming to stay with you the day after tomorrow."

"Don't you think you had better leave your decision about that until after you have seen your bride?" Charles Holstead suggested.

Lord Meridan got up with such violence that the glasses shook on the table.

"Come on!" he said. "Let us get this farce over and get back to sanity. All this tattle of love and marriage makes me feel sick."

He walked determinedly out towards his carriage, followed by Charles Holstead, who was laughing.

Their journey started again, but by this time they were hopelessly late. It was nearly three o'clock before the carriage drew up outside the village church.

Lord Meridan alighted unhurriedly and was quite unaware of the whisper that rustled round the congregation, nor did he know that as one of the ushers bent to tell Lady Belvil of his arrival she reached for her smelling salts. Sheer relief almost made her swoon.

There was the usual crowd of villagers clustered round the path to the church.

Lord Meridan walked slowly through them, making no response to their cries of "Good luck!"

In the porch he saw a little group of people waiting and noticed that among them was an extremely pretty girl with fair hair, blue eyes and an angelic sort of face which would make any man pause in admiration.

Unused to weddings, he thought, as she turned towards him, that she must be the bride.

Then she curtsied, her hand was outstretched and a soft voice said:

"I am Hester—your future sister-in-law."

Behind him he heard Charles Holstead splutter, as if he was surprised, and thinking he wanted to be introduced Lord Meridan turned and said:

"This is my best man—Colonel Charles Holstead."

"How do you do?"

Hester held out her hand, and Charles took it in his.

"I saw you once," he said, "last year. Must have been at Almack's because I never go to the Society balls! I remembered you, but I never learnt who you were."

She smiled at him a little shyly.

"I am Hester Belvil," she said, "The bride's sister."

"And does your sister look like you?" Charles Holstead asked her. "I heard she was a stunner. I suppose she was in London the same time as you?"

"No, my sister has never been to London," Hester answered.

She was far too guileless to realize that Colonel Holstead was staring at her in astonishment, remembering that once the engagement was announced everyone in London had been only too willing to say how beautiful Sir Edward's daughter was and that they had always been convinced that she would marry well.

"Do we go in?" Lord Meridan was asking rather disagreeably.

"Yes—yes, of course," Hester said.

She introduced a pink-faced young man who was acting as an usher and who escorted Lord Meridan and Charles Holstead up the aisle and seated them in the front pew.

The church was packed, and Lord Meridan was conscious of feeling suddenly very tired. He had not got to bed until the early hours of the morning, and he had drunk a lot of brandy. Usually the two things combined to make him sleep like a log, but last night he had tossed and turned and found it impossible to compose himself.

When he was called by his valet drawing back the curtains on a fresh spring day he had a sudden uncontrollable longing for Meridan Park.

He stifled an impulse to order a horse and ride there immediately as he would have done on other occasions. Often when he felt nauseated with the riotous life of London he retreated to Meridan and found all the company he needed with his horses.

This mood never lasted long and he was soon back in the gay life again, and he knew now that it was not so much a yearning for Meridan as a dislike of what lay ahead of him.

He had not wanted a wife—he had never intended to

get married. And now that damned Committee at Almack's had forced him into it—egged into their decision, he was quite certain, by that tigress Lady Jersey, who had never liked him because he had not responded to her very obvious invitations to become her lover.

Oh well! he had decided, he would call her bluff and arrive at Almack's with his wife and reinstate himself. And although it was a nuisance to be saddled with such a creature, it would doubtless make very little difference except for the bother of having had to come to Hertfordshire today and marry her.

At least, he thought, as he sat with his back to the fluttering and whispering congregation, she would be good-looking.

If the girl he had met in the porch was a sample of what he had to expect he would certainly have no complaints on that score, and, what was more, she would be young enough to do what he wanted and respectful enough to be worthy of bearing his name.

After all, he philosophized, it might be worse, and he did not have to put up with these country bores. Having made it quite clear that he was not going to listen to embarrassing speeches at a wedding breakfast, they would leave for London immediately the ceremony was over.

He saw Charles pull his watch from his vest pocket and look at it with some perplexity, and realized that they had been sitting there for nearly fifteen minutes.

Damn it all! He had been late enough as it was, without having to hang about now he had arrived!

He bent forward to whisper in Charles's ear.

"What the devil are we waiting for?"

"The bride!" Charles answered, with a twinkle in his eyes.

"Why is she late?"

"She had the good sense not to wait here for you!" Charles whispered back. "I wonder who put her up to that one?"

"Damned impudence!" Lord Meridan growled.

"At least you will not start your married life with recriminations," Charles told him.

His friend gave him a look as if he thought he, too, was being impertinent.

And then there was a rustle at the end of the church and a turning of heads, and the organ, which had been played softly and rather badly, now played loudly and exceedingly badly.

"Here she comes!" Charles said in jubilant tones.

Lord Meridan got very slowly to his feet. He wondered to himself what on earth he was doing here. It was too late now to get out of it, but he had a feeling that someone had set a trap for him and he had fallen into it.

The clergyman was waiting at the steps of the chancel. The bride was coming up the aisle.

Without turning his head Lord Meridan was conscious that the bride was approaching and moved forward so that she could stand beside him.

"Gracious!" he heard a woman exclaim behind him. "What can Lucinda be wearing on her head?"

Curiosity was too much for him. Lord Meridan turned.

She was nearer than he thought and he found himself looking into a pair of very dark, curious eyes.

It was a small face—not beautiful, not at all what he was expecting. And it was crowned by a wreath of vivid red roses, which made her look not in the very least like any bride he had anticipated—or ever seen in his life before.

4

Lord Meridan threw himself back in the corner of the coach with an air of disagreeableness and irritability.

One of the rose petals which had been thrown at the bride and bridegroom as they came from the church had stuck to the lapel of his coat and he flicked it off with a distasteful finger.

There were cries of "Good luck!" and "God bless you!" from the crowd gathered in the churchyard and smiles from the guests who were pushing their way out of the church and who did not as yet know that this was the last glimpse they would have of the happy couple.

The villagers, tenants and the employees on the estate, all in their best clothes, waved their caps or handkerchiefs and the children threw rose petals and rice, the latter making Lucinda's face sting as she sought sanctuary in the coach.

In the vestry, when they had gone to sign the register, there had been an uncomfortable exchange of words between her father and her husband.

"I received your letter, my Lord," Sir Edward said aggressively. "I hope I am mistaken in thinking that you wish to leave for London immediately?"

"There is no mistake," Lord Meridan replied.

"A wedding breakfast is prepared at my house," Sir Edward insisted, "and Lucinda would wish to change into a travelling gown."

"If Lucinda wishes to follow on afterwards that is her concern," Lord Meridan replied loftily. "I regret if it causes you inconvenience, but I have matters in London which require my urgent attention."

"I cannot imagine anything more important today than the fact that you are marrying my daughter!" Lady Belvil interposed.

Lord Meridan bowed in her direction, but he said nothing and it was quite obvious from the implication he made by his silence that he did not agree.

"Please don't worry about me," Lucinda said. "I am prepared to travel as I am."

She would have said more, but her mother drew her aside.

"How dare you put that ridiculous wreath on your head?" she asked. "You look utterly absurd—who ever heard of a bride wearing red roses?"

"Who ever heard of a bride marrying a man she had never met and leaving for London immediately after the ceremony?" Lucinda asked.

Lady Belvil stared at her in astonishment.

"Really, Lucinda! It seems that your new position has already gone to your head!" she said sourly.

It was Hester who broke the tension.

"I think the organist is ready to play the 'Wedding March'," she said, apparently quite oblivious that her father and her new brother-in-law were talking in voices that were gradually being raised higher and higher and that her mother and Lucinda were staring at each other angrily.

At the sound of Hester's voice Lord Meridan turned round and stared at her.

She looked very lovely in her full muslin dress with its white fichu and a wreath of lillies-of-the-valley on her fair curls.

She carried a bouquet of the same flowers, and it seemed to Lucinda that Hester's beauty would always be an inescapable memory of her wedding day.

She turned towards her bridegroom, saw the tightening of his lips and guessed with a sudden perception that this was something he invariably did when he was angry.

"Let us go at once," she said quickly. "I am ready."

She kissed her mother perfunctorily and clung for a moment to her father.

He, too, was annoyed. She could feel it in the stiffness

of the arm he put about her and knew it by the way he muttered something derogatory as he kissed her cheek.

Then she put her fingers on Lord Meridan's arm and they were walking down the aisle to the strains of the "Wedding March" and encountering the curious, envious and amused glances of those who had attended the ceremony.

As the coach moved off, Lord Meridan, his lower lip more prominent than ever, stared straight ahead of him. He was trying to sort things out in his own mind. He had the uncomfortable feeling that he had been done.

He recalled Charles Holstead's conversation with his sister-in-law and echoing back into his mind came Hester's words: "My sister has never been to London." That was the whole key to the question—he was certain of it.

He remembered Lady Jersey speaking to Sir Edward of his beautiful daughter, and the innumerable people who, after his engagement was announced, had told him how lovely his future wife was and how much they had admired her the previous Season.

The pattern was falling into place.

It was not Hester he had married, but it was Hester he had intended to make his wife! Instead he had been palmed off with Lucinda!

He realized that he had not been sufficiently alert to escape the trap which had been set for him and into which, catching him irrevocably with its pronged teeth, he had fallen so neatly.

He knew now that he should have refused to marry Lucinda as she reached his side at the chancel steps, directly he saw a small white face with dark hair when he had been expecting someone pink and white and gold.

It was all that damned drink he had consumed last night. He had been what his friends called bosky when he got to bed, and the only way that he could get himself into shape so that he could travel to the wedding ceremony was by a hair of the dog that bit him.

Brandy had pulled him together, but it had left him—as he knew himself—rather slow in his reactions, while the inferior wine they had drunk at the coaching inn had done nothing to clear his brain.

Fool that he was! If he had acted at once he could have

walked away from the church a free man—and yet that would have meant that he had gone through all this palaver for nothing and would have to start again at the beginning.

He must have groaned aloud and put his hand to his forehead, because a voice beside him said:

"Does your head ache? I am not surprised—mine does, too. I think I will take off my wreath and veil."

Lord Meridan gave his bride a sour glance. She certainly would not grace the family jewels, as everybody had expected.

He tried to find words in which to express his suspicions and his anger at what had happened.

While he was thinking how to begin, Lucinda said:

"I hope you did not mind my wearing a wreath of red roses. Mama was scandalized, as I knew she would be! And I expect everyone in the church had something rude to say about it, but I looked so terrible all in white—just like a ghost—and who wants to look like a ghost on their wedding day?"

"You have never been to London?" Lord Meridan said accusingly.

Lucinda, turning round a little in the coach to look at him, saw by his expression exactly of what he was accusing her.

"How did you know?" she asked.

"Your sister—Hester, I think her name is—told Charles Holstead, who was acting as my best man."

"So you guessed?" Lucinda said.

He did not pretend not to understand her.

"No," he said. "I did not realize what was happening until I saw you. From what everyone had said, I expected someone who looked very different."

"You expected Hester?" Lucinda said simply. "She was already engaged."

There was a pause, and then Lucinda added almost defiantly:

"You just wrote, . . . *Your daughter* . . . If you wanted Hester you should have said so, and then, of course, Papa would have had to refuse your kind offer."

There was a hint of sarcasm in her voice which Lord Meridan noticed.

"Your father must have known my intentions. He was there when Lady Jersey mentioned how beautiful your sister was. She could hardly have meant you, if you have never been to London."

"Papa was in a fix," Lucinda said lightly. "It was my idea, actually, that I should save the family fortunes and get myself a husband at the same time. They had not much hope that I would find one otherwise!"

Even Lord Meridan was startled by such frankness.

"What do you mean?" he asked. "What's wrong with you?"

"Look at me!" Lucinda said.

He looked as she suggested and found it rather difficult to make out exactly what she did look like in the shadows of the coach.

She was pale and rather sallow, he thought, and her hair was most unbecomingly dressed and rather untidy now that she had taken the wreath from it.

There was nothing very wrong, except that she was not the type of wife whom people would envy him having, and he knew now that he wanted to be envied when he produced the new Countess of Meridan—just as he was envied for his horseflesh, his pictures, his furniture, his magnificent houses and his position in Society.

"Well, it is done now!" he said almost savagely, more furious with himself than with Lucinda.

He could see now it was entirely his autocratic manner of doing things which had brought him to this. If he had had the sense to see the girl even once before the ceremony he would have called the arrangement off.

That old fool Sir Edward Belvil could have been made to cough up the thirty-five thousand pounds he owed him and it would have been easy enough to ask any of the great London hostesses to find him a suitable bride.

"Yes—it's done!" he heard Lucinda say with a little sigh. "I feel in a way it was rather a shabby trick; at the same time, it is your own fault! I cannot imagine a man buying a horse without seeing it—let alone a wife!"

"I don't think that is the sort of thing you ought to say," Lord Meridan remarked, and was astounded at himself for feeling shocked.

"Why not?" Lucinda asked, turning towards him with

61

wide eyes. "You have bought me, haven't you? All that money . . . you have washed out Papa's debts . . . and they were large enough, in all conscience! And now the fifty thousand pounds you have settled on me! Perhaps you would like to take that back?"

"Good God, no!" Lord Meridan ejaculated, feeling that this conversation was the last thing he had expected of his bride, and yet not knowing quite how to cope with it.

"I think it is best to be frank with each other," Lucinda said. "After all, I know why you married me—I am really your ticket to Almack's, aren't I? I expect at the same time you are feeling I am rather an encumbrance, especially as I shall not look the part at the head of your table as Hester would have done."

Lord Meridan stared uncomfortably.

"I didn't say that," he said.

"No, but I have," Lucinda answered. "I have got no illusions about myself. I have always been a disappointment to my parents. As a child they were always punishing me, and now they are always finding fault. Mama, especially, felt she would never turn me into a lady—rather funny, if you think of it!"

"It is not the sort of joke which makes me laugh," Lord Meridan said sourly.

"No—of course not," Lucinda agreed, "and I expect you will find me a dead bore after all those exciting women you go about with in London. I have heard about Juanita da Riva—is she very lovely?"

Lord Meridan gave an exclamation which was almost like a pistol-shot and sat up abruptly.

"Good heavens!" he exclaimed. "Where have you heard such things? How do you dare to speak of them? Have you no elegance of mind? You are my wife, remember. And you will try and grace the position."

"I am sorry," Lucinda said humbly. "Shouldn't I have said that?"

"Most certainly not!" Lord Meridan said, and then felt more astonished at his own reaction than at Lucinda's words.

The coach came suddenly to a standstill and Lucinda, bending forward, saw they were at the crossroads just a few miles from her home.

"Why are stopping here?" she asked, and saw to her surprise that Lord Meridan looked almost shamefaced.

"Well, it is like this," he said. "Charles Holstead has to get back to London, so I sent my phaeton for him. He will be just behind us and I—I thought a little fresh air would be pleasant, coaches are always stuffy."

Lucinda's eyes lit up.

"Oh, what a splendid idea!" she exclaimed. "I, too, hate coaches . . . they always make me feel sick. I was only hoping that I would get to London without being ill. A phaeton would be much more fun, and much quicker."

She stared out of the window and gave a cry of excitement.

"There it is! What magnificent horses—and perfectly matched! I have always longed to drive in a phaeton as high as that!"

Before Lord Meridan could say more—indeed, before the footman could step down from the box and open the door—she had sprung out into the road and was hurrying towards the black and yellow phaeton with its shining accoutrements which was drawn by two perfectly matched horses.

Lord Meridan put his hand to his forehead again.

It was impossible, he thought, to explain to this impulsive child—for she was nothing more—that he intended her to drive sedately to London while he and Charles rolled ahead in the phaeton.

He had the uncomfortable feeling that if he insisted that she should do as he planned she would defy him.

Perhaps for the moment, at any rate, it was best to let her have her own way—although, heaven knew, he would have to put his foot down sooner or later!

He was just about to dismount when Lucinda came back. She was holding up the train of her white satin dress and showing, he noted disapprovingly, a most unconventional amount of ankle as she did so.

"I forgot my cloak," she said cheerily. "It is a good thing I brought it, isn't it? I did not put it on when we left the church because it is rather old and shabby and there was no time to buy a new one! But it is there on the seat in front of you. If you could just help me . . . it is an awful nuisance having to hold my skirts up."

Meekly, because he could think of nothing to say, Lord Meridan stepped from the coach and put the cloak over her shoulders.

It was blue, but of a cheap, coarse material, he noticed, and, as Lucinda had said, it was very shabby.

The colour seemed, however, to be reflected in the excited eyes which were turned up to his.

"You were quite right," she said, a note of warm approval in her voice, "this is much more fun than a wedding breakfast . . . and all those heavy speeches."

She moved away from him, and he noted, again with disapproval, that she clambered up on the phaeton without waiting for the footman to assist her.

She seated herself beside Charles, who was holding the reins, and she evidently expected to drive to London between the two men—her husband and his best man.

Lord Meridan collected his hat and moved very slowly from the carriage to the phaeton.

The horses were champing a little and Charles called out to him:

"Hurry up, Sebastian! They are hard to hold!"

Lord Meridan climbed on to the seat beside Lucinda.

She gave a little gurgle of delight as he settled himself and said:

"This is indeed wonderful! I do wish Mama could see me—she would swoon away at the horror of it!"

"Then hadn't you best travel in the carriage?" Lord Meridan asked.

"As though I would want to do such a thing!'" Lucinda replied scornfully.

"Do you wish to take the ribbons, Sebastian?" Charles asked, "or shall I take them the first part of the journey?"

"We will change at Potters Bar," Lord Meridan replied.

"Very well, then," Charles said.

He flicked the whip, the groom released the horses' heads, ran and jumped up at the back.

Lucinda felt the wind brushing against her face and knew that the pins put in so painstakingly by Agnes were falling away and her hair was tumbling over her shoulders.

It did not seem to matter—she was enjoying herself! She felt free and untrammelled—a strange thing, she thought, to feel on one's wedding day.

"Faster! Faster!" she cried, and Charles looked down at her and laughed.

"We are going as fast as I dare take them," he said. "We will give them a rest at Potters Bar. I expect Sebastian could do with a drink—I know I could."

"Now I think about it, I am hungry," Lucinda said. "I did not have any breakfast this morning, there seemed to be so much to do."

"I expect you were excited," Charles suggested.

"Not really," Lucinda answered. "I felt rather solemn— not exactly afraid of what lay ahead, but rather apprehensive."

She paused for a moment and then added:

"No, I suppose that is not truthful. Nat says everyone is afraid before they go into a fight."

"A fight?" Lord Meridan ejaculated, speaking for the first time. "Is that how you look on your marriage?"

She smiled at him almost apologetically.

"Well, it is almost the same thing, isn't it? At least, that is what Nat thought."

"And who might Nat be?" Lord Meridan asked, an ugly note in his voice. "Your beau? I should have thought you were too young to have started affairs of the heart. Or perhaps that was one of the reasons why you were so keen to get married?"

He was being so unpleasant that even Charles looked at him in surprise.

But Lucinda only threw back her head and laughed.

"I don't think you would suspect Nat of being my beau if you saw him," she said. "He will be sixty this year! He is our groom and the best judge of horses in the whole of Hertfordshire . . . even Papa says so, and he is often annoyed because Nat knows more than he does."

"*Touché*, I think, Sebastian," Charles said softly.

Lord Meridan flashed him an angry glance before he said:

"So this groom—Nat, or whatever you call him—told you that your marriage was going to be a fight?"

"He did not mean it like that," Lucinda said. "It was just that we were talking about courage and what a man felt like before he went into a mill. You see, Nat was a champion in his own class for many years."

"I can see your achievements, Sebastian, are going to nave a lot of competition where Nat is concerned," Charles said with a hint of amusement in his voice.

"I think perhaps it would be a good idea if we found other opinions for my wife to quote rather than the prattling of a stable-hand," Lord Meridan said sourly.

Lucinda looked from one man to the other in perplexity and then because she did not quite understand the turn which the conversation had taken relapsed into silence.

There was no need to talk. She was enjoying every moment of their rush through the countryside—the narrow road winding away beneath the horses' hoofs; and the pace which left her breathless and brought the colour flooding into her cheeks.

They passed through the village of Hatfield and then ahead of them saw the green undulating fields which led to Potters Bar.

As they neared the hamlet there was on an open common a crowd of people. From the height of the phaeton Lucinda could see over their heads.

There was a rough ring around which horses were being led, and a large number of animals of all sizes and descriptions—some being groomed by gaitered farmers, some being held on a string by ragged boys whose dark eyes and wild hair proclaimed them to be gypsies.

"It's a horse fair!" Lucinda exclaimed. "I had forgotten that it would take place today."

"I am sure if you had recollected it you would have postponed our wedding," Lord Meridan said.

"It would be a pity to miss the fair," Lucinda answered. "You get better bargains at Potters Bar than practically anywhere else—Nat said so and it is here that he bought Seagull, a mare which has already won back her price a dozen times in prizes."

"Not quite the same as Tattersall's," Charles said with a taunting smile, "but, all the same, Sebastian, would you be interested in inspecting the nags?"

"Oh please, let us do that!" Lucinda cried. "It would be a pity to miss something really good, wouldn't it? Please stop!"

"Quick, Sebastian—make up your mind," Charles said,

and then without waiting for Lord Meridan's answer drew the horses to a standstill.

The groom ran to their heads. Charles stepped down and turned to assist Lucinda to alight.

She was too quick for him and jumped to the ground. As she did so, the last remaining hairpins fell from her hair and it tumbled over her shoulders and down to her waist, a dark blue-black cloud which she threw back impatiently.

She pulled the train of her gown off the ground, holding it up under her cape with a gesture of annoyance which was unmistakable.

"Come with me!" she said eagerly. "I know where we can see best. It is no use trying to force our way through the crowd . . . we must go where the horses come into the ring."

She did not wait for the men to agree with her, but sped ahead, winding her way in and out of the slow yokels, the fat, well-fed farmers and the crafty-eyed thin little men who had obviously come down from London for the pickings.

They caught up with her at the entrance to the ring.

"That one might be got up to scratch," she said, pointing to a young stallion which was being led by a vacant-looking butcher's boy who was receiving his instructions from a fat middle-aged owner.

"I will tell you why it is being sold," she continued, lowering her voice. "I bet that heavy-fisted old man cannot hold him."

"We will go into the ring," Lord Meridan said loftily. He and Charles, with a delighted Lucinda following them, moved forward past the attendants at the opening and stood in the centre watching the horses parading around them.

"Can I be of any assistance, my Lords?"

It was the usual cunning-faced agent who appeared at every horse fair, his smile too ingratiating, his eyes too shifty, and Lucinda distrusted him on sight.

Lord Meridan did not deign to answer him, but Charles Holstead said sharply:

"We will do our own bargaining, thank you."

"If you do need me, my Lords, I shall not be far away."

The man bowed himself to the ringside. Lucinda stood looking at the horses—quite unaware of the attention she was causing by her flowing hair and peculiar clothes.

Lord Meridan and Charles began to discuss the merits of the stallion she had first noticed, and it was then outside the ring that she saw the foal.

It was rearing a little, frightened by the crowds and the proximity of the horses, but even at the first glimpse she had of it she knew its quality and saw how beautiful it was.

Without bothering to explain that she was leaving, she hurried out of the ring towards it.

It was a lovely small creature and she knew at once that it was well bred and had all the spirit which was necessary in a horse which was born to be raced.

Its bridle was held by a boy of about fifteen. Without really thinking of it, she realized that he came of good yeoman stock, the kind of boy who in the future would make a good farmer.

She talked to him and found out how the horse was sired, and she realized by the pride in the boy's voice that he was not lying when he said the dam had won a dozen races before she had had this foal.

"How much do you want for him?" Lucinda asked at length. She felt, as she asked him, it was the sort of question which Nat would have told her to work up to gradually, but she was in a hurry and she somehow felt that the boy was honest and would not take advantage of her.

"Ten pounds—or more, if we can get it."

Lucinda gave a little sigh. Ten pounds was a lot of money for a foal.

And then suddenly she remembered that she was rich! —sufficiently rich to buy the horse if she wanted, although how and where she was to keep it she had no idea.

She flashed the boy a smile.

"Do not sell it to anyone else," she said. "I will not be a moment," and ran back across the field towards the ring.

Lord Meridan and Charles had just missed her and were coming out to look for her, feeling rather apprehensive that Lady Meridan should not be left unattended at a horse fair of this description.

"Come and see what I have found!" Lucinda said

quickly, in her excitement putting her hand in Lord Meridan's arm and giving him a little pull in the direction in which she wished him to go.

"Where have you been?" he asked angrily. "You must not wander about here alone."

"I am all right," Lucinda answered, and then remembered something she had forgotten for the last quarter of an hour—that she was a married woman with a position to keep up.

"Oh, I am sorry," she said hastily, "but nobody knows me. They have no idea that I am your wife, so it really does not signify. Come and see this foal! It is going to be a winner, I am sure of it. Oh, if only Nat were here!"

"Perhaps our opinion, although not equal to the incomparable Nat's, might be helpful," Lord Meridan suggested.

"Yes . . . of course," Lucinda said. "I would like you to see what you think. He is only ten pounds. I know it is a lot of money, but could you . . . do you think you could . . . lend it to me? Papa did say that I was to have the income of what you had settled on me, and I would like to buy this horse more than anything else . . . if that is all right with you, of course."

Her small flushed face was turned up to Lord Meridan confidently, then she heard Charles laugh.

"Ten pounds, Sebastian—can you possibly afford it?"

"I will have a look at the animal first," Lord Meridan said. "In this place it is almost certain to be worthless."

He felt Lucinda draw her hand from his arm and knew with a strange instinct that he had not possessed before that she was not annoyed with him doubting her judgement but merely afraid that he knew so little himself that he would persuade her not to have the animal.

Far down in the depths of his memory something struggled to his mind.

He had been small, perhaps not more than six or seven, and his father had taken him to the stables and told him to choose what was the best horse. He had pointed to the one he liked best, and even now he could hear their laughter. It had hurt his pride, although he was not going to show it, but he had never quite forgotten the pain he had felt at the time.

"Where is this hope for the future?" he asked, his voice

kinder, and because of it Charles checked a quip which was already moving his lips.

They came to the boy and the foal, but the agent who had approached them in the ring was there before them.

"Oh, my Lord, I thought you would find the one jewel among the dust," he said. "It is an animal really worth having—a piece of horseflesh which even your Lordships might see running under your own colours at Newmarket."

"Get off!" Lord Meridan said. "I am not dealing with you."

"As your Lordship pleases," the man said, but Lucinda saw the look he gave the boy as he walked away.

"He will make him pay almost everything as commission," she said in a low voice, and then to the boy: "How much did that man say you had to give him?"

"He said we were to go halves," the boy said.

"But it isn't fair!" Lucinda exclaimed.

"I'll have to pay him," the boy said unhappily. "If I don't he'll hound I one way or t'other."

"What did you want the money for?"

" 'Tis the mortgage," the boy answered. " 'Tis due the first of the month and we've had a hard winter. I didn't want to sell Sir Galahad yet, but my father can't find the money, and so he has got to go."

"Sir Galahad," Lucinda said softly. "Is that what you call him?"

"I heard the name when I were at school," the boy told her. "It seemed to stick in m'mind."

Lord Meridan and Charles were inspecting the foal, and Lucinda knew by the expression on their faces that they thought well of him.

She waited until they had finished and then asked apprehensively:

"Can I buy him?"

"You found him first," Charles said. "If you do not want him I will have him."

"It is as Lucinda wishes," Lord Meridan said.

She smiled at him.

"You mean . . . that you will advance me the money?"

"Of course," he answered.

He drew his purse from his pocket.

"Wait a minute," Lucinda said, and glanced over her shoulder.

The agent was not far away. He was pretending he was watching the horses in the ring, but she knew he was alert to every move.

"You told him that you had asked me ten pounds?" she said to the boy, knowing he was too honest to have lied.

He nodded.

"What you have left—will it pay the mortgage?" she asked.

"Not all of it," he answered, "but it'll help."

Lucinda drew Lord Meridan to one side.

"Listen," she said. "If we give him fifteen pounds he will have ten for himself and five for that horrible man."

"You are being very generous," Lord Meridan told her.

"Please . . ." she said. "I want the horse, but I also want to help the boy."

"It is your money," he said gravely. "Are you quite sure they are not in league?"

Lucinda hesitated a moment.

"I do not think so," she said. "The boy is like his horse . . . true and honest. There are no tricks about him . . . you can see it in his eyes."

"Do you always judge people by their eyes?" Lord Meridan asked unexpectedly.

She laughed up at him.

"I am not going to be caught by a question like that," she said. "No, I look people all over, just as I look at a horse, and I make very certain that they are not gone in the wind."

She laughed at her own joke, and to his astonishment Lord Meridan found himself laughing too.

Then he held up his finger to the boy.

"Come here, boy," he said. "Here is five pounds for you. Take it to that crooked fellow over there and tell him he is damned lucky to get it. And then take your horse home and I will send one of my grooms to fetch it. I am Lord Meridan. The groom will bring you the rest of the money, and, thanks to this lady, perhaps a little more. In fact, if you keep your mouth shut you need not worry about the mortgage for this year, at any rate. Is that clear?"

"I understand, m'Lord. Thank you very much indeed—and thank you, m'Lady."

"Now where do you live?" Lucinda asked practically.

"Bell Farm," the boy answered. "Anyone around here will tell you where it is."

"Very well," Lord Meridan said. "The groom will be there tomorrow. Do not let anyone harm the horse—remember it belongs to her Ladyship."

"I will keep him as careful as careful, m'Lord," the boy promised.

Lord Meridan did not wait for his reply. He had already turned away and started to walk back across the field towards his phaeton.

He felt a small hand clutching his arm and looked down to see Lucinda's face raised to his with eyes soft with happiness.

"Thank you . . . thank you," she said. "I had no idea that anyone could be so kind . . . so very generous. That boy was grateful. And now for the first time I have a horse of my own."

"Fifteen pounds is a lot of money," Charles said, and she did not realize that he was teasing her.

"Indeed, it is a lot," she agreed seriously, "but you do see that if we had not given the boy the extra five pounds they would have been unable to clear the mortgage."

"And that is a thought which would undoubtedly have kept us all awake at night," Lord Meridan said.

"The farmers have had a very bad winter," Lucinda replied. "I expect you have found that on your estate, haven't you?"

She wondered why Lord Meridan did not answer, or why Charles, looking at him out of the corners of his eyes, said:

"You have found that, of course, Sebastian. I know how deeply it has concerned you."

"Shut up, Charles!" Lord Meridan said sharply.

They had reached the phaeton and he helped Lucinda on to the high front seat.

"I wonder if a year from now," he said, "you will be as satisfied with such a purchase, or think fifteen pounds such an immense sum?"

"A year from now is a long time away," Lucinda said,

and as the two men settled themselves on either side of her, and Lord Meridan took the reins, she added: "But I shall remember my wedding day every time I look at Sir Galahad."

"And what could be a better reason for remembering it?" Charles said mockingly, and he looked at Lord Meridan across Lucinda's head.

5

It was late in the afternoon when they reached London.

They had stayed longer than was intended at the coaching inn in Potters Bar, talking to some of the horse dealers who had come from various parts of the country to the fair, and finding by the time they had finished that there was quite a surprising number of strangers in the private sitting-room where Lord Meridan had commanded they should eat their meal.

It had all been amusing and interesting to Lucinda, but it was nothing to the excitement of seeing London for the first time. She noticed how the herds of cows and sheep blocking the roads gradually became less, and, instead, their places were taken by carts bringing fresh vegetables and fruit to the markets.

Intermingled with smart coaches with emblazoned coats of arms on their painted doors were the phaetons and curricles driven by smart young gentlemen—their hats at an angle—whom Charles told her were called Corinthians. There was also a motley collection of pedestrians, some of whose appearance nearly caused Lucinda to fall out of the phaeton, she was so astonished by them.

"Look at that monkey dancing with a tambourine in its hand!" she exclaimed breathlessly. "And do look . . . there is a bear! Oh, poor thing! I hope it is not going to be taken to some dreadful pit where it will be baited by dogs!"

" 'Tis a sport I never could abide," Charles Holstead assured her. "Don't you agree, Sebastian?"

Lord Meridan, who seemed preoccupied with his own thoughts, turned at the question.

"It is certainly not something I should expect my wife to watch," he said.

"No, of course not," Charles Holstead said quickly. "But, then, if it comes to that, she should not be watching any sports—ladies don't, you know."

"You mean to say that I will never be allowed to go to a mill again?" Lucinda exclaimed in tones of horror.

"Are you telling us that you have attended one already?" Lord Meridan asked.

"But dozens!" Lucinda replied. "Of course, Mama and Papa did not know—Nat took me. And very exciting they were, too! I cheered myself hoarse at the last one!"

"I have never seen a lady of quality at one," Charles Holstead said. "But perhaps Sebastian will be able to smuggle you in disguised."

"I shall do nothing of the sort," Lord Meridan said somewhat aggressively.

There was an edge to his voice which told Lucinda it was better not to argue. He had now taken the reins and they drove very swiftly in and out of the traffic which was getting thicker as they progressed further into the city.

Now there were shops, and she leant forward eagerly to look at their bow windows and wondered what it would be like to be able to buy the very latest and most modish costumes instead of having to rely on pictures torn from the *Ladies' Gazette.*

She was still thinking about this when the shops were left behind and they entered a grand square of houses, passed through it and came to another.

"You are home!" Charles remarked, and then gave a sudden exclamation. "Good God, Sebastian, look what's outside your house!"

Lord Meridan reined in the horses and they paused for a moment at the top of the square, looking down to where, on the right-hand side, a resplendent carriage waited with attendants wearing a green and gold uniform which Lucinda guessed instinctively proclaimed a Royal owner.

"Prinny, for a certainty!" Charles cried softly. "A reception committee, Sebastian!"

"Damn it!" Lord Meridan said. "I did not expect H.R.H. to offer his congratulations in person."

75

"I do not suppose he is alone," Charles said in a voice which, somehow, seemed to hold a note of warning.

"No?" Lord Meridan replied uncommittedly, then he shrugged his shoulders. "Well, we had best go in and face him—although I would rather see a glass of wine than the Prince at this moment."

"But, Sebastian, you cannot introduce Lucinda like this!"

Lucinda turned her head swiftly and saw the expression on Charles Holstead's face.

It was then she realized for the first time what she must look like—her wedding gown crumpled and muddy at the hem, her old cloak thrown over her shoulders, her hair streaming down her back and tossed by the wind around her face, making her look a very untidy romp.

She put up her hands to try to smooth her hair into place.

"I could not meet the Prince like this," she said miserably.

"It is not the Prince—it is who is with him," Charles said quietly.

Lord Meridan's face darkened.

"What does it matter?" he said with an air of bravado.

He whipped up the horses and Charles gave a sudden cry.

"Do not be cork-headed, Sebastian! It would be all over London tomorrow that Lucinda had spent her wedding day at a horse fair. Think what the Committee at Almack's would say! It is doubtful they would let her in—let alone you! Drive round to the stables first. Lucinda and I will enter the house the back way."

For a moment it seemed to Lucinda that Lord Meridan was going to refuse. She knew subterfuge and pretence went against the grain; and yet at the same time she was wise enough to know that what Charles was saying was reasonable.

"Damn it!" Lord Meridan said angrily. "This comes of having a wife and trying to be a respectable married man!"

Charles laughed at him.

"This is only the beginning, Sebastian. Respectability is

going to hang heavy on your shoulders. But you've had a good run for your money."

"Shut up!" Lord Meridan commanded him.

Nevertheless he drove the horses skilfully round to the mews at the back of Berkeley Square and drew up with a flourish.

Charles and Lucinda got down, and with a perfunctory lift of his hat Lord Meridan drove off, leaving them standing in the mews.

"Who is with the Prince of Wales?" Lucinda asked curiously, as soon as the phaeton was out of sight.

"Oh, I just thought that the Prince might have brought some friends with him," Charles said evasively.

She had the feeling that Charles was not telling her the truth. He led her through the stables, telling her severely that there was no time now to see the horses, and down a covered way which led into the house behind. It skirted an ornamental garden and then Lucinda found herself in a rather dark passage off which a flight of stairs led upwards.

"Come on," Charles said. "I will take you up the back stairs. I think I know which bedroom you are likely to have."

They went up the stairs. feeling, Lucinda thought, like conspirators.

Then Charles opened a door and she found herself on a broad landing with rooms on either side of it and behind she could see a grand staircase obviously winding up from the floor below.

The furniture, pictures and chandeliers were all magnificent and a little overpowering. She stared about her for a moment while Charles opened one door, shut it again and opened another.

"Oh, here's your bedchamber!" he exclaimed. "Look— they have already brought up your trunk. The coach must have got here hours ago."

Lucinda, glancing past him, could see her trunk on the floor and two maids busily unpacking it, their white mob-caps with starched streamers making her remember almost with embarrassment the untidy appearance of the village girls who had been maids at her home.

Charles shut the door again and turned and smiled at her.

"Cheer up!" he said. "You are looking rather like a lost puppy that has been left out in the rain!"

"That is exactly how I feel," Lucinda said. "I wish we could have stayed at the fair and not have had to come on here."

"You'll be all right," Charles Holstead said kindly. "It is all a bit strange at first—I can understand that."

It seemed to Lucinda that he was trying not only to cheer her up but to forewarn her against what lay ahead.

It was then that she heard voices and she said quickly in a whisper:

"I must go and look at the Prince. Is he really as handsome as they say he is?"

She tiptoed towards the top of the stairs and crouched down by the banisters to peep through them into the hall below.

Against the black and white squared marble floor, with its rich Persian rugs and white and gold panelled walls, was standing a resplendent, if slightly ridiculous, person, who bore little resemblance to the pictures she had seen of him or to her own imaginings.

And yet she recognized him and knew at once that this was the fabulous, romantic, extravagant, incredible Prince of Wales, about whom the whole country had heard so many extraordinary stories. It was hard to know where truth ended and fantasy began.

One thing was inescapable—the Prince was fat. Despite his tightly laced stays, despite his spasmodic efforts at fasting, he was undoubtedly stout, and with every promise of becoming stouter still.

His stomach bulged over his very tight pantaloons and his exquisitely tailored coat of blue satin only managed to retain its place because the two front buttons, set with diamonds, were linked together.

His snowy cravat concealed some of his chins and yet the face above it was handsome, with fine features and bright, intelligent eyes.

All in all, Lucinda thought, there was something overpowering about him, and his voice, rich and deep, was exactly what she had expected.

"I am desolated, my dear Meridan," the Prince was saying, "that we must leave without having seen your bride, but I have a party at Clarence House tonight and I cannot be late for my guests."

"No, indeed, Sire," Lord Meridan agreed. "And my wife will be greatly mortified to think that she has missed your kindly and most gracious visit, but the ceremony and the drive here proved rather too much for her. I am afraid she has a headache."

Lucinda glanced up at Charles and stifled a giggle.

"Well, let us hope that such an indisposition does not spoil your wedding night," the Prince said, and Lucinda's amusement was suddenly checked as she imagined, although she could not see it, the slight leer in His Royal Highness's eyes and the smirk on his lips.

At that moment a woman came into the hall.

"Heavens—that would be disastrous!" she said, and Lucinda could hear the insincerity in her high voice, and looking down, saw her lay a white gloved hand on Lord Meridan's arm.

It was then she saw the smartest and one of the most beautiful women she had ever beheld, dressed in a gown such as Lucinda had never imagined could exist.

The new *directoire* fashions had just reached London from the Continent and the low square-cut neck, the tiny puff sleeves, the high waist-line throwing into prominence the fullness of the breasts, were all revolutionary.

But what made Lucinda gasp was that the dress, of finest muslin, was transparent, and the wearer's slim but very feminine body was completely revealed.

If the lady wore anything under the dress it was not noticeable, but her fair hair was crowned with a magnificent tiara set with turquoise which matched her necklace and the ribbons on her gown.

The newcomer was, for want of a better expression, as lovely as an angel and yet 'angel' was not quite the right word.

There was something very sophisticated, very polished, about this woman and something in her voice—low, caressing and yet at the same time aristocratically haughty —which to Lucinda could be expressed in one word— dangerous!

The Prince had moved towards the door and yet his companion made no movement to follow him.

Instead, she stood looking up into Lord Meridan's face, and Lucinda could see very clearly the long dark lashes which half veiled her eyes.

"Has it been so tiresome?" she asked softly. "Never mind, Sebastion, you are married and Almack's is open to you again."

"It is not Almack's that matters—you know that," Lord Meridan replied.

He spoke in a very low voice and yet Lucinda could just hear what he said.

"Yes, I know," the woman answered. "But as a member of the Committee I had to be careful while you were in disgrace. Now we can start again."

"Can we?"

The question must have surprised her, for her eyes opened suddenly, and then Lucinda saw that they were not blue as she had somehow imagined, but green, flecked with curious little shades of amber which gave her almost a feline expression.

"But, of course, Sebastian," she said sweetly, with an underlying meaning in every word. "Call on me tomorrow."

His lips touched her hand and then she was moving exquisitely, her body almost naked against the light, over the marble floor and out through the front door to join the Prince of Wales in his coach.

Lord Meridan stood staring after her, then turned and walked through the door of the room they had all just left.

Lucinda got to her feet. Her eyes were enormous in her pale face and when she spoke she stammered a little.

"Wh . . . who is s . . . she?" she asked.

"I told you you should have gone to your bedchamber," Charles said sharply. "Prying and peering over the banisters—it is not becoming in a lady."

"I am not a lady," Lucinda said crossly. "I am someone who knows nothing and nobody—a country bumpkin, so tell me . . . who is she?"

"If you are referring to the lady with His Royal Highness," Charles said uncomfortably, "she is Lady Devereux. Her husband is a lord-in-waiting to His Royal Highness."

"And she is one of the hostesses at Almack's?" Lucinda said.

The pieces were beginning to fall into place in her mind. It had seemed extraordinary that someone with Lord Meridan's reputation should have been so keen to get back into what, after all, was really a social club, a meeting place for those members of Society who considered themselves smart and respectable.

"Does he love her?"

She asked the question without thinking, and saw the astonishment in Charles Holstead's face.

"Really, Lucinda!" he said a little pompously. "You must not ask me questions like that."

"Who else is there to tell me?" Lucinda enquired. "I knew about Juanita da Riva—but not about Lady Devereux."

"You knew about Juanita?" Charles Holstead repeated almost stupidly.

Lucinda nodded.

"But . . . Lord Meridan said I was not to speak about her."

She could not bring herself to say 'my husband' and there seemed no other way to refer to him.

"I should think not, indeed!" Charles Holstead retorted hotly. "I thought you said you were a country maiden— quiet and out of touch with the *beau ton*—how can you have heard of—a fancy piece like that?"

A dimple suddenly appeared on each side of Lucinda's mouth.

"As a matter of fact," she said, "I overheard one of the coachmen talking to Nat. He had brought some people to call on Mama—people who had never taken the slightest interest in us before—so I crept away and went down to the stables. Just as I got there, before they saw me, I heard the coachman telling Nat what Lord Meridan had spent on horses for Juanita da Riva. 'And she's worth the pair o' them!' he said. 'There's a woman who's all fire and spirit! I sees her a-dancin' at Covent Garden and wouldn't have minded giving her a couple of nags myself!' "

Charles looked shocked.

"I hope you didn't tell Sebastian that," he said.

"No—no. I merely asked him if she was very lovely," Lucinda answered.

"It must have given him quite a shock that you knew about such—such things," Charles said severely.

"But no one told me about Lady Devereux," Lucinda complained a little piteously.

"Now look, Lucinda," Charles said anxiously, "Sebastian is a law unto himself. You are not expecting him to have sported a lily all his life, are you?"

"No, of course I am not," Lucinda replied. "But she is so beautiful and so smart. I shall look like a freak beside her. It will be like living with Hester all over again."

"Oh, it's your appearance that is worrying you," Charles said, as if he were relieved. "Well, you must get yourself up to crack. Get some new gowns and have your hair done in a fashionable way—you cannot walk about with it hanging down your back."

"Of course not," Lucinda agreed. "But where does she get her clothes—Lady Devereux, I mean?"

"Damme, how should I know?" Charles began, only to check himself. "But I do know! I remember she kept me hanging about one day for an hour—and the horses as restless as though they were walking on hot bricks! Madame Bertin—that's the place—it is in Bond Street. And Madame is, I am told, an old battle-axe who dresses half the fashionable women in London."

Lucinda smiled.

"Thank you—I will go there."

"You will find her cursed expensive," Charles said; "not that that will worry Sebastian—his pockets are deep enough."

The door at the end of the corridor opened, and an elderly woman dressed in black silk and with a chatelain of keys hanging from her waist came bustling towards them.

She stopped at the sight of Lucinda and curtsied hurriedly.

"I must apologize, m'Lady," she said in an anxious manner, "for not having been told before that you had entered the house. I had instructed one of the footmen to let me know immediately of your Ladyship's arrival, but unfortunately he neglected his duty."

"It is not the footman's fault," Lucinda said. "Colonel

Holstead and I came in the back way. I did not think I looked tidy enough to meet His Royal Highness."

"Oh, that was how it happened, m'Lady—now I understand! Your Ladyship's bedchamber is ready for you."

"Thank you, Mrs. . . . ?" Lucinda hesitated.

"Mrs. Watson, m'Lady. I am the housekeeper and I have been here nearly twenty-five years, first with his Lordship's mother and now with his Lordship. If you will come this way . . ."

She gave Charles a disapproving look as if he should not be there. He took the hint and held out his hand to Lucinda in a friendly gesture.

"I must go now," he said. "Good luck—and do not fret."

"When am I going to see you again?" Lucinda asked.

"Not tonight," he answered; and Lucinda remembered as he said it that it would be unseemly for a bride and bridegroom to invite a third party to dinner the very night of their wedding.

"Good-bye," she said a little regretfully, and thought to drop him a curtsy before she turned and went into her room.

It was nearly two hours later when, having bathed and dressed, Lucinda walked down the broad staircase to the library where she had been told Lord Meridan would be waiting for her.

She had put on the prettiest of her new evening gowns, one of pale peach satin, but even so she knew it was woefully out of date and bore no comparison to the gown which Lady Devereux had worn.

Nevertheless, with her hair piled high on her head and wearing the diamonds which Lord Meridan had sent her, she hoped that she looked at least presentable.

She glanced at herself in the mirror just before she left the room and had a sudden longing to ask Mrs. Watson what was wrong with her. But then she knew that it would not be at all the right thing to say, and it was unlikely that the housekeeper, with her old-fashioned ideas, would have any suggestions to offer.

Already she was late for dinner and Lucinda knew that she could linger no longer but must go downstairs to face her husband.

It had been one thing to chatter away unconcernedly at the horse fair, and in the phaeton, with Charles Holstead there to laugh and tease Lord Meridan, Lucinda had forgotten her looks, her strange wedding and even the fact that she was a bride.

But now, in this big, quiet house—so overpoweringly luxurious, with an abigail helping her to dress and footmen waiting outside every door—it was quite a different thing to walk downstairs to meet a man whom she had never set eyes on until they were joined together as man and wife.

Two footmen flung open the twin mahogany doors and she walked into an enormous salon lit by hundreds of gleaming candles.

Lord Meridan was standing at the far end with his back to the lighted fire. He had changed into an exquisitely cut evening coat of grey silk, and Lucinda thought that she had no idea until that moment how handsome he was—and, at the same time, how awe-inspiring.

He was scowling as she advanced towards him; and she felt with a sinking heart that he was resenting the fact that he must stay at home and dine with her rather than join the Prince and Lady Devereux at Clarence House.

"I hope my servants have looked after you properly," Lord Meridan remarked as Lucinda reached the hearthrug.

"They were very kind, thank you," Lucinda replied. "I am sorry if I am late for dinner, but . . . my hair had got so tangled by the wind that it took a long time to get it brushed and arranged in what the maids told me is a new fashion."

"Yes, of course," Lord Meridan said.

He was not in the slightest interested in her hair or anything else about her—she realized that—and was thankful when the door opened and the butler announced dinner.

They went down a passage into a very large dining room where on the long, brilliantly polished table there was a profusion of gold ornaments.

There were orchids, too, grouped around the base of the golden candelabra and trailing in an elegant arrangement around the ornamental centre-piece and the shell-shaped comfit dishes filled with chocolates and peppermint creams.

Lucinda had never seen a dining table before which had

not been covered with a white tablecloth. She had heard that the Prince had introduced a new-fangled notion of dining off a polished table, but this was the first time she had seen one.

It was pretty, she thought, but knew that her mother would have considered it unconventional.

The butler pulled out a chair for her at the far end of the table. She realized that she would have to raise her voice to address Lord Meridan.

And quickly, because if she waited she felt her courage might not be equal to it, she said:

"I do not want to sit here—so far away from you. May I sit at the side so that we can talk? There are a lot of things I want to ask you, and it is so embarrassing to have to shout."

Lord Meridan looked astonished, but he replied courteously:

"You may sit where you wish."

Her place was moved and she sat beside him.

"That is better," she said. "It is too formal to be so far apart, and I wanted to speak with you about Sir Galahad."

This was the one subject she thought they both had in common, and soon they were talking quite easily of Lord Meridan's country house in Sussex where Sir Galahad was to be trained.

They discussed the other yearlings he had picked up at the sales and which had or had not proved their worth, and the inevitable difficulty of getting the right people to train the right horses for the right races.

Dinner passed off easily and then because Lord Meridan said he did not want any port, he moved, when Lucinda did, upstairs to the big salon which the butler said had been got ready "specially for her Ladyship."

This room was filled with flowers, all of them white, and the scent of the lilies and carnations wafted towards them as they entered the salon.

The walls were covered with the palest blue brocade and the pillars were of white with their capitals and bases of gold. Blue curtains embroidered with gold thread draped the windows.

It was a beautiful room, meant for a reception or an assembly, and Lucinda felt small and insignificant as she walked over the Aubusson carpet to sit beside the fireplace on a satin-covered sofa.

"Did your mother decorate this room?" she asked, looking around her in admiration.

"No—it was done recently," Lord Meridan replied; "in fact, I had the whole house redone. It had got old and shabby and was completely out of date."

"But what wonderful taste you have!" Lucinda exclaimed. Then she saw the expression on his face and knew, even as she said it, who had chosen the things for him.

Pale blue . . . white and gold . . . the soft pastel tones in her bedroom—she might have guessed, she thought, what a background they would make for someone like Lady Devereux, with her gold hair.

"It was extremely expensive," Lord Meridan said, "but worth it, I think. I am considering doing up Meridan Hall —that has not been touched since my father died."

"I am glad about that," Lucinda said.

He raised his eyebrows, and she added:

"I mean I . . . I would like to see it as it is. In a way, I hate changes. I think everyone does."

She was talking to prevent the silence which she sensed was going to come between them—but now it had come.

Determinedly she rose to her feet.

"I think I will retire to bed," she said. "It has been a long day and I expect you want to go out and join your friends."

"No—no—I am not going to do that," Lord Meridan said. "I am going away tomorrow."

"You are?"

There was a note of surprise in her voice; she had not expected this.

"Yes, I am visiting Charles Holstead," Lord Meridan replied. "He asked me a long time ago. It will only be for a night or two."

"Will you stay at his house near Newmarket that he was talking about this afternoon?" Lucinda asked.

"Yes," Lord Meridan answered.

"Are you racing or is there going to be a mill?" Lucinda asked.

"Perhaps both," Lord Meridan said with a slight smile.

"Oh, I wish I could come, too!" Lucinda exclaimed.

"I am afraid it is a bachelor party," Lord Meridan informed her. "That means men only—not that they are all unmarried."

"Yes, I know," Lucinda answered. "But it does seem unfair that men should have all the fun."

"You will be all right, won't you?" Lord Meridan said, as if he had just thought about it. "I expect people will come to call as soon as they know you are here—you will make new friends and there will be shopping, or whatever women do to pass the time."

"Yes, there will be shopping," Lucinda agreed. "And I suppose, as you say, I shall have to make new friends—but I do not like women very much. I suppose there is no chance of Colonel Holstead inviting me too? I could keep out of the way and perhaps no one would notice I was there."

"That is absolutely impossible," Lord Meridan said gravely. "I think, Lucinda, I should make it quite clear to you that you have got to behave very circumspectly in your new position. This afternoon was different—no one knew you at the horse fair, and, anyway, I had planned for you to come back in the carriage."

"Do you think it is really going to matter all that much?" Lucinda asked. "After all, what you wanted was a wife—they did not say what sort of wife."

"They?" Lord Meridan questioned.

"The Committee at Almack's."

"Oh, I see what you mean!" he said. "But I expect my wife to be circumspect and acceptable not only at Almack's but everywhere else in Society."

"It sounds rather dull!" Lucinda exclaimed.

"You cannot know until you have tried it," he said. "And, anyway, there is no alternative. I am sure you will soon find your feet."

"I expect so," Lucinda said dolefully.

She saw Lord Meridan's eyes go to the clock.

"It is half past ten," he said. "How long does it take you to prepare for bed?"

She turned round to face him.

"So that is why you are staying in!" she said; ". . . why you are not joining your friends . . . I was so stupid, I did not understand. But now I do! And I want . . . I . . . want to say this: You have married me because you wanted a wife who would get you into Almack's; but I am not going to be your wi . . . wife . . . your real wife . . . until we know each other better."

Lord Meridan rose to his feet. He was frowning and he looked so formidable that Lucinda felt her heart pounding.

"Am I to interpret from that slightly incoherent speech," he said, "that you have taken a distaste to me?"

"No, of course not," Lucinda said, "but you are a stranger . . . I have never seen you until today . . . and I have married you because I could not let Papa sell up our home, estate and everything we own. We have both . . . I think . . . had something to gain from our . . . marriage. But that does not mean that I want to get into bed with you . . . with someone I have hardly met!"

Lord Meridan walked across the room and back again.

"I am sure you should not be talking like this," he said. "I thought you were a young, innocent girl who did not know of such things."

"Of course I know that people sleep together when they get married," Lucinda said. "Mama and Papa always sleep in the same bed. And I know what happens to the country people . . . th . . . they have . . . babies. I am not as green as not to know that. But I know something else as well."

"And what is that?" Lord Meridan asked, almost curiously.

"It is that most people when they get married are . . . in love," Lucinda said, her chin high, her eyes very bright. "Perhaps not the smart people you know who circulate round the Prince of Wales. But, amongst ordinary people like Hester and Nat's family, a man loves a girl and a girl loves a man and they want to touch each other . . . to kiss each other and then to sleep together and have children. I do not believe it is right to . . . do that . . . unless you really want to . . . unless you l . . . love one another."

"A young girl's dreams!" Lord Meridan said scornfully.

"Is love only for those who are not in Society?" Lucinda asked. "Haven't you ever been in love?"

Her eyes met his, and she thought that if his skin had not been slightly tanned she might have seen his flush.

"I thought myself in love many times," he replied honestly.

"Then you have some idea what it is like," Lucinda said, "and you know that you are not in love with me, even though I am your wife."

She paused and added:

"I will try and behave as you wish; I will try to be worthy of bearing your name . . . but I won't bear your children because you think it is the right thing to do. And nobody . . . neither you nor any other man . . . shall sl . . . sleep in my bed unless I love him."

Her voice broke on the last two words, and without looking at him again she turned and ran from the room, shutting the door sharply behind her.

She reached her bedchamber and to her relief found that although the candles were lit there was no abigail waiting for her. She closed the door and locked it and stood trembling a little just inside the room.

For a moment she contemplated bursting into tears. Then the self-control which she had exercised over her emotions ever since she was tiny made her walk across to the dressing table to sit down and stare at her reflection in the mirror.

Her heart was thumping and her lips felt dry.

"Have I done the right thing?" she asked aloud, and knew that in saying what she had she had followed the dictates of her heart rather than the logic of her mind.

It was a question which she was still asking herself as the hours of the night went slowly past, and the question was still in the back of her mind when morning came and she saw the sun trying to shine through the heavy curtains which were pulled over her window.

She felt stifled and she rose to pull them back and open one of the windows.

The window she had chosen overlooked the square, and she saw below her a sudden flurry at the front door and a high phaeton with two magnificent horses being brought from the stables.

She pulled the curtains slightly to, so that no one should see her watching, and she stood there waiting, knowing that at any moment Lord Meridan would appear.

It was still very early and one of the grooms at the horses' heads was yawning.

Then across the red carpet which had been run over the

pavement Lord Meridan appeared. He was beautifully dressed as usual—his coat fitted without a wrinkle; his hat was set at an angle, and his boots gleamed like black diamonds as he hoisted himself into the driver's seat.

He held the reins with a confidence which was unmistakable, then the groom had taken a flying leap and the phaeton moved off.

Lucinda watched her husband go.

His profile was stern and uncompromising and there was no smile on his lips.

She wondered what it would have felt like if he had agreed to her suggestion to take her with him, to sit beside him in the phaeton.

And then she knew that she had craved the invitation not for the pleasure of his company but because of her loneliness and what was almost fear of being left alone in London with no one to guide or help her or even to show her around.

But irrepressibly the thought came to her that she was free—she could do as she liked! There was no mother to find fault and scold her; there was no Hester to be shocked at her suggestion of playing truant or omitting one of the many duties which had always fallen to her lot; there was no husband to tell her she must keep up her position.

She was free—free to do as she liked! And for the first time in her life she had money to do it with.

She turned from the window and got back into bed.

For a long time she lay staring at the ceiling and making plans, turning things over and over in her mind. When finally she rang the bell it was decisively and without any hesitation.

When the maid came Lucinda ordered breakfast in her bedroom, and while it was coming she bathed and dressed herself so that immediately she had eaten she was ready to go out.

"Can I have a carriage?" she asked the housekeeper.

"But of course, m'Lady. I will send for one immediately. Will your Ladyship be going far?"

"No, only to the shops," Lucinda answered.

"Is there anything I can get for you?" Mrs. Watson asked politely. "Or would you like a maid to accompany you?"

"No, I would rather go alone, thank you," Lucinda said.

She swept downstairs when the carriage was announced, forcing herself to walk with dignity, although she had a desire to run and jump with the sheer excitement of what lay ahead.

The carriage was a small one, but emblazoned with the Meridan crest and upholstered inside with the softest of seats.

As the horses moved off, Lucinda thought of the old uncomfortable coach which her mother used at home, and longed for her parents to see the contrast in the type of vehicle she could command for her special use.

She told the footman that she wished to go to Madame Bertin's shop in Bond Street, and as he made no comment she assumed that either he or the coachman knew the right number.

As they moved along she pressed her face to the carriage window, looking at the fine houses they passed, the shops, and, of course, the passers-by on the street. Everything she saw was exciting and she only wished she had someone to whom she could comment on all she observed.

Madame Bertin's establishment was not as large as Lucinda had expected from the outside, but as soon as she entered the soft carpeted, heavily draped showroom she was conscious of an atmosphere of expense and luxury that she had never before encountered in a shop.

There were two other ladies talking to a *vendeuse* and one glance at their gowns and gaily feathered hats made Lucinda very aware of her own badly cut dress and unimportant bonnet.

She waited for some moments until the ladies left and had been bowed ingratiatingly from the door, then the *vendeuse*, stopping on the way to tidy the shop, moved towards her and said in a high autocratic voice:

"Is there anything I can do for you, Madame?"

"I wish to see Madame Bertin," Lucinda answered.

The *vendeuse* shook her head.

"I am afraid that is impossible—Madame Bertin only sees very special clients."

Her glance at Lucinda's dress said all too clearly that Lucinda could never come into that category.

"I think, if you ask Madame Bertin, she will see me,"

Lucinda said firmly. "My name is the Countess of Meridan. I wish to speak with her privately."

"The Countess of Meridan?"

The *vendeuse* repeated the name incredulously, and added hastily in another tone altogether:

"I will enquire, my Lady, if you will be so kind as to wait a moment?"

She moved towards the far end of the salon and disappeared through a door which was marked "Private."

As if interested in some materials which had been draped on a stand nearby, Lucinda moved towards the door which had been left slightly ajar. She could hear voices inside and she quite shamelessly eavesdropped.

"There is a lady here, Madame," she could hear the *vendeuse* say, "at least, she is little more than a girl and dressed in the most dreadfully dowdy gown, who says she is the Countess of Meridan. She demands to see you."

"The Countess of Meridan? Yes, I heard that he was about to be married," an old, rather thick voice with a French accent replied.

"But, Madame—Lady Devereux's account—why, she was here only yesterday and she ordered half a dozen new gowns, and all to be made in material from France!"

"I am sure Lord Meridan will meet his obligations," the elderly voice said. "I should like to see the new Countess —show her in."

Hastily Lucinda moved away from the door, and was staring at a reticule made of a brocade which had obviously been smuggled across the Channel when the *vendeuse* came to her side.

"Madame will see you, my Lady," she said.

Lucinda put down the reticule and inclined her head.

"Thank you," she said.

She was led back to the private door. The room into which she was shown was small and rather stifling; everywhere there were rolls of silk, satin, brocade and lamé. There were sprig muslins and French batiste and gaberdine all piled together one on top of the other in the corners, making a kaleidoscope of colour.

In the very centre of the room, sitting in a low armchair beside a table littered with patterns and ribbons, and looking rather like a very ancient and lined Buddha, was Madame Bertin.

She was over seventy; she dressed all the quality of London and had done so for fifty years.

When she was very young she had come to England from France as a lady's maid. She had been seduced by her employer's husband who had set her up in a small house of her own. Bored when he was not with her, she started as a milliner, going from house to house of other women like herself who had protectors, and then to the wives of rich shopkeepers.

But her talent was too obvious to remain unnoticed by the quality. A famous beauty appeared in St. James's in a hat which set the town talking, and little Bertin became a vogue.

Money was lent her to open a small shop, her clientele grew until she had moved not once but several times. When she reached Bond Street there was no reason to be ambitious any longer.

Everyone flocked to her, the great hostesses and their daughters, the famous play-actresses, the mistresses of the nobility—there was really no one left except those who couldn't pay the price.

Madame Bertin had grown old and bored.

There were few women, she decided, worth the bother of creating anything new and sensational. Everyone who was anyone came to her as a matter of course and, as there was little competition, Madame Bertin found it difficult to arouse much enthusiasm for a new fashion and a different material.

She very seldom saw her clients now; she found their chatter tiring, and it was really only curiosity which made her want to see the wife of the Earl of Meridan, from whom she had received a great deal of money one way or another during the past ten years.

She looked up as the door opened, making no attempt to rise because, having grown fat and heavy with the years, it was an effort to get out of her chair once she had got into it.

She saw standing looking at her, a child—for she was little more—wearing a badly made dress in a hideous shade of beige with an ugly bonnet, appallingly trimmed with cheap ribbons, perched on her dark hair.

It was a strange, rather appealing little face, Madame Bertin thought at first glance. And then two big eyes looked into hers and a soft voice which was unexpectedly musical said:

"I have come to you, Madame, because you are the only person who can help me. Could you contrive to make me smart—and, if possible, beautiful?"

6

The traffic in London presented no problem to Lord Meridan. He drove his curricle at what some considered a dangerous speed, but because of the excellent way in which he handled the reins he actually constituted a far less danger than the slower-moving phaetons and carriages.

With his high hat set at a jaunty angle, Lord Meridan was feeling pleased with himself.

He had spent a most enjoyable time with Charles Holstead, he had made money at the races and at the cockfighting, and he had discovered what he believed to be a new champion fighter to whom he had extended his patronage.

The weather had been good, and the visit could not have been more pleasant or amusing from the time he had arrived at Charles's country house until today, when they had left another country mansion where they had spent the night after a riotous dinner party.

The visit which had been intended to last only a few days, had extended to nearly a fortnight. But, then, who could have anticipated that the Prince of Wales would turn up at Newmarket with Lady Devereux in his party? But he had, and Lord Meridan had left Charles's house to stay a few days with the Prince's host and had, gone on from there to another bachelor party at which the 'ladybirds,' as Charles called them, had been even more luscious and enticing than he himself had provided at Holstead Towers.

"You are well in pocket, Sebastian!" Charles said now as they swung round a narrow corner and missed a heavily laden dray by inches.

"Pleasantly so," Lord Meridan answered. "You are an excellent host, Charles—I hope you will invite me again."

"It will be some time," Charles said a trifle grimly, "unless I can win back at Brooks's what I lost at the races."

"You should have taken my tips, my dear fellow," Lord Meridan said indifferently. He was so wealthy himself that he had little idea of how gaming losses could so easily cripple a man when it came to entertainment or doing the things in which he was most interested.

"Another time I will," Charles said; "if there is another time."

"What do you mean?" Lord Meridan asked quickly. "Is it as bad as all that?"

"Not as far as I am concerned," Charles said, "but I think you have forgotten something these last two weeks."

"Have I?" Lord Meridan asked. "What?"

"Lucinda," Charles replied.

"Good gracious! Whatever makes you say a thing like that?" Lord Meridan asked in genuine surprise. "I had not forgotten her, and she will have been all right. After all, London can be most entertaining at this time of the year."

"I had really forgotten her myself," Charles said honestly. "There were so many other things—and so many other women, if it comes to that—to think about. But now I am remembering our last drive into London when she was with us. It seems a bit callous to have left her alone in a city she had never visited, with no relations and no friends as far as we know."

"Oh, she would manage," Lord Meridan said easily. Charles did not answer, and after a moment he broke out angrily: "Damn it all, Charles! What do you expect me to do? Be a nursemaid to a girl who doesn't know her oats? She'll have to grow up on her own—or I'll get someone to teach her."

"Who, for instance?" Charles asked, and added mischievously: "Lady Devereux?"

Lord Meridan frowned. He never thought it amusing to be teased about his love affairs.

"But seriously, Sebastian," Charles went on, before he could speak, "I think you will have to do something about

Lucinda. Haven't you got a sister, an aunt or someone, who could help the child over her first hurdles?"

"I haven't many relations, except in the grave, thank God," Lord Meridan replied. "And if they were alive they would be of little use. They always were miserable types and talked about me as 'poor Sebastian' as if I were an imbecile or a cripple."

Charles threw back his head and laughed.

"I wish I could have heard them!" he cried. "There are not many people who refer to you as 'poor Sebastian'."

"That's why I resented it," Lord Meridan answered grimly.

"And so you have been showing them ever since that you are nothing of the sort," Charles said, with a sudden flash of perception.

"Damn it all!" Lord Meridan exclaimed. "Stop criticizing me, Charles—I won't have it! And stop fussing about Lucinda—she will be all right, I'll see to that."

"I wonder what she has done these last two weeks?" Charles said reflectively. "You know, Sebastian, she might not be bad-looking if she were properly gowned."

"I am not prepared to discuss my wife," Lord Meridan said, and he used his coldest and most awe-inspiring voice.

Charles chuckled.

"Trying to set me down, eh, Sebastian? Well, I'll not have it! I will take Lucinda out myself and buy her a new bonnet."

"If you do I shall call you out," Lord Meridan said sharply.

"A duel? Really, Sebastian, you are getting quite old-fashioned! All the smart ladies accept presents these days from their beaux—and who should know that better than you?"

Lord Meridan flicked his horses with the whip, which made them start forward at an even quicker pace.

"Curse you, Charles!" he said, and this time he sounded really angry. "If you won't be quiet I will set you down here and make you walk home!"

They were passing Buckingham Palace, driving towards Hyde Park Corner.

"Let us see who is in Rotten Row this evening," Charles

said. "I feel that I have been away so long there might be a few new faces."

"Don't you believe it!" Lord Meridan replied. "The same old lot will be there—simpering, scheming and intriguing, just as they always have done. Wasn't it Beau Brummel who said that Society was a cock-fight fought by hens?"

"Sounds like him," Charles replied. "I never could stick the fellow, even though he is the vogue."

They swung round Hyde Park Corner and entered the Park by the Achilles Statue. Here were gathered all the carriages and vehicles of the social world, their occupants gossiping while they stared at the passers-by.

Charles and Lord Meridan tipped their hats half a dozen times and drove on, looking at the elegant figures of the women escorted by the fobbishly dressed, high-hatted men with their gold-topped canes.

"There you are—the same old lot!" Lord Meridan muttered beneath his breath; and then surprisingly felt Charles nudging him.

"Look," he exclaimed, "who's that?"

Ahead of them there was a lightly built curricle drawn by two perfectly matched horses which brought an exclamation of surprise to Lord Meridan's lips.

"What a pair!" he ejaculated. "Now where the hell can they have come from? There was nothing like that at Tattersall's last week—no, damn it! I wasn't there last week, but the week before. God, what I must have missed!"

The two horses were jet black with long tails and silky manes. Their harness was ornamented with silver, but the leather was black and matched the paint on the glistening curricle which had not a touch of colour on it.

"A natty turn-out!" Lord Meridan muttered, and then felt Charles's elbow nudge him again.

"Look who is sitting beside the driver," he said. "It's Kingsclere! I'd know the back of his head anywhere."

"It can't be," Lord Meridan contradicted. "I offered him any wage he'd like to ask if he would come to me two years ago, and he merely said he was comfortable where he was."

"It's Kingsclere," Charles repeated stubbornly. "The

best handler of horses in the whole country—and yet he's not driving them. Who the hell is she, Sebastian?"

For the first time Lord Meridan looked at the driver of the curricle.

He saw that it was a woman, that she was extremely elegant and her waist was very small. But it was the effect she created which not only made him stare but kept the heads of everyone they were passing turning towards her.

While the curricle and her horses were black, she herself wore a vivid coral-coloured driving coat made of some thin material which revealed rather than concealed the perfection of her figure.

On her dark hair, piled high on her head so that it showed her long graceful neck, she sported at an impudent angle an absurd and daring little hat trimmed with cocks' feathers of the same coral as her coat.

She looked bizarre, and at the same time the whole ensemble was outstandingly chic and arresting.

"Who the hell is she?" Charles asked again, as Lord Meridan manœuvred his horses forward to draw alongside.

As if the vision ahead of him realized his intention, she suddenly whipped up her horses and drew ahead at a fast pace, causing Lord Meridan to grit his teeth and force his own pair to a greater effort.

Unfortunately, his chestnuts, magnificent though they were, had already done a long and tiring journey, while the ebony pair ahead were obviously fresh.

"She's getting away from us!" Charles said almost in an agony. "I must know who she is, Sebastian!"

"And I want to know where the devil she got those horses," Lord Meridan replied.

"Not only did she get the horses but she's got Kingsclere as well," Charles complained.

"I won't believe it is Kingsclere until I have spoken to him," Lord Meridan said.

"You haven't much chance of doing that unless you get some more speed out of those mules of yours," Charles said tauntingly.

"If you ever call my horses mules again I will flog you within an inch of your life!" Lord Meridan retorted.

"Well, let them prove they are decent horseflesh by catching up that vehicle in front," Charles challenged.

Perhaps because the lady they were pursuing did not intend to elude them completely, they drew alongside her by the time she had reached Knightsbridge Barracks.

As they passed, she turned a laughing face towards them and drew in her horses.

"Stop—for God's sake stop, Sebastian! She's ready to speak to us!" Charles said, raising his hat and turning his face eagerly to the left.

And then as Lord Meridan brought the horses hastily to a standstill he realized, as he, too, turned to look, that Charles, sitting beside him, was silent and open-mouthed.

The vision in the flame coat and impudent hat bowed to them politely.

"Good day, Colonel Holstead! How are you . . . m . . . my Lord?"

She stammered a little as if she had meant to say "Sebastian" and then lost her nerve.

"Lucinda!" Lord Meridan ejaculated, the name coming between his lips in what was almost a gasp.

"I had no idea you had returned," Lucinda said. "It is delightful to see you. What do you think of my new pair?"

"What do I think of them?" Lord Meridan replied, finding his voice at last.

But words failed him, and he stared for a moment at the horses and then back at Lucinda.

"You didn't choose these," he said at length, accusingly, "Kingsclere did?"

"But of course," Lucinda smiled. "I have engaged him to build me up a stable. You don't mind, I hope?"

"Mind!" Lord Meridan growled, almost speechless, and furious with himself because he could not find the right words with which to answer such a statement.

"Kingsclere can't have left the Duke," Charles Holstead said almost pathetically, as if such a course was utterly impossible.

"Oh yes, he has," Lucinda said.

"Now what magic did you use to entice him away?" Charles asked. "We have all been trying to do that for years, haven't we, Kingsclere? And you refused us all. Aren't I right?"

100

"Quite right, Sir," Kingsclere said woodenly.

He was a thin, wiry little man of about fifty, with hair that was just beginning to turn grey and shrewd blue eyes that twinkled.

His reputation as regards horses was so high that rumour had it that the Prince of Wales had commanded the Duke of Melchester to give him Kingsclere as a Christmas present; and the Duke was reputed to have replied that the Prince could have his wife, his house and any of his damned children—but he was not parting with Kingsclere, even if he had to cross the Channel and serve under Bonaparte!

"Why, in God's name, have you gone to her Ladyship?" Charles asked, coming, as usual, to the point, but speaking in a manner which was not in the least offensive.

"Her Ladyship knows the answer to that," Kingsclere said solidly.

"Nat had asked him to help me," Lucinda said. "You will remember, my Lord, that I told you about Nat?"

"Of course—your groom," Lord Meridan said, "the one who informed you that marriage would be a fight."

"Well, Kingsclere is Nat's first cousin," Lucinda said, as if that explained everything, "and when I told him how hopeless I felt about buying the right horses and building up a stable he offered to come to me."

"That was very agreeable of him," Lord Meridan said sourly, as though Kingsclere were not there.

"We seem to be blocking the way," Lucinda said, glancing over her shoulder. "I think we had best be moving."

"But, Lucinda . . ." Charles expostulated, only to find that the words were spoken to the air and that already Lucinda with her magnificent pair of horses had moved away from them.

"Go after her, Sebastian!" Charles said urgently. "There is so much more I wish to hear."

"You will doubtless meet again," Lord Meridan replied in a cold voice.

He turned his horses round and headed in a different direction from that Lucinda had taken. As he drove back through the crowds, his mouth was set in a tight line. He looked neither to right nor left, nor made any effort to raise his hat to his acquaintances.

101

"Damn it all, Sebastian, this is the outside of enough! I can't get the hang of it at all—horses, Kingsclere—and did you see Lucinda? By God, she is a beauty! Somebody's altered her."

It was just what Lord Meridan was thinking, but he was not going to say so.

Charles went on talking.

"She has done something to her skin, for one thing—it was white! And her eyes . . . ! Of course she's got her hair up. But she's different—different altogether. And, the devil take it, to get hold of Kingsclere . . . !"

Charles found he was talking to himself.

There was no response from Lord Meridan, who was riding with grim determination towards Berkeley Square. When they arrived there he said:

"I don't suppose you wish to come in—the groom will take you home."

Charles Holstead, who was longing above all else to get inside the house and find out more, knew by the very surliness of the invitation that he was not expected to accept it.

And so, reluctantly, more from a sense of tact rather than because he was afraid to defy his friend, he let the curricle drive him away to his rooms in Curzon Street.

Lord Meridan entered his house with a frown on his brow which his servants knew all too well. The major-domo bowed, but made no effort to speak until he was spoken to.

"Brandy!" Lord Meridan said sharply, and, walking through the hall, entered the library and threw himself down in a chair beside the hearth.

He felt he wanted time to think, to consider what had happened.

When the footman brought the decanter of brandy and set it beside him on a silver tray he looked up and said:

"Is her Ladyship in the house?"

"I don't think she has returned, m'Lord," the footman replied.

"Inform her Ladyship when she does return that I am back and wish to speak to her."

"Very good, m'Lord."

The footman withdrew, closing the door behind him

quietly. Outside he made a grimace at his fellow footman which told him most expressively exactly the mood the master was in. Then he went to find the butler, to tell him to relay the message to another footman, who would carry it to Lucinda's lady's maid, who would, in her turn, pass it to Lucinda.

All this took time, and while the correct procedure was running the gauntlet of the correct hierarchy of the servant's hall, Lucinda had come into the house and gone upstairs to her room.

She guessed that Lord Meridan was back and she had no wish to see him at the moment. Going to her bedchamber, she took off her driving clothes and was actually in her bath by the time Lord Meridan's message arrived.

About ten minutes later, by the same process of a message passing from servant to servant, the butler, entering the library, said quietly:

"Her Ladyship presents her compliments, my Lord, and regrets that as she is at the moment changing she is not able to be with your Lordship immediately."

"Very well," Lord Meridan said. "Bring me some more brandy."

It was nearly an hour later and Lord Meridan had drunk a considerable amount from the second decanter when the door opened and Lucinda appeared.

He looked up at her and there was quite an appreciable pause before he got slowly to his feet.

She came into the room and as she smiled at him a little uncertainly he realized that his first impression of her had been, "My God, what a wonderful figure!" and, his second, a considerable feeling of irritation that his wife should be so scantily dressed.

Lucinda wore a robe of transparent gauze which showed very clearly the soft, exquisite curves of her body—the tiny waist, the small pear-shaped breasts and an almost Grecian line from the hip to ankle.

She was dressed for the evening with her dark hair piled elegantly by a master hand high on her head. Jewels from the Meridan collection glittered around her ears and in her hair.

Round her neck was a magnificent necklace of emeralds, accentuating the strange whiteness of her skin, which seemed to have a velvet texture that reminded Lord Meridan of something. Then he remembered a magnolia—and found himself wondering whether, indeed, it felt like one.

Lucinda came nearer until she stood beside him.

He had forgotten how tiny she was, and now as she looked up at him he saw how large her eyes were in her small, pointed face—and that her lips were red, far redder than he had ever remembered them to be.

They neither of them said anything for the moment.

Then, as if the words were being jerked out of him, he said:

"What have you been doing to yourself?"

"While you have been away?" Lucinda asked, which they both knew was not what he had meant.

"While I have been away," Lord Meridan repeated, almost stupidly, he thought.

"It's been a long time, hasn't it?" Lucinda said artlessly. "But I expect you were enjoying your visit. I heard you acquired a fighter—is he up to scratch?"

"Who told you that?" Lord Meridan asked in astonishment.

"Oh, I have forgotten who it was," Lucinda said. "Someone who had been at Newmarket and seen the fight."

"I hope he turns out to be worth the money I have staked on him," Lord Meridan said.

"I expect you are a good judge," Lucinda said—a trifle doubtfully, Lord Meridan thought, as if she was saying it more from politeness than conviction.

"Hell take it!" he said suddenly. "I don't want to talk about fighters—I want to talk about you. Where have you been and what have you been doing? Where did you get those clothes?"

"I bought them," Lucinda said sweetly. "I hope you do not mind my taking the jewels from the safe. Your secretary told me that your mother left them to be worn by all the future Lady Meridans."

"I want to know more than that!" Lord Meridan said.

Lucinda's eyes went towards the clock on the mantelpiece.

"I do wish I could relate all that has happened since

your departure," she said, "but I should be late for dinner."

"You are dining out?" Lord Meridan asked.

"I am afraid so," Lucinda answered. "You see, I had no idea you were returning tonight, otherwise I would have made other arrangements."

"Damn it all, you can make other arrangements now!" he said almost roughly. "I can send a groom with a note to these—these friends of yours, whoever they may be. Tell them the truth and say your husband has returned and wishes to dine with you."

"I wish I could do that," Lucinda said, "but unfortunately my host might be offended. And you, of all people, know how an empty place at the table might upset him."

"Who are you talking about?" Lord Meridan asked, but knowing almost as soon as he asked the question what the answer would be.

"His Royal Highness the Prince of Wales," Lucinda said. "He most graciously asked me to dine at Clarence House tonight. I expect he will be delighted to see you, if you can spare the time to drop in later on."

She turned towards the door, her figure moving with an almost feline grace beneath the soft green gauze of her dress.

"Wait! Wait!" Lord Meridan cried, as she reached the door. "You cannot go to Clarence House alone. Surely you know that!"

"But of course I can't," Lucinda said, "and Mr. Brummel has most kindly undertaken to escort me. He is waiting now, I believe, outside in his carriage."

"Mr. Brummel!" Lord Meridan exclaimed. "Beau Brummel?"

"Of course," Lucinda answered. "He has been so very obliging—in fact, he chose my curricle for me. I do hope you liked it."

Lord Meridan glared across the room at her. He was well aware that he had been about to say that the curricle was too *outré* for someone in her position.

It seemed that she realized that this was at the back of his mind, and now with a smile which seemed to light up her whole face she waved her hand at him and was gone.

He heard the soft tap of her shoes moving across the hall—Beau Brummel to escort her and waiting outside!

Lord Meridan poured himself another glass of brandy and drank it down without even tasting it.

In the coach Lucinda sank down beside Mr. Brummel and he raised her hand perfunctorily to his lips.

"My husband is back," she said. "I met him with Colonel Holstead in the Park this evening. When they saw the curricle, the horses and Kingsclere, their mouths fell open. Charles actually looked like a surprised goldfish!"

Beau Brummel laughed.

This child amused him more than anyone he had met for a long time. She had an ingenuous manner of saying things which he had thought was his particular perquisite, but sometimes she seemed to beat him at his own game.

"I saw you," he said. "You looked magnificent! The whole Park was talking about your turn-out."

"You have been so kind," Lucinda said. "I could never have achieved it without your advice and help."

"I am not always destructive," Beau Brummel said; "in fact, I only destroy those who thoroughly deserve it."

"I have always found you the kindest person one could possibly imagine," Lucinda said with deep sincerity.

Her words made Beau Brummel look a little uncomfortable; he preferred people to be against him rather than for him.

But the story of Lucinda had touched his heart—if, indeed, he had one. He had remembered his own struggle for social recognition, the time when he had been nobody and everyone had seemed intent on making him feel insignificant and a nonentity. Well, he had proved to the world that he was not that!

And because he had seen a little of himself in Lucinda he had helped her.

That old witch Madame Bertin had told him about her. He had gone into the shop with the reigning toast of St. James's, and was fingering the ribbons which had just been smuggled across the Channel, when Madame Bertin had called him into her room and told him about Lucinda.

He was quite certain she had done the same thing to a dozen important hostesses, because, overnight, as it were, Lucinda became the rage.

There was never a woman born who did not like to patronize someone who was young and unfledged—so long as she was likely, ultimately, to be a success. And there was no doubt about the latter.

Lucinda, dressed by Madame Bertin, but armed with her own wit and an unquenchable spirit of adventure, had amused and intrigued the *haut ton*.

But this would, perhaps, have not been enough if there had not been a double, underlying motive behind it.

To "take up" Lucinda was a chance to get even with that odious, stuck-up Lord Meridan. He was treating his new wife badly, was he? Well, they would show him! He had been too long in the Prince's favour not to arouse the jealousy, hatred and malice of those in whose way he stood. And there were quite a lot of women, too, who resented his preoccupation with others of their sex, who were only too willing to champion the injured wife.

"This is your first visit to Clarence House," Beau Brummel said reflectively.

"Yes, and I am longing to see it," Lucinda told him.

"Hope you won't be disappointed," the Beau answered. "It is rather like Prinny himself—too ornate, too flashy and too luxurious."

"You are unkind!" Lucinda said. "It is very obliging of him to invite me."

"I told him he would be missing something if he didn't," Beau Brummel said.

"Then it's due to you!" Lucinda exclaimed, turning her big eyes upon him. "Oh, thank you—thank you, dear Mr. Brummel! It's like a fairy-tale to be dressed like this, and going with you to dine with the Prince of Wales. Do you think I look all right?"

She asked the question anxiously with a childishness which made the most sophisticated and *blasé* man in London smile.

"You grace the Meridan jewels," he answered, and saw by the sudden flash on Lucinda's face that he could not have said anything that could have pleased her more.

He had spoken deliberately. He had heard only too often what had been said about Lord Meridan's intended bride when all the world had thought he was marrying Hester.

"Thank you," Lucinda said in a very slow voice. "'I can't explain . . . but it's the most wonderful compliment I have ever had in my whole life."

"Don't be humble," Beau Brummel said sharply. "Never be humble to anyone. You have got to force them to admire you, force them to notice you. They will never do that if you crawl about on your stomach."

"Was I doing that?" Lucinda asked.

"Yes," he replied.

"Then I won't do it again," Lucinda said. "If they don't compliment me . . . I . . . I'll spit in their peepers!"

The stable-boys' slang made Beau Brummel laugh. He was still laughing when they stepped out under the white portico of the doorway of Clarence House.

Lord Meridan, arriving about eleven o'clock, not having allowed himself to come sooner, found a whole stream of people being set down in their carriages and pushing their way towards the great staircase.

"It's one of the Prince's big occasions!" he thought wryly, remembering how usually he made every effort to avoid them.

Tonight, he told himself, Lucinda would doubtless be very glad to see him. Even if in some mysterious manner she had got herself invited to Clarence House it was unlikely she would know many people—and this, he supposed, was as good an opportunity as any to introduce her to some of the people she ought to know.

Despite these righteous feelings, he was not in a particularly good mood, and having snapped at two or three acquaintances who asked him how he was, he passed into the big gold and yellow salon where the Prince was holding court, surrounded by his favourites, rather like a sultan dispensing favours in the harem.

The Prince greeted Lord Meridan with outstretched hand.

"I thought we should see you here tonight," he said. "How did that filly run in the last race? I was sorry I could not wait to see her."

They had a short talk on racing, and Lord Meridan, seeing Lady Devereux making her way towards him through the crowd, moved deftly in the opposite direction, feeling that this was not the moment to find himself entangled with the lady of his fancy.

He moved through the various rooms, but there was no sign of Lucinda. Perhaps, he thought compassionately, the poor child had gone home.

And then from the Chinese Room he heard a burst of laughter and saw a crowd of dandies, many of whom he despised. Looking over their shoulders he could see to his astonishment and deep annoyance that the centre of interest was Lucinda.

She was chattering away, and Lord Meridan realized to his chagrin that she was describing a mill in graphic detail amid bursts of irrepressible laughter from her audience.

" 'Lord save us, but 'e 'as the devil's trident in 'is 'and!' Battling Belcher said, and down he went for the count. . . ."

Lucinda, with an instinct for dramatization, paused.

Lord Meridan pushed his way through the spellbound audience and said sharply:

"Lucinda! I have been looking for you everywhere!"

"Well, now you have found me," Lucinda said happily.

"Oh, Lord Meridan, you could not deprive us of the end of the story!" someone ejaculated with a foreign accent, and Lord Meridan saw that the speaker was a man he particularly disliked.

Comte Jacques de Falaise was one of the refugees from the Revolution who had escaped to London. He was an extremely good-looking, polished French aristocrat who managed to fascinate every woman on whom he turned his glance.

He and Lord Meridan had often been rivals for the hand of the same lady, and it was regrettable, but true, that several times the Frenchman had beaten the Englishman to the bed!

"I wish," Lord Meridan said stiffly to the Comte, "that my wife should accompany me."

He held out his hand to Lucinda.

"You are a spoil-sport, Meridan!" one of the dandies complained. "Pay no attention to him, Lady Meridan— let's hear the end of the story!"

"Another time," Lucinda replied.

"No! No!" several other gentlemen cried.

But Lord Meridan, his face dark with anger, drew Lucinda away, muttering as they walked from the room:

"You are making an exhibition of yourself!"

His feelings were not soothed by hearing behind him a certain rather raucous laughter which he knew was directed against himself.

"You are very late," Lucinda said. "We finished dinner a long time ago."

"I had other things to occupy me," Lord Meridan said loftily.

"At Brooks's?" she asked teasingly.

Lord Meridan did not deign to answer her.

They were walking rather quickly through the rooms, and she wondered where he was taking her until she realized they were making for the main staircase.

"We are not leaving?" she asked in consternation.

"Why not?" he enquired. "You have seen all there is to see here."

"But I haven't!" she expostulated. "Besides, I cannot go without saying good-bye to the Prince. It would be rude after his kindness to me."

Lord Meridan stared at her.

"I wish to take you home," he said. "I want to talk to you."

"Tomorrow will be time enough for that," she said. "You are cross—I don't know why, but I suspect it is because you haven't had a good dinner! It's your own fault . . . if you had told me you were coming I would have told the chef to cook something very special. But please don't spoil my evening . . . I am enjoying myself so much. There are lots of rooms I haven't seen. And . . . don't you think it is rather a good thing that people should see us here together? There have been remarks about my being left alone so soon after our marriage."

Lord Meridan could not believe his ears. If one of the statues around the room had come to life and told him how he should behave he could not have been more astonished. This child—this chit—to tell him what he should do and what he should not do was intolerable!

He opened his lips to answer Lucinda sharply, then there was a heavy hand on his shoulder and a thick, plummy voice which he knew so well in his ear.

"She's enchanting, Sebastian—exquisite! Already she's the toast of St. James's."

It was the Prince, and Lord Meridan knew now there was no escape.

"Oh, Sire," he heard Lucinda say, "please, please show me the new picture that you bought at Christie's yesterday! Everyone's talking about it, and I am longing to see it."

There was no surer way to Prinny's heart, Lord Meridan thought drily, than to ask him to talk of his treasures, and that he was always prepared to do interminably.

"I was just taking my wife home," Lord Meridan began, and then suddenly saw Lucinda's eyes looking up into his beseechingly. It reminded him of a dog longing for a walk, hoping that his master would not deny it to him.

Almost despite himself, he found the words that were on his lips altered into something else.

"I was just—going to ask you where this new acquisition was hidden, Sire," he said.

"Come along—come along, both of you," the Prince said, delighted.

He led them back into the crowded drawing-room, and Lord Meridan, moving instinctively nearer to Lucinda to guide her through the guests, felt the pressure of her fingers on his arm.

"Thank you," she said softly.

And although he tried to glare back at her, it was, as a glare, somewhat unsuccessful.

7

Lord Meridan rose before noon, feeling surprisingly fresh because he had gone straight home from Clarence House the night before, and had not, as was his usual custom, gambled until the early hours of the morning.

He dressed carefully, tying his high, snow-white cravat into an exquisite shape at the first attempt, which drew an exclamation of admiration from his valet, and with his tasselled boots gleaming he walked slowly down the stairs to the hall.

It was a warm sunny day, and waiting for him outside the open front door he could see prancing at the restraining hand of the groom a bay mare which he had bought at Tattersall's the week before he left London and which he had not yet ridden.

It put him in a good humour and as he set off for the Park he was smiling, so that the two footmen watching him go raised their eyebrows a trifle quizzically and would have made impertinent remarks had not the butler been within earshot.

Already the carriages were sweeping their way to Rotten Row, bearing occupants sporting the very latest fashion in bonnets and carrying small, lace-trimmed parasols to protect them from the sun.

The majority of men were on horseback—it was considered rather effete to drive in the morning—and by the time Lord Meridan reached the Achilles Statue there were a large number of his acquaintances cantering either in front or behind him.

He did not stop to gossip at that well-known rendezvous

but passed on to where he saw, as he expected, an elegant open carriage drawn up at the side of Rotten Row, and a very fetching bonnet trimmed with blue feathers turned towards him as he approached.

He swept his tall hat from his head and bent from the saddle to kiss the white gloved hand which Lady Devereux held out to him.

"I did not imagine you would be here so early," he said.

She raised her amber-flecked eyes to his.

"It was the only chance to see you alone," she murmured almost beneath her breath.

"You are looking very lovely," he told her.

She was, in fact, a picture in her white muslin dress trimmed with blue ribbons, and the smile which she gave him for the compliment was intimate and caressing.

"You did not speak to me last night," she complained, pouting a little, which she knew drew attention to her cupid-bow mouth.

"There were so many friends to whom I must introduce my wife," Lord Meridan replied.

"Your wife . . . ah yes!" Lady Devereux said, and there was a sudden chill in her voice. "As soon as I returned to London I learnt that she has become the talk of the town."

"Indeed?"

Lord Meridan's response was abrupt, but Lady Devereux continued:

"I saw her this morning, but she seemed too preoccupied with the gentleman who escorted her to notice me."

Lord Meridan looked up the Row.

"Lucinda is here, then?"

"She passed me on horseback perhaps ten minutes ago," Lady Devereux replied. "How strange that she did not tell you that she was riding! Or perhaps she had very good reasons for keeping it a secret. . . ."

There was no disguising now the cat-like tone in Lady Devereux's voice.

Lord Meridan drew himself up.

"I will go and join my wife," he said. "Your servant, madam."

He bowed, set his hat at a jaunty angle on his head, but now he was frowning and there was no longer a smile on his lips.

Lady Devereux watched him ride away. He was, without doubt, the most handsome man in the whole Row—and the look in her eyes was very feline.

Lord Meridan rode on. A number of friends waved or raised their hats to him, but he ignored them and continued searching the crowds for one particular person.

It was some time before he saw her, and his attention was taken first by the horse she rode—an incomparable grey, such as he knew only Kingsclere could have procured.

Then he saw Lucinda's companion, and his face darkened.

There was no mistaking the foppish over-elegance of the Comte Jacques de Falaise. He was well mounted, for he did not ride his own horses—which he could not afford—but there were always friends prepared to let him exercise their animals.

He was a good horseman, and he was managing to keep quite a spirited mount in check while he leant from the saddle towards Lucinda.

"You are entrancing—you make me dream of spring," the Comte had said to Lucinda when she met him a little earlier; and Kingsclere, who was in attendance, had moved in a well-trained manner out of earshot.

"You always say the most delightful things to me," Lucinda answered. "Even if you don't mean them, I like hearing you say them."

"That is not the correct manner in which to receive a compliment," the Comte said with a smile.

"I know," Lucinda answered. "But I have never received compliments before—so now, when I go to bed, I count them up one by one."

"Then I shall tell you, so that you can recall it tonight, that you are the smartest and most elegant rider in the whole Park," the Comte said suavely.

She laughed at him, her teeth like pearls against her red lips.

"That's something I really want to hear," she said. "It would indeed be shameful, with such a fine mount, if I couldn't handle him."

"But you ride like a goddess!" the Comte exclaimed. "I have never seen a woman like you!"

"Kingsclere says that either one is born for the saddle or one is not—and there is nothing one can do for those who are not," Lucinda said.

"I am not interested in Kingsclere's opinion," the Comte replied; "I am interested only in you. You are a very evasive lady! I have tried to capture you like a butterfly in my net. But you slip through my fingers, you elude me—it's exciting, but at the same time it is very frustrating!"

"You talk a lot of nonsense, you know!" Lucinda smiled. "What do you mean . . . that you have tried to capture me?"

"Shall I try and explain?" the Comte asked softly.

Lucinda's eyes dropped before his. There was some knowledge she decided that she did not want to learn.

"No . . . thank you," she said quickly. "Tell me about yourself. Do you miss France . . . your own country?"

"I miss nothing when I am with you. I just want to go on listening to you—to look at you."

He saw the sudden gleam in Lucinda's eyes and asked:

"Why does that please you so much?"

"Because you said you like to look at me," Lucinda answered. "Nobody before has ever looked at me, except in disgust."

"That I will not credit!" the Comte exclaimed.

"It's true," Lucinda replied. "You see, my sister is so beautiful . . ."

"But you have so much more than mere beauty," he interrupted. "You have character and intelligence in your face—and a figure that is beyond words! How is it that no one has ever told you these things before?"

"They . . . it's a long story," Lucinda answered, "but, I promise you, they did not."

"Then I must compensate for such omissions of good taste," the Comte said. "Shall I tell you just what you look like to me? Shall I tell you what emotions are aroused within my heart when I see you?"

There was an ardour in his voice which made Lucinda drop her eyes—which was why she did not see Lord Meridan approach.

The first thing she knew was that his horse was beside hers and his voice—sharp, clear and authoritative—said:

"Good morning, Lucinda. I might have hoped that you

would have waited for me before coming into the Park. But, now I am here, we can ride together."

She turned her face towards him and he saw the flush on her cheeks.

He ignored the Comte, and Lucinda, somewhat flustered, turned to hold out her hand in farewell. The Comte raised it to his lips. There was a pressure on her fingers which she understood.

Then she found herself riding quickly up the Row, away from the more fashionable parts, towards the Kensington end of the Park.

Kingsclere was following them, and, as they drew in their reins, Lord Meridan spoke over his shoulder:

"I will see her Ladyship home, Kingsclere."

"Very good, m'Lord."

The groom wheeled his horse and cantered away.

For a moment Lord Meridan's attention was taken by the animal—it was better than anything his grooms had the privilege of riding.

"How did you do it?" he asked, and his voice was not so frosty as it had been before.

"How did I get Kingsclere?" Lucinda asked, grateful for the diversion. "So many people have asked me that. I think he was delighted with the idea of having a free hand. Besides, as you already know, he is Nat's cousin, and was glad to do him a favour."

"One hardly expects people of Kingsclere's calibre to change their positions for such a personal reason," Lord Meridan said drily.

Lucinda gave a little laugh.

"I very nearly went down on my knees to him, as well," she confessed. "Mr. Brummel told me that only Kingsclere could give me what I wanted."

"And what was that?" Lord Meridan asked.

"A stable of my own—as good as, if not better than, yours," she replied.

He looked at her in astonishment.

"But who put such an ambition into your head?"

"It's something I have always craved, really," she answered, "although there was never any chance of attaining it. But when I came to London I realized that as I could never be as beautiful as Hester . . . and . . . well, other

116

people, I had to have something which they hadn't got—horsemanship, for one thing."

"What an extraordinary girl you are!" Lord Meridan said, staring at her.

Lucinda did not answer, and he remembered that there was something which he wished to say to her.

"Now, listen to me, Lucinda . . ." he began.

She touched her horse with her spur and started to move away from him.

"Pray do not say that!" she said. "I always know, when people start a conversation by telling me that I must listen to them, I am going to hear something unpleasant. Papa always prefaced his lectures with those words, and so did Mama."

Lord Meridan found that he had to push his horse to keep up with her.

"But, deuce take it, Lucinda! There is something I have got to say to you!"

"I know what it's going to be," Lucinda said, turning her head over her shoulder. "It's going to be don't do this, and don't do that . . . I have been listening to such strictures all my life!"

Again that wicked little spur touched her horse, and it sped ahead so that Lord Meridan was forced to spur his own horse into a gallop.

It was all most unfashionable and would certainly not have been approved of by the *haut ton* which they had left behind them, for now they were racing each other, galloping over the grass with Lucinda two lengths ahead and Lord Meridan using all his experienced horsemanship to keep up.

She could ride superbly—he had to give her that. And he was too well versed in feminine charms not to realize that her green velvet riding dress, which showed off her figure, and her high hat with its green veiling floating behind her like transparent wings, was a smarter turn-out than anything he had seen before.

He caught up with her after about a mile of hard riding, and even then he was not certain that she had not purposely slowed her horse a little.

They were both panting as he drew alongside and

117

reached out his hand to grasp the bridle of her horse, drawing it as well as his own sharply to a standstill.

"Damn it all, Lucinda!" he began, only to find her face laughing up at him—her eyes sparkling, her cheeks delicately coloured from the exertion.

"That was fun!" she gasped a little breathlessly. "If only we had room really to let them go! Oh, Sebastian, let us race when we are in the country . . . my horse against yours! I swear I will have a chance of being the victor!"

"Let us hope nobody saw us," he said, noting with satisfaction that they were still in a very unfashionable part of the Park. "Such a romp is not done, Lucinda—it's just not done!"

"People will talk, whatever I do," Lucinda replied, "so I might as well give them something to talk about."

Lord Meridan drew his brows together, and would have opened his mouth to speak, but Lucinda, detaching his hand from her bridle, turned her horse round.

"We will go back," she said in a quiet voice, "and I promise that I will behave myself. But please don't lecture me . . . it spoils the whole morning."

"I am sorry if it annoys you," Lord Meridan said, "but I must speak to you about the Comte. He is not a fit companion for you."

There was a moment's silence, and then he saw that Lucinda had raised her chin a little.

"And who is the judge of that?" she asked.

"I think anyone would agree with me," Lord Meridan said heavily.

"Such as the patronesses of Almack's, I suppose?" Lucinda said.

"Most certainly," he replied. "Comte Jacques de Falaise has a reputation as a lady-killer . . ."

"My dear Sebastian, so have you," she answered.

He stared at her for a moment, hardly believing his ears.

"But . . . didn't you know that?" she enquired. "I wouldn't wish to tell you what indiscretions people credit you with when they think I am not listening—and sometimes when they think I am."

"I will not—" Lord Meridan said in a voice of thunder,

"—I will not, Lucinda, be compared with Comte Jacques de Falaise! You will please understand that, as my wife, you will not be seen with him—and I do not wish him to be invited to my house!"

"Merely because he is a lady-killer?" Lucinda asked in almost child-like tones.

"Because he is an undesirable acquaintance for a young woman," Lord Meridan said. "Anyone would tell you the same."

"Anyone?" Lucinda asked. "For instance . . . Lady Devereux?"

The name seemed to put a certain constriction on Lord Meridan. But after a second's pause he answered:

"I am sure Lady Devereux would agree with me."

"But she introduced me to the Comte!" Lucinda said sweetly. "It was the very first night I appeared in London. Lady Jersey invited me to her reception; and Lady Devereux went out of her way to present the Comte to me, saying she was certain he would do his best to entertain me while my husband was out of town."

There was a long silence, broken only by the jingle of the horses' bridles.

Lucinda had spoken in an artless tone of voice, but there was a suspicion in Lord Meridan's mind that she knew exactly what she was saying.

And then before he could collect his wits, before he could think what else to say, Lucinda gave a sudden cry and wheeling her horse away from him galloped across the grass.

For a moment he could not think where she was going until he saw in the distance a man with a large stick beating a very small donkey.

He turned to follow Lucinda, but two nannies pushing perambulators got in his way and by the time he arrived Lucinda had dismounted from her horse and she and the man were shouting at each other.

"Don't you dare touch that donkey again!" she cried. "If you do you will be sorry for it!"

"And 'ow will a gentry-moit mike me sorry?" the man asked aggressively.

He was a big, burly, middle-aged man. His breath smelt

119

of alcohol, and it was obvious to Lord Meridan, if not to Lucinda, that he had been drinking.

"Yer shove orf an' keep yer sneezer out o' me business!" he shouted to Lucinda. "This be my donkey—an' if I wants ter beat it, nobody ain't a-goin' ter stop me!"

"I'm going to stop you!" Lucinda said. "Hit that animal once more, and I'll hit you!" She raised her thin riding whip and at the same time the man raised the stick in his hand.

As they glared at each other a voice behind them said sharply:

"Stop that immediately! Put that stick down, my man, or it will be the worse for you."

Lucinda looked up at Lord Meridan and he saw the relief on her face.

"Oh, Sebastian, stop him from ill-treating this donkey in such a manner! Look at the weals on its back—and its neck is bleeding!"

"I ain't a-hurt it," the man said in a whining voice. " 'Tis an obstinate beast wot won't do as it be told."

"It is half-starved, that is why," Lucinda said accusingly. "Look at the manner in which its ribs are showing."

"I can't give it no food if I don't earn any, can I?" the man asked truculently. "Wot child'd want ter ride a lazy beast wot won't move?"

"It is too old and ill to carry children when it is in this state," Lucinda said.

" 'Tis me livelihood, lidy," the man answered, with a sidelong glance up at Sebastian.

Lucinda also looked up at her husband, her eyes wide and beseeching.

"Please, Sebastian . . ." she faltered.

Reluctantly Lord Meridan drew a guinea from his pocket and chucked it contemptuously on the ground.

"There you are, my man," he said. "Take it—and be grateful that I have not given you the hiding you deserve!"

The man bent down, snatched at the guinea and was gone without another word.

Lucinda, no longer interested in him, was patting and caressing the donkey, which seemed to realize that something strange had happened in its life and was standing quietly, accepting the caress of her soft hands as if they were a gift from heaven.

"And now what do we do?" Lord Meridan asked, with a hint of laughter in his voice.

"What do you mean?" Lucinda asked.

She had one hand on the bridle of her horse to prevent him straying and the other on the donkey's neck.

"I was just wondering," Lord Meridan said, "How you intend to travel with your latest purchase? Shall we carry it home, or do we lead it on a string down the Row, perhaps setting a new fashion?"

Lucinda's hand went up to her lips.

"Oh, I never thought of that!" she said. "And . . . and where will you put it?"

"That is your problem," Lord Meridan answered. "I daresay Kingsclere will welcome another addition to the stable."

Lucinda was suddenly overcome with helpless laughter.

"Can't you see Kingsclere's face?" she cried, and Lord Meridan found himself laughing too.

"Tell him you bought something on your own," he said. "I feel sure he will appreciate your choice!"

Lucinda patted the donkey on the nose.

"Well, we can't leave it here," she said. "Besides, if we did, the man would come back, claim it and torture it all over again."

"Then what is your suggestion?" Lord Meridan asked.

"I just do not know," Lucinda said. "Oh, please, Sebastian, think of one!"

It somehow pleased him that he could provide a solution.

He looked round and beckoned to a group of boys who had been watching the drama enacted before them. The eldest amongst them was a sensible-looking lad of twelve or thirteen.

"Come here, my boy," Lord Meridan said.

The boy, ragged and unkempt, had, Lucinda decided, an honest face. He listened attentively as Lord Meridan asked:

"Do you know your way to Berkeley Square?"

The boy hesitated a moment and then said:

"Yes. Guv'nor."

"And the stables behind it?"

"I thinks so, Guv."

"Well, lead this donkey there. Ask for Lord Meridan's stables, and you will find that you are expected. There will be a half-sovereign for you if you deliver the animal there within the next hour."

"I'll do that, Guv.," the boy said, his eyes bright at the thought of so much wealth.

"But do not hurry," Lucinda admonished. "Take him slowly, as he is old and ill and has been so very badly treated."

"I'll be careful with 'im, Lady," the boy promised.

"You aren't to ride him, you understand that?" Lucinda went on. "You are too heavy for him."

"Naw, I'll walk him," the boy said. He reached out his hand and patted the donkey's neck.

"If you are kind to him," Lucinda said, "I know he will do what you want. It is just that he has always been ill-treated. He's frightened, and a frightened animal has to fight, just as we all do."

"I'll get 'im there," the boy said. "Lord Meridan—were that the nime?"

He mispronounced it, but it was clear enough, Lucinda thought.

"That is right. And thank you for being so obliging."

The boy and the donkey walked slowly away and she turned towards Lord Meridan.

"Thank you . . ." she said, "thank you so much."

"I am wondering what the next thing is that you will foist on me," Lord Meridan said.

"I know it is inconvenient . . . and not at all the thing . . . we should have bought," Lucinda said hesitatingly, "but there was really nothing else we could do, was there?"

"We could, of course, have pretended not to see it," Lord Meridan replied, with an accent on the pronoun.

Lucinda shook her head.

"You would not have done that," she said, "now would you?"

"Wouldn't I?" Lord Meridan asked, speaking more to himself than to her. "No—perhaps I wouldn't."

He looked down at her, so tiny beside the two big

horses. He seemed about to say something, then changed his mind.

"I will help you mount," he said.

"Oh no, it is quite unnecessary," Lucinda answered. "I am so used to riding by myself."

It seemed to him that she sprang into the saddle as if she were borne on wings, only having a little difficulty in arranging the folds of her new dress; and in a few seconds they were cantering back towards Rotten Row and the crowds perambulating up and down for the admiration of each other.

Lady Devereux's carriage was where Lord Meridan had last seen it, and he would have passed by, just raising his hat, if she had not called out to them and it was impossible to pass without speaking.

"So you found your wife, Sebastian?" she said with a smile; then turning to Lucinda: "I was just telling your husband that you had become quite the talk of the town since he had been away."

"That is a compliment from your Ladyship," Lucinda answered, "for everywhere I go, people talk about you."

The words were innocent enough, but something in the direct gaze of Lucinda's eyes made Lady Devereux draw in her breath.

"I am so glad that Sebastian found you, my dear," she said sweetly. "I told him that you already had an escort— but like all good husbands he hurried in search of you."

"He not only found me," Lucinda assured her, "but he has given me a most delightful present—one I particularly wanted."

"Indeed?"

There was a glacial quality about the single word, and then Lady Devereux added:

"But he is always most generous! Aren't you, Sebastian?"

That, Lucinda thought to herself, was definitely round two to Lady Devereux. She touched her horse with her spur and made him prance a little.

"I am afraid my mount is rather restless," she said politely. "How wise your Ladyship is to take your exercise in a more sedate and less exhausting fashion! But I expect you rode when you were my age."

Without waiting for an answer, she moved away as if she could no longer hold her horse in check, and Lord Meridan, with a muttered word of "Good-bye," followed her.

Lucinda forced the pace and there was no possibility of further conversation until they reached Berkeley Square. There she darted in ahead of Lord Meridan to find Kingsclere and tell him about the new addition to her stable.

"What have you done to yourself?" Charles Holstead asked her. He had dined that evening in Berkeley Square before they all went on to a reception at Devonshire House.

He asked his question in a low voice, and before she answered it, Lucinda glanced over her shoulder to see if their other guests were out of earshot.

There were only a dozen of them, who had been invited at the last moment when Lucinda had told Lord Meridan that they were expected at Devonshire House. He had then found a number of his special cronies were in the same position as himslf in not having arranged a dinner party beforehand.

The result was that there were only two other women besides Lucinda—both rather nice, quiet wives, with dashing, fashionable husbands—and the rest were Lord Meridan's bachelor friends, several of whom had been staying with Charles Holstead at Newmarket.

"Tell me, Lucinda," Charles said. "You may pretend to the others, but not to me. I saw you on your wedding day, and I swear that it was almost impossible to recognize you when we came upon you in the Park!"

"Is there really such a difference?" Lucinda asked.

"You know full well there is," Charles answered. "Come on, Lucinda, tell me who waved the magic wand?"

"As a matter of fact, it is all due to you," Lucinda told him.

"To me?" he asked in astonishment.

"Yes, indeed," Lucinda replied.

She left his side for a moment to ask one of the ladies if she would like more coffee, and he watched her move across the room, her dress of strawberry pink gauze, fashionably transparent, showing off not only her superb figure but also the snowy whiteness of her skin.

When she had returned to his side Charles put his hand up to his forehead.

"I begin to think I am dreaming," he said, "when I recollect a sallow-faced little brat with extremely untidy hair, wearing a very dirty wedding gown."

"I have not forgotten her," Lucinda said. "Sometimes in the night I get out of bed, light a candle and stare into the mirror, just to make quite sure that I have not been dreaming . . . all this."

She indicated with her hand the people sitting around talking in the white and gold salon, and then her fingers came to rest on the magnificent diamond necklace she wore.

"You're real enough," Charles told her. "How have you done it?"

"It was Madame Bertin," Lucinda answered. "Oh, Charles, I cannot tell you what those first days were like! She never let me out of that overcrowded, stuffy little room of hers. A thousand materials were fitted on me, the pins stuck into me until I began to think I was being tortured. Then she sent for a colleague of hers who painted my face with some extraordinary concoction which made me look like a clown."

Lucinda smiled at the memory before she continued:

"It took away all the sunburn that I had acquired throughout the years. It hurt and was so uncomfortable that at times I could not bear it. But when she scraped it off, my skin was as you see it now."

"Did you never realize that you had such skin?" Charles asked. "It is like a camellia—I have never seen anything to compare with it."

"I had no idea," Lucinda answered. "You see, I was always riding and walking about without a hat—not that Mama did not try to make me wear one. And I only wore Hester's dresses that she had outgrown or for which she had no further use; and, as Hester was fair, they were always white or very pale colours—which Madame Bertin says made my skin look sallow. Now she designs my gowns only in strong, vivid colours."

"Did you know you have set a fashion already?"

Charles asked. "All the women in London are dyeing their muslins."

"I heard that!" Lucinda said. "Isn't it exciting?"

"Dash it, but you're a marvel, that's what you are!" Charles said.

"And it is all due to you," Lucinda answered. "I would like to throw my arms around you and hug you!"

"For God's sake, don't!" he said hastily. "Think of the scandal! And Sebastian would blow a hole in me—he is a much better shot than I am!"

"You are safe, Charles, don't worry," Lucinda said. "I was only speaking metaphorically—or whatever the word is."

"Damme, I'm proud of you, that's what I am!" Charles said. "We brought you to London, a little harum-scarum creature whom no one would look at twice. And now here you are the belle of the ball—because that's what you will be tonight."

"Do not forget his Lordship's Ladyship will be there," Lucinda said with a small grimace.

Charles glanced towards Lord Meridan, hoping he had not heard.

"For heaven's sake, Lucinda . . . !" he began.

But Lucinda had moved away from him and he heard her laughing at something one of Lord Meridan's other guests had said.

There was the usual crush at Devonshire House, which meant that having once lost the members on one's party, one never found them again.

The reception rooms were magnificent, but even they seemed hardly sufficient for the huge throng of people crowding up the stairs.

There were thousands of lighted candles; a string band whose music was almost lost in the chattering voices; flunkeys in velvet carrying on gold salvers crystal glasses filled with champagne—and a general atmosphere of tension, intrigue and snobbery.

The Duke's stern and unsmiling face was ably compensated for by the wit and beautiful smiling countenance of the Duchess.

Everyone who was anyone crowded into Devonshire

126

House, and the Duchess's invitation was the most prized of the whole season.

Lady Devereux was one of the outstanding beauties in a dress embroidered all over with tiny forget-me-nots. But those who were watching decided that by far the most striking gown was that worn by the new Countess of Meridan.

The strawberry pink gauze stood out even amongst the kaleidoscope of colour moving slowly round the dance-floor, and the Meridan diamonds—the tiara with its huge pear-shaped stones and matching necklace—had few rivals amongst the profusion of glittering gems.

It was not only the colour of Lucinda's dress—it was the way she wore it and the perfection of her figure which drew the eyes of the men.

"She's not exactly beautiful," one old roué growled to another, "but there's something about her which makes you want to look at her again."

"By Jove—devilish attractive woman!" his friend ejaculated, while another man, known as a cynic, said to himself, "Her eyes are like a child's at a party!"

But perhaps the real reason Lucinda attracted attention was that there was something untouched and innocent about her. Something which made the other women look old and rather heavy as she seemed to float past them—so tiny, yet somehow significant.

It was about midnight when Lord Meridan realized that he had not seen his wife for some time. He had been prevailed upon by Lady Devereux to take her down to supper, and when he came back to the ballroom there was no sign of Lucinda.

He saw Charles Holstead talking to someone and sauntered across the room to them.

"Have you seen Lucinda?" he asked casually.

"Not for an hour or two," Charles answered. "Thought she was with you."

"I've been down to supper," Lord Meridan explained.

"And left Lucinda to starve, I'll be bound," Charles said accusingly.

Lord Meridan had the grace to look slightly ashamed.

"I saw Lady Meridan about twenty minutes ago," said the man to whom Charles had been talking.

"Where was she?" Lord Meridan enquired.

"She was going up the stairs to the floor above," the man answered. "That French cove was with her—Comte Jacques something-or-other—and I heard him say something about showing her some pictures."

Lord Meridan's lips clamped together like a vice. Without a word he strode through the doorway and up the stairs.

"The little fool!" he muttered to himself. Surely Lucinda knew that when a man of de Falaise's reputation asked her to go and look at the pictures away from the ballroom he meant something very different?

How could she be so stupid, so unsophisticated, as to leave the ballroom in the company of a man with a reputation like that?

But then he remembered she was not well versed in social behaviour and knew that Charles was right, he should not have gone down to supper without seeing that his wife had an escort.

This thought did not make him feel any better-tempered as he reached the floor above.

There were a number of rooms opening off a broad corridor. He entered the first and found there a study well stocked with books. A man and a woman were whispering together in one corner—but there was no sign of Lucinda.

Three other rooms produced the same result, then, as he almost reached the end of the corridor, he saw her come through a doorway.

He was just going to call out her name when she turned, inserted a key in the lock and turned it. Then she started to walk very rapidly towards him.

He stood still, astonished at her behaviour and curious to see what she would do.

Just as she reached him she raised her head. Her face was very white and her eyes were frightened.

"Sebastian!"

It was a cry of relief which seemed to come from the very depth of her being.

"Oh, Sebastian, thank God you have come! I was just going in search of you."

"Why?" he asked harshly. "What have you been doing?"

Lucinda glanced over her shoulder and dropped her voice a little.

"I had to find you," she whispered. "You see . . . I have . . . killed a man!"

8

Lord Meridan took one look at Lucinda's white face and without questioning her he opened the door of the room nearest to him and looked inside.

There was no one there.

"Come in," he commanded, and when she had entered he closed the door behind her.

"Now tell me what has happened," he asked gently.

She looked up at him, her eyes wide.

"I . . . I think he is . . . dead," she faltered.

"Who?" Lord Meridan asked, knowing the answer.

"Comte . . . Jacques de Falaise," Lucinda replied.

Lord Meridan's expression did not alter.

"How did you kill him?" he enquired, and then before she could answer he added hastily: "Tell me from the beginning exactly what happened."

Lucinda clasped her hands together like a child trying to remember its lesson. Her voice was low and her sentences broken.

"I . . . danced with the Comte," she said, "and then he suggested that he should show me . . . the pictures upstairs. He said there was a very fine collection and described some of them . . . to me."

"Go on," Lord Meridan said grimly. "It is a trick as old as Hades, but you wouldn't know that."

"I did not wish to leave . . . the ballroom," Lucinda continued, "but he was so insistent that it seemed rather . . . rude to refuse."

"So he led you up on to this floor?" Lord Meridan supplied.

130

"Yes," Lucinda agreed. "We looked into the first room we came to and there were some quite nice pictures there, but there were other people looking at them and the Comte kept . . . urging me further down the corridor."

She paused a moment and swallowed and said in a low voice:

"You must think me very . . . foolish. I cannot conceive why I did not realize that I should not have gone with . . . him as . . . he suggested."

"The Comte is very experienced and convincing—where young women are concerned," Lord Meridan said wryly.

"I . . . know that . . . now," Lucinda answered, "but I did what he . . . wanted. When we came to the last room I entered ahead of him and saw there were not many pictures. It was a writing room with a desk in the centre of it. I turned to ask whether we had made a mistake and then . . . I . . . I saw . . ."

Lucinda paused and took a deep breath.

". . . I saw he was locking . . . the door."

"I told you that man was an outsider!" Lord Meridan exclaimed. "Go on."

"For a moment I thought . . . I must be mistaken!" Lucinda continued. "I said, 'There are not many pictures in this room, I think it would be best for us to return to the ballroom' . . . and then . . ."

She put her hands up to her face.

"Then?" Lord Meridan prompted relentlessly.

"He . . . he came towards me and . . . put his arms around me . . ."

Lucinda was trembling, but with an effort she went on:

"He was . . . saying something about he had known me for so long and yet we had never been . . . alone together. He was trying . . . to . . . to kiss me . . . I backed away from him, but I found myself against the writing desk. I . . . I could escape no further. I tried to struggle . . . but he was so . . . strong and somehow it was . . . impossible for me to . . . move."

She stopped and her hands went out towards Lord Meridan appealingly.

"It was horrible!" she cried. "I knew then that I hated

131

him . . . I didn't want him to touch me . . . but it was too late . . . his . . . his lips were on . . . mine and I could not . . . escape . . . !"

She gave a little sob at the memory.

"But how did you escape?" Lord Meridan insisted.

"He . . . forced me against the writing desk," Lucinda continued in a quivering voice, "and was kissing me so . . . frighteningly . . . that I felt I might swoon. I have never felt like it before. And then . . . then my hand, which had dropped on to the desk, touched something."

"What was it?" Lord Meridan asked.

"A candlestick . . . a heavy brass candlestick," Lucinda answered. "In an instant . . . almost as if somebody had told me . . . I knew what to do. I picked it up and brought it down with all the force I could on the back of his head. It seemed to stun him for the moment: he released his hold on me and sort of fell forward on to my shoulder."

Lucinda shuddered as if what had occurred was almost too nauseating for words.

"I hit him again," she whispered, "and . . . again and again—I do not really think I knew what I was doing, except that I hated him . . . I wanted to hurt him. It was only when he fell to the floor and . . . didn't move that I realized what . . . I had done."

Lucinda looked up at Lord Meridan with her eyes full of tears.

"I . . . I am sorry, Sebastian," she murmured, ". . . sorry that I should have done . . . done this, because I know it will make a scandal . . . it will mean trouble for . . . you . . . oh, why did I strike him?"

He put his hand on her shoulder.

"You did the only thing you could do," he said. "The swine deserved it."

"But Almack's . . ." Lucinda cried, "the Prince . . . and everyone else . . . what will they say?"

Lord Meridan seemed to be thinking for a moment. Then his hand closed over his wife's cold fingers.

"You have got to be brave, very brave, Lucinda," he said, "and you must do exactly as I tell you."

"You do not want me to go . . . back into the room and . . . and look at him?" Lucinda asked with a tremble in her voice.

"No, of course not," Lord Meridan replied. "I want you to go downstairs to dance and behave as though nothing has happened."

She did not answer, but stared at him wide-eyed.

"Do you understand?" he said. "You must not be involved in this. Leave the rest to me."

"Sebastian . . . it was my fault. . . ."

"I hope it's not going to be anybody's fault," Lord Meridan said, "but we can't stay here talking. Look in the mirror, Lucinda—straighten your necklace and tidy your hair."

Automatically she crossed the room to obey him.

But as she stared at her reflection in the gilt framed mirror it was hard to believe that she was a murderess. She looked chic and elegant and the jewels in her hair and around her neck flashed mischievously as if they were taunting her.

She turned to Lord Meridan.

"I cannot let . . . you take the blame . . . for what I have done," she told him.

"Nobody is going to take the blame if I can help it," he answered, "except the man who deserves it—the Comte himself. Trust me, and now you must give me the key of the room where you left him."

Lucinda gave it to him, and he held out his arm.

"Come, Lucinda," he said, and added gently: "Keep your chin high."

He led her out into the corridor. As they walked down the stairs she tried to do as he had commanded her. By the time they reached the crowded ballroom they were talking together in what Lucinda hoped was an animated and amusing manner.

They entered the salon, its huge candle-lit chandeliers sparkling above the dancers, glittering with jewels, and Lord Meridan caught sight of Charles Holstead.

"Charles!" he said urgently. "I want you."

Charles sauntered towards them. He was looking exceedingly elegant in a coat of plum satin which fitted him so tightly that he might have been poured into it.

"At your service, Sebastian," he said a trifle mockingly. "Do you desire me to have the honour of escorting Lucinda?"

"I desire you to come with me. It is of the gravest import."

Charles's eyes widened. Lord Meridan looked round the room as if in search of someone.

"Whom do you know?" he asked Lucinda in a low voice.

Before she could answer there was the sound of voices coming up the stairs and amongst the guests hanging around the door a reverent hush which always proclaims the arrival of royalty.

The Prince of Wales, resplendent and bejewelled, had arrived.

Before they could move he had seen them.

"Ah, Meridan," he said genially. "I thought I should find you here. And Lady Meridan—it is a pleasure. I am late and I am sure I have missed a great deal of excitement. Come with me and tell me what is happening and who, besides yourself, is in beauty this evening."

Lucinda sank into a deep curtsy.

"I shall be honoured, Sire," she answered.

"Strictly *entre nous*," His Royal Highness went on, "you can tell me if Devonshire gives a better party than I do—and I shall be exceedingly hipped if you say he does!"

"It is unthinkable, Sire," Lucinda answered and added mischievously: "Even if such were the case neither I nor anyone else would be brave enough to tell Your Royal Highness the truth!"

It was an impudent reply which seemed to amuse the Prince, and as they went on talkng, perambulating slowly across the ballroom in search of the Duke and Duchess of Devonshire, who had long since given up receiving their guests, Lucinda knew that Lord Meridan and Charles had disappeared.

She tried not to think about them, tried to concentrate on amusing the Prince and letting everyone see how apparently gay and unconcerned she was.

She was not certain then or afterwards what she said, but whatever it was it entertained both the Prince and those in attendance on him. She kept them all laughing—and somehow slowly but inevitably the time passed.

Centuries later, it seemed to Lucinda, she saw Lord Meridan wending his way through the dancers.

The Prince was deep in conversation with a member of the Diplomatic Corps and Lucinda was able to move from his side towards her husband.

She did not dare say the words which her eyes asked him. He slipped a consoling hand under her elbow.

"I think it is time we went home," he said gravely, "if you are willing to forgo any further dances."

"It must be very late," she answered.

They made their formal farewells to the Prince, their host and hostess, and a number of other people who all seemed to want a word either with Lord Meridan or with his already famous wife.

The fact that Lucinda had been at the Prince's side ever since he had arrived at Devonshire House had not gone unnoticed; and as Lady Meridan was obviously going to be as popular with their heir to the throne as her husband, it was essential for anyone with social ambitions to be her friend.

Lucinda could not help thinking that they almost had to fight their way downstairs to the entrance; how very different her reception would have been if she had appeared in one of the dresses which her mother had bought for her trousseau. And, more important, if she had not been fortunate enough to be sponsored during her first week in London by Mr. Brummel and the Countess of Jersey!

If they only knew, she thought despairingly, all these people who were anxious to gain her approval, that she was a murderess and had left a man dead in a room upstairs.

They waited while the linkman called their carriage and then at last they were alone and the horses were carrying them the short distance to Berkeley Square.

"What happened?" Lucinda asked breathlessly.

"It is all right," Lord Meridan replied soothingly. "It was not as bad as you thought."

"He is not dead?"

For a moment Lucinda thought she might burst into tears, the relief was so poignant, so overwhelming. Then she remembered that men, and especially Lord Meridan, hated scenes. With an effort that was almost superhuman she fought back the tears, biting her lips so that the pain gave her back her self-control.

"No, he is not dead," Lord Meridan repeated. "But stap me, Lucinda, I had no idea you were such a little tiger-cat! He might have been in a mill! It will be a deuce of a time before the wounds in his head heal!"

"But he is alive?" Lucinda questioned, as if she could hardly believe what she had already been told.

"He is alive and damned sorry for himself!" Lord Meridan said.

"Oh, thank God! How did you get him away? Where is he? And what happened?"

"Charles and I carried him down the back stairs," Lord Meridan answered. "He lodges in St. James's Place, so we called a carriage and took him home. Anyone who saw us would think he was foxed. When we got to his lodgings we had to carry him up the stairs and put him on his bed."

"Was he unconscious?" Lucinda asked.

"Not after we had given him a glass of brandy. We told his valet to send for a physician. We spun the man the yarn that he had fallen downstairs in his cups. The valet believed it and I don't think the Comte will be in a fit state to contradict the story until it is too late—anyhow, he won't want to."

"Supposing he tells the truth?" Lucinda asked.

Lord Meridan smiled.

"No man would admit willingly to being knocked out by a woman—especially someone as small as you. He would be the laughing stock of every club in London. No—there's nothing dishonorable in being drunk."

"So nobody will know . . . about me, I mean?" Lucinda asked.

"Not unless you talk, my dear," Lord Meridan replied.

"Oh, thank you! Thank you! How clever of you to . . . to save me!"

In her gratitude Lucinda longed to throw her arms round Lord Meridan, or at least to touch his hand, but again the tears pricked her eyes and she forced herself to stare straight ahead and hold herself severely in check.

"I thought you were going to say 'hide the body'," Lord Meridan was saying. "It is what Charles and I went upstairs to do, and what we thought we would have to do when we first saw him."

136

"And if the Comte really had been . . . dead, would you have got rid of . . . of him?" Lucinda asked.

"I have not got to answer that question," Lord Meridan told her. "The situation has not arisen, thank God! Another time, do not strike to kill, Lucinda. One blow would have been enough—the other half-dozen were unnecessary."

"It will never happen again," Lucinda said quickly. "I will not be so bird-witted, for one thing."

"I warned you," Lord Meridan said.

"Yes, I know you did," Lucinda answered. "It was silly of me not to listen to you, but . . . you don't know how . . . exciting it was to . . . to be told that I looked lovely . . . that I was so . . . smart and . . . elegant." She paused. "No one had ever said those things to me before."

"Well, after your success with the Prince there are plenty of people ready to say them!" Lord Meridan said drily.

"Apparently," Lucinda answered. "But in future I am not going to listen to them."

"You will," Lord Meridan said. "All women like flattery —I dare not suppose you are any exception."

"Men also enjoy flattery," Lucinda retorted. "In fact, I suppose every man and woman wants to be praised."

"I expect you are right," Lord Meridan said with a yawn. "Anyway, here we are—we're home. There is one thing about you, Lucinda, you manage to relieve the dullest party from being a dead bore."

Lucinda was not certain whether he was being sarcastic or not. She glanced at him a little uncertainly before she alighted from the coach and went into the house.

The candles were all lit and there were half a dozen tired footmen waiting up for their arrival.

Lucinda wondered what would be said if she suggested that perhaps just one person could wait up for them and that the rest should go to bed.

She was certain that such a revolutionary suggestion would shock the butler, who was asking them now if they wanted anything to eat or drink.

"A glass of wine," Lord Meridan said. "What about you, Lucinda? I recollect you had no supper."

"I am not hungry," Lucinda answered, feeling that

137

the mere idea of food after what had happened made her feel sick.

"Tell the chef to send up a cold collation," Lord Meridan said sharply.

"Very good, my Lord."

They moved into the library. Lord Meridan threw himself down in one of the deep armchairs.

"Have something to eat," he said kindly. "You will feel better in the morning. Or would you like a glass of wine?"

"I really do not want anything," Lucinda said. Then, thinking she sounded ungrateful, she added: "But I will try and eat something when it comes."

She moved across the room and put down her gloves and fan.

Lord Meridan watched her go and said:

"Did you never realize what a good figure you have?"

"I did not have much chance of thinking about it until I left home," Lucinda replied with a little smile. "Besides, Mama would be shocked that anyone should mention anything so delicate."

"I suppose she would," Lord Meridan agreed, "and rightly. We have grown very loose in our talk, as in our acceptance of what is second rate. That is why people like the Comte are accepted in decent Society."

Lucinda moved towards him and stood for a moment with her hand on the mantelshelf. She looked as elegant as the Sèvres vases which ornamented it.

"I enjoyed myself tonight," she said reflectively, "until all that happened. I can understand why people get obsessed by Society and why it matters so much. I thought it was all nonsense when Mama and Hester used to talk about it—but it is rather fascinating."

"Personally the whole caboodle bores me," Lord Meridan said.

Lucinda shook her head.

"That is not true. You would hate it if you were not invited to Clarence House—if you were not accepted everywhere for people to admire—and at the same time fear—you. You are rich! You are successful; you are part of the *haut ton*. Have you ever thought what it must be like for those who want so much to do the things that you can do, but who are not eligible?"

"You are quite eloquent, Lucinda," Lord Meridan said sarcastically.

"I was thinking about tonight," she continued, as if he hadn't spoken, "when we were trying to come away from Devonshire House and everyone was wanting to talk to us, that if Papa had not lost that money to you I might never have got married . . . I might never have come to London."

"And would that have mattered so very much?" Lord Meridan asked, watching her.

"I suppose I should never have known what I had missed," Lucinda said. "But now—I am glad of the experience. You may think that I am very stupid, but I am learning . . . I am learning a lot of things."

"What an extraordinary girl you are!" Lord Meridan said for the second time.

"In other words, I am not the wife you expected!" Lucinda exclaimed.

"I did not say that," he answered.

"But you are thinking it," she said accusingly.

"I don't know now quite what I did expect," he answered; and she knew he was speaking in all sincerity. "Certainly not someone who would go about murdering their too ardent beaux."

"And now you are being unkind to me," Lucinda said.

"Am I?"

He gave her a curiously sweet smile and added:

"At least I have a wife who is not only a social success but has an original turn of behaviour."

Lucinda's eyes met his and for a moment there was silence as if something passed between them—although she could not quite determine what it was.

Then the door opened and the spell was broken.

A footman entered, carrying a tray laden with cold dishes of every sort and description.

There was wine, coffee or chocolate, and by the time they had both been served Lucinda was aware that she felt desperately tired and knew it was the reaction after what had happened.

"I think I will retire," she said, handing her plate, from which she had taken only half a dozen mouthfuls, to the attentive footman.

"I should," Lord Meridan answered; "and I have a good mind to turn in myself, although Charles is waiting for me at Brooks's."

"Is it not rather late?" Lucinda asked, glancing at the clock.

"The *habitués* will be gaming until dawn," Lord Meridan replied.

"Then good night, my Lord," Lucinda said with a small curtsy, "and thank you once again."

There was no chance to say more with the servants in the room.

He raised her hand perfunctorily to his lips.

She went up to her bedroom, conscious that, above all things, she wanted to sleep and forget what had happened.

She slept late—so late that she could not help wondering what her mother would say if she knew that it was midday before she stirred and rang for the maid to bring her a cup of chocolate.

"Has his Lordship gone out?" she enquired.

She did not know why, but she thought that he might have left a message for her, perhaps suggesting they might do something together.

She had a feeling that the events of the night before might have bound them closer together so that he would have been sufficiently interested to invite her to go driving with him.

"I think his Lordship has departed for Ranelagh," the maid answered.

With a little sigh, Lucinda turned to her writing desk where there were piles of invitations.

She had been invited to assemblies, receptions, masques, tea parties, At Homes, luncheons and dinners—in fact there were dozens of white cards, all bearing the names of well-known hostesses.

"What a tangle these are in!" Lucinda exclaimed.

"I am sorry, your Ladyship," the maid said. "I forgot to tell you that his Lordship's secretary sent you a note in which your Ladyship's engagements are listed day by day."

"Oh, that will be helpful," Lucinda answered.

She took it from the maid and saw it was written in the secretary's clear, precise handwriting.

It seemed to her that there were far too many things she could do—and she had no desire to do any of them.

"I cannot make up my mind," she said, impatiently putting the list down. "I think I will visit Madame Bertin. Send a message to Kingsclere before the carriages comes round that I want to see the horses and . . . and my donkey before it leaves for the country."

Kingsclere had found a home for the donkey with an elderly relation of his who, for a small sum of money, looked after animals who were too old for work but whose owners did not wish them destroyed. The donkey would be happy and well cared for, Lucinda was assured of that.

She smiled at the thought, and suddenly the fact that she was alone did not matter. There were always the horses. Perhaps Kingsclere would have heard of a new mare or stallion which he would want her to buy for riding, or maybe another pair for her new phaeton which was being built at the coachbuilders in St. James's.

"I am spending a lot of money," Lucinda thought guiltily, adding to her extravagance the cost of the presents which had gone back to Hertfordshire for Hester, her father, mother and, of course, Nat.

Then she remembered her first visit to Madame Bertin and the six new gowns for Lady Devereux! She shrugged her shoulders.

Going down the stairs on her way to visit the stables, Lucinda met a footman hurrying up towards her with a note on a salver.

"This has just come for you m'Lady."

Lucinda picked it up indifferently, expecting it to be another invitation, but this time a more intimate one written by the hostess herself and therefore more difficult to refuse.

But the letter, strangely scented, when she opened it, was engraved with an address in Half Moon Street, and it read:

My Lady,

If you care for Your Husband and wish Him to remain in Good Health, I beg You to Visit me immediately for I have Something of Import to relate to You.

Do not Speak of this to Anyone, or it might prove Dangerous—both for Him and for You.

The writing was ill-formed and the spelling erratic, but there was no mistaking the flowing signature at the end —*Juanita da Riva*.

Lucinda read the note through twice.

"Who brought this?" she asked the footman.

"I think it was a manservant, m'Lady, but he has not waited for an answer."

"Thank you," Lucinda said.

She put the letter into the reticule which she carried on her arm.

"Cancel the carriage," she said. "I shall not want it for the moment—I am going to walk."

"Do you wish someone to come with you, m'Lady?"

"No. I will go alone."

She went out into the sunshine and started to walk the short distance towards Half Moon Street.

She had a feeling that Lord Meridan would not wish her to go—and yet if he was in danger she could not afford the risk of not hearing what this woman had to tell her.

What danger could it be? she wondered. And from whom?

She knew it was an unprecedented step for the mistress of a man to write to his wife. She knew it was outrageous and unthought of that a wife should visit her husband's mistress.

And yet neither of these things worried Lucinda. If Sebastian was in danger it was only right that she should warn him.

Stopping only to give some money to an organ-grinder whose monkey held out beseechingly a small red cap to passers-by, she wended her way to Half Moon Street.

She pulled the doorbell, wondering whether anyone could see her and what they would think. Then she was inside Juanita da Riva's small, rather stuffy hall and being led up the stairs to the sitting room on the first floor.

The house was decorated in a flamboyant Spanish style which might have been expected. But the flowers which graced the sitting room were obviously a tribute to the opera dancer, and were magnificent.

Juanita, in a gown trimmed with emerald ribbons, with a small necklace of uncut emeralds round her neck and her red hair falling over her shoulders, looked more beautiful than even Lucinda had anticipated.

There was a vivacity about the dancer, making every gesture expressive and compelling attention. Her huge liquid eyes and sensuous red mouth were as much a part of her beauty as her low, musical voice.

"So you come, Madame!" she exclaimed in surprise as Lucinda was shown into the room.

"You did not expect me?" Lucinda asked.

"*Sí, Sí!* I was certain you not refuse," Juanita replied. "Please to sit down."

Lucinda took a seat on a sofa covered in a rich brocade and wondered if Sebastian had paid for the furnishings, which were overcrowded and over-ornate.

"Madame, you are not as I—how I say it?—I make picture of you," Juanita said, with a frown between her eyes.

Lucinda realized that while she had been looking at the room her hostess had been inspecting her critically and that there was something curiously akin to hatred in her large, dark eyes.

"What did you expect?" Lucinda asked.

"Someone from the country, someone quiet and—and as the English say—lady-like. But you different. People they talk about you."

"Do they?" Lucinda asked. "But I have not come here to discuss such matters. You said in your note that my husband was in danger."

"I wish very much to see you," Juanita said, as if she had not spoken. "They say you verry chic and the fashion after one, two weeks in London! I think they lie!"

Juanita was speaking in a strange foreign way which sounded almost threatening.

"I have also heard about you," Lucinda replied. "You dance delightfully, I am sure. I hope one night to see you at Covent Garden."

"Me-Lord, he has talk about me?" Juanita enquired.

"No, indeed, my husband has not mentioned you," Lucinda said.

"Then why—why he not come to me?"

Lucinda took the letter she had received from her reticule.

"You sent me this, Señorita," she said, severely, holding up the letter. "You told me that my husband was in danger. I am here to talk about that—and nothing else. If he is in danger I want to know why, and from whom."

Juanita bent forward and snatched the letter from Lucinda's fingers.

"I tell you I want to see you," she said. "I want to ask you why you keep him from me. I did not believe you come here, but I think perhaps you come quick if I say he in danger."

"So it was a trick, was it?" Lucinda asked.

Juanita tore the letter into a thousand pieces and threw them on the floor.

"You not understand!" she said, stamping her foot. "Every man in London—everyone of import—have mistress! But wife not come between, you understand? Wife not interfere. But you—you interfere! Me-Lord not come to me—not once since you marry him."

"Indeed?" Lucinda said, "And that, you think, is unusual?"

"O' course it unusual!" Juanita stormed, her eyes flashing and her full bosom heaving. "Before, Me-Lord come many times—now never."

"You think it is my fault?" Lucinda asked.

She was not in the least frightened or even embarrassed by this woman. It suddenly struck her that Juanita was exactly what she had expected her to be like—tempestuous, fiery—but, underneath it all, ineffective—a common woman who managed because she was beautiful to get the luxurious things of life out of men.

She had the feeling that Juanita had never really held Sebastian's heart—she might have amused him—but she was not, with all her vibrant beauty, half as dangerous as the pink and white Lady Devereux.

"I write Me-Lord—I send him note—I send message—but he not come," Juanita screamed. "Why? Why? Unless you . . . you stop him?"

"I assure you that my husband does exactly as he pleases," Lucinda said.

144

"Verry well," Juanita stormed, her eyes flashing. "He tired of me. Now I kill him—or I die!"

She picked up a long stiletto from the table of *objets d'art*. It shone and glittered wickedly in her hand—and Lucinda wondered if she herself might not be the victim.

Suddenly an idea came to her.

"I see that I must tell you the truth, Señorita," she said quietly. "Put down that very dangerous weapon and listen to me."

"I tell you he not go another woman!" Juanita cried. "I swear it! A wife—she nothing, unless she make trouble! And Me-Lord—he promise a wife make no difference—not come between us!"

"My . . . my husband promised you that?" Lucinda asked.

"*Sí, sí*—he promised—a vow, you understand? He love me—he love me so much—me, Juanita, who can have any man—any man I choose. But I chose Me-Lord because I love him—an' he love me."

"You love him so very much?" Lucinda asked softly.

"More than life!" Juanita answered dramatically.

"Come—sit down and let me talk to you," Lucinda said. "I have something to tell you."

Juanita looked wary.

"Is bad news?"

"Yes," Lucinda said with a sigh. "I am afraid it is bad news."

Almost reluctantly, as though she had enjoyed her performance, Juanita put down the stiletto on the table from which she had taken it and sat down beside Lucinda, looking at her a little apprehensively, her red mouth pouting.

"What I am going to tell you," Lucinda began, "must, of course, remain a secret between us. You must swear to me that you will not mention it to anyone, because the information I am about to convey to you could only have emanated from me. It would therefore be very embarrassing if you were to reveal what I am about to tell you. You promise?"

"I promise," Juanita said, "but if it affect the love of Me-Lord, then I not keep this promise."

Her eyes were suddenly suspicious.

"You having a baby? That what you tell me?"

"No, of course not," Lucinda replied. "It is nothing like that—but if you will not promise to keep a secret, then I must remain silent." She rose to her feet. "There is really nothing more to discuss, Señorita."

"No, no—do not go!" Juanita exclaimed. "The secret—I promise I not speak. You tell me—yes?"

"I will tell you," Lucinda said. "But you must promise on something you hold sacred."

She glanced at the mantelpiece and saw at the corner of it there was a rosary.

"You are a Catholic?" she asked, and Juanita nodded.

Lucinda picked up the rosary and held it towards her.

"Swear on this," she said, "that you will not reveal to my husband what I am about to tell you."

Juanita hesitated a moment, then she took the rosary in her hand.

"Sacremento!" she said sulkily. "I swear."

Lucinda sat down again on the sofa.

"This is the secret," she said quietly. "My husband has lost nearly all his money."

She heard Juanita give a little gasp and went on:

"Of course, as you speak so movingly of your depth of affection for his Lordship, this disaster will make no difference, to you personally. He will not be able to provide you with so much money . . . with horses, with more jewels . . . but as your tenderness is above such paltry trifles, you can still be his mistress and he can count on your help and loyalty in his affliction."

"Sí, sí, that I can understand," Juanita said.

"We have only just heard," Lucinda replied, "that a solicitor whom my husband trusted has absconded with a large amount of his fortune. But nobody must know—it would not be wise, you understand, for his creditors to realize that they may have to wait for their money."

"Sí, sí, that I can understand," Juanita said.

"His Lordship is very distressed, as you can imagine," Lucinda went on, "but he does not want anyone to learn of his misfortunes. And it is only because you have expressed your devotion so sincerely that I have entrusted you with his secret."

146

"This is the truth?" Juanita asked. "I told that his Lordship was verry rich—one of the most rich gentlemen in all England."

"He was," Lucinda said with a sigh, "until the last few weeks. Disaster has come upon him."

"That is bad fortune," Juanita said, "verry bad fortune."

Her tone changed. She rose briskly to her feet, her eyes on the clock on the mantelpiece.

"Soon I go to Covent Garden," she said. "But first I do something. I write a note—yes!"

"Not to my husband, I hope?" Lucinda said quickly. "You know what you promised."

"No, no. Not to Me-Lord—to a gentleman who ask me out to supper—a verry charming, verry rich man. I not give him my answer. Now I tell him, yes, we have supper —you understand?"

"I understand," Lucinda said.

"It is not that I no longer love Me-Lord," Juanita continued. "I love him verry much—but a woman must look after herself, you understand."

"I understand," Lucinda said again.

"I think Me-Lord verry lucky to have such a verry charming, verry elegant wife," Juanita smiled. "And you lucky, too—he—how you say in English?—irresistible. I have loved him verry much."

Lucinda noticed the past tense. She held out her hand with a smile.

"Good luck, Señorita," she said. "I hope one night that I shall see you dance."

"You let me know when you come Covent Garden," the dancer said, "and I dance my verry, verry best—just for you, yes?"

"I should enjoy that very much," Lucinda said.

The dancer opened the door.

"I like to say—'Give my love to Me-Lord', but I know you not tell him you have seen me."

"No—he must never know that," Lucinda said earnestly.

"I never tell him, I promise," Juanita said. "But be kind to him, because he is so very irresistible. You love him, yes?"

She spoke lightly; but Lucinda hesitated before she answered.

Then, in a voice which seemed to come between her lips without her consciously willing it to do so, she heard herself say:

"Yes . . . I love him."

9

"I love him . . . !"

Lucinda repeated the words to herself over and over again as she walked back along the sunlit streets to Berkeley Square."

". . . I love him!"

The sound of the horses' hoofs, the wheels of the carriages, seemed to be saying the same words—"I love him" . . . "I love him" . . .

It seemed nonsensical that the dancer's question should have made her realize her love when it had been there all the time.

She must, she thought now, have fallen in love when she first saw him—so smart and debonair, his beaver hat at a rakish angle as he cursed her and Nat from his high phaeton and forced them to move from the place they had been occupying for several hours, determined to get a good view of the mill.

She had thought then that she hated him! He had seemed like a satyr from another world, his many-caped riding coat of dark green, the high exquisitely tied cravat, his hands adeptly holding the reins of his magnificent horses.

"How dare he!" she had grumbled to Nat—and yet in her heart of hearts she had admired him for the ruthlessness which had made him get what he wanted, disregarding the feelings of other people.

She saw now that when she offered to marry Lord Meridan in Hester's stead there had been little sacrifice in her action.

She had been sorry for her father, and she wondered if it had been a question of marrying anyone else whether she would have been quite so eager.

She wanted to see the autocratic stranger again . . . to look at that handsome, scowling, sardonic face.

Of course, she had not realized it was love; she had never known what love was . . . until now.

It was not, she thought, the sentimental droolings of Hester and the limp, rather ineffective Colin; it was not the easy, comfortable mating of Joe and the rest of Nat's family.

She had always believed in her heart that love was like this—a tempest, a fire—something which would sweep her off her feet, overwhelm her and bring in its train not only joy and ecstasy but perhaps fear as well. In her girlish dreams she had wanted a man—and now she had one!

She stopped for a moment at the corner of Berkeley Square and put her hands to her eyes. Somehow it did not seem possible that she had lost her heart completely and irretrievably. And yet she knew that, in truth, that was what had happened.

She knew now why she had looked forward so eagerly to Lord Meridan's return from the country; why she had been able to endure the pain and the torture of having her tanned skin sloughed away like a snake's skin; and why she had stood uncomplaining hour after hour while Madame Bertin's gowns were fitted on her.

It had not really been because she wanted to be a social success; it was not only because she hated being plain and unattractive, the ugly duckling of the family. It was, although she would hardly admit it to herself, because she wanted to look attractive in her husband's eyes.

She could see again the astonishment in his face when they had met in the Park; she could see something which she believed to be admiration when she had come into the room later in the evening and told him that she was dining at Clarence House.

"How can I make him love me?" she asked wordlessly of the pigeons fluttering across the road in the gardens of Berkeley Square.

At least he was conscious of her—she supposed that she should be grateful for that. And now she had been daring

150

enough to eliminate—or at least partially eliminate—one of his mistresses from his life.

She felt her heart beat a little faster both with fear and anxiety lest she had made a mistake.

She had gone to Juanita da Riva out of curiosity and an urgent desire to know what this woman was like who could hold the interest, if not the heart, of anyone so mercurial as Lord Meridan.

But now that she had told her lie, and perhaps been instrumental in persuading Juanita not to bother Lord Meridan, she was not certain that she had gained very much.

It was Lady Devereux in whom he was interested. She had known that from her wedding day, when, peeping over the banisters, she had seen them together.

She had known it by the way Sebastian's eyes lingered on that beautiful pink and white face, and by the manner in which his courtesy was a little more impressive, a little more meticulous when it was applied to Lady Devereux.

"I hate her!" Lucinda told the pigeons. And then her heart, aching suddenly with an intensity such as she had never known before, added: "But I love you . . . I love you . . ."

The footman flung open the door almost before her hand had touched the bell-pull.

She entered the hall and saw that Lord Meridan's secretary was waiting for her.

He was a middle-aged, quiet little man with grey hair and grey clothes, who was so unobtrusive that he seemed to have no character at all. And yet Lucinda had learned that the smooth-running of Lord Meridan's two houses was almost entirely due to him.

He moved towards her with a note in his hand and said in his gentle, polite voice:

"I deeply regret bothering your Ladyship, but a groom has just arrived with a note. I thought that you would wish to have it at once."

"But of course," Lucinda smiled. "How are you, Mr. Greystone? As busy as usual?"

"Very busy, your Ladyship."

"Let us hope that this is not more work for you to do," Lucinda said, opening the note.

She saw the handwriting, and her heart gave a sudden leap even before she saw the signature. She would have known that strong, virile script anywhere, although she had only seen it on a letter to her father and in the register on her wedding day.

The note had no beginning, and she read:

I forgot when I left the House this morning that it is the Opening Night at the Opera. It is Customary to use the Family Box. Lady Devereux has graciously Consented to be one of our Guests and I would be Obliged if You Will Invite perhaps Seven Other People for Dinner and to accompany us Afterwards to Covent Garden.

I trust this will not Inconvenience You at so Short a Notice.

Sebastian

Lucinda read the note carefully and she looked up at Mr. Greystone and smiled.

"I am sorry, it is extra work!" she said. "His Lordship wishes a dinner party of ten tonight before we go to the Opera. He has aleady invited one guest—a lady."

Mr. Greystone was, Lucinda thought, the perfect secretary. He remembered from whom Lucinda had taken hospitality; who would be likely not to be already going to the Opera, and with whom it was easy to get in touch so that they could have an answer immediately.

Lucinda went into the library and wrote the notes, and Mr. Greystone, thinking of everything, persuaded her to write two extra in case those invited were already engaged.

"I will keep them, my Lady, until the groom returns," he suggested, "and then I will not have to trouble your Ladyship again."

"You think of everything," Lucinda said. "We shall need an odd man, so I hope Colonel Holstead is free."

"The Colonel usually makes himself free if his Lordship requires him," Mr. Greystone said simply.

"Yes, of course," Lucinda answered. "I cannot conceive what we would do without Colonel Holstead. I hope he likes opera!"

It was somewhat ironic that she had just come from Juanita. She had not expected to see her dance so soon.

152

She wondered if Juanita would realize that they were in the audience!

When Mr. Greystone had left the library Lucinda walked across the room and looked at herself in a carved mirror which was set over an exquisite marble-topped Charles II table ornamented with cupids.

She still found it difficult to recognize herself; her hair coiled high on her head, the diamonds flashing in her small ears, the dazzling whiteness of her skin seemed to belong to another person altogether.

"And yet I am the same," she murmured aloud. "I am Lucinda whom nobody loves and nobody wants."

It seemed to her that she could see Lady Devereux standing behind her—pink and white and gold—her eyes fringed with dark lashes, bright red mouth pouting a little.

"Does Sebastian really love you?" Lucinda asked the imaginary figure. "And do you love him? Or are you just like Juanita—out for what you can get? Would you love Sebastian if he were poor, if he could not give you those magnificent dresses, if he were not *persona grata* at Clarence House and one of the most envied men in London?"

Lucinda gave a deep sigh.

She wondered what Lord Meridan would say if he found out what she had told Juanita da Riva? The opera dancer had been stupid enough to believe her; but she was certain that in dealing with Lady Devereux far more subtle tactics would have to be employed.

Lucinda felt small and helpless. It had been frightening to enter the social world by herself; but now to try and win her husband's love—surely that would be an impossibility?

Then she remembered Beau Brummel's advice: "Don't be humble: force them to notice you!"

Still watching herself in the mirror, she flung up her head. Now the expression on her face was no longer worried and miserable, but resolute, alive, her eyes sparkling a little as she knew a man's eyes would sparkle before he went into battle.

Nat had told her so often, "You're not beaten until after the count."

"I will win him!" Lucinda told her reflection.

She picked up her feathered bonnet from where she had thrown it when she had come into the library and put it on her head.

This was the first time that Lady Devereux had come to the house since her wedding day. They had not met on that occasion, but tonight she should have no reason to ignore or overlook her hostess.

Lucinda was quite certain that it was Lady Devereux who had made Lord Meridan remember the opening night of the Opera. She would have reminded him and suggested that they might all dine together.

Lord Devereux was very likely to be in waiting on the Prince or had perhaps had to go to an official dinner to which wives were not invited.

Whatever it was, it was not chance that had made Lady Devereux decide to dine with Lord Meridan and his wife this evening! Perhaps she was showing her power to the rest of Society; perhaps she thought that if Lord Meridan saw her and Lucinda together it would be quite obvious who would eclipse whom.

Lucinda tied the ribbons under her chin with a firm hand and swept from the library.

"My carriage, please," she said to one of the servants in the hall.

"It is outside, my Lady."

Lucinda walked out into the sunshine. It did not take the horses long to swing into Bond Street.

There was the usual crowd of carriages outside Madame Bertin's but Lucinda walked straight through the salon and into Madame's private room.

The old woman was sitting at the table with the designs and patterns laid out in front of her.

Her face lit up when Lucinda entered the room, and she held out her hand eagerly.

"*Bonjour, chérie!* I not expect you this morning."

"*Bonjour, Madame,*" Lucinda said, and bent to kiss the wrinkled old face.

"I have a problem, Madame . . ."

Lucinda broke off to utter an exclamation of sheer delight, for lying on the table was the most beautiful dress she had ever seen in her life.

"Whose is it? Where did it come from?" she asked.

Madame put out her hand and drew the dress towards her.

"It arrive last night," she said, and lowering her voice, although they were the only two people in the room, she continued: "From France, of course."

Lucinda by now knew where Madame Bertin obtained the embossed velvets, exquisite gauzes, embroidered brocades and cobweb-fine lace. Such things were only made in France, and despite the war there was almost continuous traffic across the Channel.

The British coastguards and Customs officers did their best, but they were outnumbered and out-manœuvred. Napoleon, who badly needed the gold that such sales brought to France, encouraged smuggling, so that only an army of dragoons and the entire British Fleet could really have brought it to an end.

There were fishing vessels which stopped in mid-Channel when they met their French counterparts; there were parcels in every diplomatic bag; there were scores of smugglers and adventurous individuals who found it very much to their advantage not only to bring brandy and tobacco from the French ports to the quiet English havens and river inlets, but also to carry materials which were eagerly snapped up by the shopkeepers who catered for the quality.

The material of every gown that Lucinda wore had been manufactured in France, but it usually came in bales or rolls of uncut material.

However, this dress was already made, and now as she touched it she thought she had never seen anything so beautiful.

It was a gown for a Princess—no, better still, for a Fairy Princess, for only someone who might have stepped straight out of a fairy-tale was really qualified to wear it.

Of the finest lace, so thin and delicate that it might have been made by spiders rather than human hands, the pattern of flowers had been traced with tiny diamanté and coloured stones of glittering blue and ruby red.

It was enchanting—a poem in itself—and the ribbons which edged the neck and cupped the breasts had picked up the colours of the flowers so that the whole effect was a symphony of colour.

"How lovely—really lovely!" Lucinda breathed.

To her surprise Madame Bertin took a piece of white tissue paper and covered the dress.

"Non! Non! Do not look!" she commanded, "To do so will make you unhappy!"

"Unhappy?" Lucinda queried. "Is it for someone else?"

"How can I tell you what has occurred?" Madame Bertin asked. *"Ma pauvre petite,* it is a tragedy and one that I cannot bring my tongue to relate!"

"But of course you must tell me," Lucinda said.

Madame Bertin gave a deep sigh which seemed to come from the depths of her large, fat body.

"The parcel *arrive* last night," she said. *"Hélas,* do not ask me who brought it! But there were no questions about the entry of *ce paquet* into England."

Lucinda smiled. She knew how proud Madame Bertin was that she could use the diplomatic bags. It gave her an almost undue feeling of importance.

"It *arrive,"* Madame Bertin went on, "just as we close ze shop. I open the box, I look, I say to myself: 'That shall be for *ma petite* Lucinda!' But I have an ache of ze head. I do no more than look. Miss Varden come in, I say to her: *'Voilà,* a gown which would sell and sell! *C'est entendu!* The cost? It must, I say, be one hundred pound!' "

"One hundred pounds!" Lucinda ejaculated.

Madame Bertin nodded.

"I tell no one, not even you, *mon petit chou,* what I pay for such a gown!"

"It is worth it!" Lucinda exclaimed. "Go on."

"Miss Varden help me into my coat, I go home. All night I dream how *ravissante* you look in ze gown—if we find just ze right occasion for you to wear it."

"The right occasion is tonight!" Lucinda cried. "We are going to the opening of the Opera . . . and . . . Lady Devereux is dining with us."

Lucinda had no secrets from Madame. She knew that her husband was paying for Lady Devereux's gowns, and after Madame Bertin's kindness she had told her what she had overheard that first day in London.

Madame, perhaps better even than Lucinda herself, knew why it was so important that Lord Meridan should see a change in his wife, should find her a very different person from the untidy, plain girl he had married.

Now Madame Bertin groaned aloud, and without meeting Lucinda's eyes went on:

"Faites attention! This morning I arrive at ze shop. I sleep *tres mal,* so I a little late. Miss Varden meet me all smiles. 'You will be very pleased with me, Madame,' she say. 'I have sold the gown! And not for one hundred pounds—but for one hundred guineas! What do you think?' "

"She had sold it!" Lucinda ejaculated.

"She had sold it," Madame Bertin repeated grimly.

"To whom?" Lucinda enquired.

Even as she asked the question she could see the answer in Madame Bertin's face.

"C'est impossible! It is Lady Devereux."

"But she cannot have it!" Lucinda cried. "Oh, Madame . . . you cannot let her have it!"

"You have not heard *la fin de l'histoire,"* Madame Bertin said. "Lady Devereux come here to leave dress to be altered. I think she not mean to get out of ze carriage, but Miss Varden, *c'est une folle* that one, invite her in. When Lady Devereux see ze dress she fetch Lord Meridan from ze carriage!"

Lucinda's lips tightened. She turned from the table and walked across to the window, looking out with unseeing eyes on to the untidy yard at the back of the shop.

"They must have been on their way to Ranelagh," she muttered.

"Lord Meridan agree to give it to Lady Devereux—as a present," Madame Bertin finished, her voice flat and despondent.

Lucinda turned around.

"She is not going to have it!"

"Ça y est! She wear it tonight!" Madame Bertin answered. "It is to be altered for her. She is too large, *la vache,* for ze gown. *Hélas,* she spoil it! Ze red ribbons to be taken off so only ze blue remain. Ze blue—so simple, so unsophisticated!"

"She shall not spoil it! It . . . it . . . is vandalism!" Lucinda exclaimed.

She pulled the piece of tissue paper from the dress and looked at it again.

"Mon Dieu, vous êtes blessée!" Madame Bertin said, a little brokenly. "You . . . who have meant so much to me. I cut off my right hand rather than let that *chienne* have it."

If Lucinda had not been so distressed she would have laughed at Lady Devereux being referred to in such derogatory terms.

"She is not going to have it!" Lucinda cried. "Listen, Madame, I have a plan, if only you will agree . . ."

Without waiting for an answer, Lucinda started to move around the rolls of material which cluttered half the room.

She thrust aside two or three dozen before she found what she was looking for. It was a lace, an English lace—which, although attractive, did not compare in any way with its French sister lying on the table.

Lucinda put it down in front of Madame Bertin and started to talk quickly. Before she had spoken a dozen sentences Madame was clapping her hands.

Miss Varden, looking apprehensive with red eyes, for she had obviously been weeping, came running into the room.

"What is it, Madame?"

"Fetch ze work-girls here—all of them."

Miss Varden hesitated.

"They are busy . . ."

"Do as I say," Madame interrupted. *"Dépêchez-vous!* All must come. Ze packers, ze matchers—*tout le monde,* you understand?"

"Yes, Madame, of course," Miss Varden said, running obediently to carry out her orders.

The clock was striking as Lucinda came down the grand staircase into the hall at Berkeley Square.

She moved slowly, trying to quell the fluttering in her breast as of a hundred butterflies. Her lips felt dry and she moistened them a little before she reached the hall and waited for the footman to open the door of the small salon. Here they were to assemble before dinner.

She glanced at the clock as she entered, hoping that her plans would not go awry.

Mr. Greystone had been bemused and puzzled by her decision earlier that afternoon to send messages to their guests that dinner was a quarter of an hour later than she had previously said.

"Your Ladyship may be late for the Opera," Mr. Greystone said a little anxiously.

"It will not matter," Lucinda told him.

Now Lucinda smiled as she heard the door of the salon open and Lord Meridan came in.

He was looking particularly handsome, she thought—or perhaps it was just because her heart leapt at the sight of him that she found him more attractive than ever.

He was wearing a coat of oyster satin which had been cut by Weston—who was, all the dandies inferred, the only tailor in London who could cut a coat without ruining it.

There was a glitter from the emeralds and diamonds which fastened his waistcoat, and his evening breeches were almost like a second skin.

He had brushed his hair in the very latest windswept style affected by the Prince—and Lucinda wondered whether all this elegance was because Lady Devereux was his guest tonight.

He walked towards her and she saw that he was in a good humour and there was no frown between his eyes.

To her surprise he took her hand and raised it to his lips perfunctorily, but with a grace which made her catch her breath.

"Have you spent a pleasant day?" he asked.

"Very pleasant," she answered. "I hope that the party tonight will be a success."

"Why not?" he said. "Though I admit at times I find the Opera a deadly bore."

"I hardly dare say it," Lucinda told him, "but I have never been to the Opera."

Lord Meridan looked astonished, then he smiled.

"In which case we must contrive to make it a memorable evening for you," he said. "Incidentally, the Duchess of Melchester has asked us to supper afterwards. Would you like that?"

"I should like it very much," Lucinda said.

He smiled at her again.

"I am glad that you are wearing the rubies," he said. "They were my mother's favourite jewels."

He did not seem to notice her shimmering, fairy-like gown. But Lucinda was not surprised at that. She had long since learned from her mother that "men seldom notice a woman's clothes". And she had privately ended the sentence with ". . . unless she does not look attractive in them."

"Some day you must tell me if you would like the jewels reset," Lord Meridan said, surprisingly gracious.

"I like them as they are," Lucinda replied, "Especially the rubies and the emeralds—I have never seen such wonderful stones!"

"They become you," he said.

She had a feeling that his eyes were telling her rather more than his lips. She glanced at him and looked away— how humiliating if he should ever guess how much she loved him!

She knew that merely the sound of his voice had the most strange effect on her so that she felt as if she were walking on air. She could still feel the little quiver that had passed through her when he had touched her hand.

"I must be careful," she thought, "very careful."

"Will you have a glass of Madeira?" she enquired. "Or will you wait until our guests arrive?"

Lord Meridan turned to look at the clock.

"They are late already," he said.

Even as he spoke the door was flung open and the butler announced in stentorian tones:

"Lady Devereux!"

She came into the room with a faint inviting smile on her lips—which Lucinda suspected she had practised in front of the mirror.

She was wearing a dress of lace embroidered with blue and red stones and with blue ribbons round the neck which tied under her breasts.

It was a pretty gown, a gown that any woman would have admired and thought most becoming and attractive— if they had not seen Lucinda's first.

Lucinda, her whole body glittering and shining in the light of the candles, with the Meridan rubies on her head and round her neck, stood in the centre of the room and waited.

Lady Devereux gave a gasp which was quite audible. The faint smile that had curved her lips vanished and for a moment her mouth fell open foolishly. Then her lips snapped to like a vice and she lost her temper.

She moved up to Lucinda, and with the words coming between her lips almost like a hiss she said furiously:

"You—you are wearing my gown!"

Lucinda's eyes opened wide.

"Wearing your gown?" she repeated. "What can your Ladyship mean?"

"I mean what I say!" Lady Devereux snarled. "That is my gown—the one I bought! I thought there was something wrong when this one arrived—it was not so well embroidered, not so chic, not so elegant as the one I saw this morning! Now I know what has happened—*you* have taken my gown and you are wearing it! How dare you defraud me in such a fashion?"

Although it was hard to take her eyes from Lady Devereux's contorted face, Lucinda stole a glance at Lord Meridan.

He was looking surprised, and yet at the same time, as she had expected, a little disgusted.

She had known that he would hate scenes, hate them as all men hate them! But above all else he would dislike a scene between his wife, who bore his name, and his mistress, who was herself a social figure.

"You and that old witch have contrived it between you!" Lady Devereux raged, her voice rising hysterically. "I bought that very gown and ordered it to be sent round for tonight—I bought it, I tell you! And I knew there was something wrong the moment I took this one from the box!"

Lucinda turned a bewildered face towards her husband.

"I think, Sebastian," she said gently, "her Ladyship must be indisposed. I have not the least idea of what she is complaining."

"You—you know well enough!" Lady Devereux cried accusingly. "And you, Sebastian, know that what I am saying is the truth! You saw the gown—I showed it to you! And now she is wearing it—flaunting it in front of me!"

Lucinda heard the door open, but she did not take her eyes from Lady Devereux's flushed and furious face.

"I am afraid your Ladyship is entirely mistaken," she said clearly, "because when this gown arrived for me the bill was inside the box—and it was made out to my husband! So there is no possibility of error. How could there be?"

As she spoke, the butler announced:

"Colonel Charles Holstead."

Charles advanced into the room, and took in, with curious eyes, the scene which was being enacted.

Lady Devereux, who seemed to have been paralysed by Lucinda's words, suddenly regained her senses. She put her hands up to her forehead.

"I am ill," she said quickly. "I must see a physician . . . Sebastian, take me home, I beg of you!"

She put out one hand appealingly to him.

Then in a cold, icy tone which only he could use so effectively, Lord Meridan replied:

"My carriage is, of course, at your Ladyship's disposal."

It was a dismissal, and Lady Devereux realized it. She raised her face to his, a sudden pallor making the patches of rouge on her cheeks stand out hideously. Then without a word she turned and went from the room, a beaten and vanquished woman.

"What is happening?" Charles Holstead asked, surprise written all over his face. "Is something amiss?"

It was such a ridiculous question that Lucinda could hardly help giggling.

She forced back her laughter and only by the sudden sparkle of her eyes did she reveal her true feelings.

"Is her Ladyship laid low?" Charles asked Lord Meridan. "Do you wish me to see her home?"

"She will be all right," Lord Meridan replied, indifferently. "A glass of wine, Charles? Or would you prefer brandy?"

"Wine, I think," Charles answered, and raised Lucinda's hand to his lips.

"You are looking magnificent," he said. "And why are your eyes shining like carriage lamps?"

"He is too perceptive," Lucinda thought, and gave him a tiny frown.

As if he realized that he had been indiscreet, Charles glossed over the momentary silence by saying:

"I cannot say that I am much looking forward to the Opera tonight, Sebastian. Last time we went you called the performers long-winded yowlers and vowed you would never sit through such misery again!"

"We need not stay long," Lord Meridan answered. "Besides, as all our guests are so late we shall not be there until it is half over."

"Late!" Charles ejaculated in astonishment. "Why, we weren't asked . . ."

There was a frantic glance from Lucinda and he realized that once again he had put his foot into it.

"You know what people are," he went on a little lamely, "they are never up to time. It is all too much of a broil, if you ask me, this bull-rushing from place to place, from party to party."

"You would be very disappointed if you were not invited," Lucinda said. "And wait until you have spent years in the country as I have, never doing anything exciting."

"It might be nice and peaceful," Charles said. "I have a mind to get married and settle down."

"Why not?" Lord Meridan asked. "It might save a lot of complications and difficulties."

He spoke enigmatically; and Charles, raising his eyebrows for a moment at Lucinda, answered:

"You set me such a delightful example of connubial happiness, Sebastian—what could be more pleasant, for instance, than seeing Lucinda at the head of the table tonight gracing the Meridan jewels and making them look even better than they are?"

To Lucinda's surprise, Lord Meridan replied:

"I have just been telling her that she does them proud."

Even as he spoke, the guests, surprisingly punctual at the time Lucinda had actually asked them, came crowding into the room.

She just had time to tell the butler in an aside that they would only be nine for dinner, and that one place should be removed, before they all moved into the dining room.

The chef had excelled himself, and Lucinda made a mental note to thank him on the morrow. She had an idea that he had made a special effort as it was her first dinner party.

163

Lucinda, because she was exhilarated, found it easy to be gay and amusing. When the port was circulating round the table she signalled to the ladies and they all withdrew.

It took some considerable time for the ladies, gossiping among themselves in Lucinda's bedchamber, to don their cloaks, the men to finish their port, and to get them all assembled and into the coaches that were waiting outside.

Lord Meridan and Lucinda were the last to leave, and Charles, having no coach, was to accompany them.

Lucinda was just leaving the house when a man stepped up to the door and said in a loud voice:

"Oi wants ter speak with th' Earl o' Meridan!"

He pronounced his name wrongly, and Lucinda, looking at his woollen pullover and rough trousers, thought that he looked like a fisherman.

"That's enough, my good man! Move away!" the butler said in an angry aside.

"Oi've somethin' for 'im," the man said.

The butler signalled to the footman, and Lucinda had the idea that the man was going to be forcibly removed from their path.

"One moment," she said quietly. "If this man has something to give his Lordship it might be of import."

"Ye're right there, loidy!" the man said.

Lucinda looked over her shoulder and saw that Charles and Lord Meridan were talking together, quite unaware of the man's arrival. She turned back.

"Sebastian," she said, putting her hand on his arm, "there is a man here—he looks like a fisherman—who says he has something to give you."

"Something for me?" Lord Meridan exclaimed.

He walked to the door where the butler and the footmen had surrounded the man, who was standing stolidly in the midst of them.

"You enquired for me?" Lord Meridan asked.

The fisherman looked him up and down.

"Be ye th' Earl?" he asked.

"I am," Lord Meridan answered.

"Then—'ere's somethin' fer ye."

The man put his hand into his trouser pocket and brought out a letter. Lucinda could see that it was written on mauve paper. He put it into Lord Meridan's hand and would have gone.

"Here, wait a minute!" Lord Meridan said. "Where did you get this letter?"

"Oi doesn't 'ave ter tell ye that," the man said. "Oi've done what Oi was a-paid for—given it Oi 'ave into yer own 'and."

"But I would like to know where you got it," Lord Meridan said.

A faint smile came into the brown, weather-beaten face of the fisherman.

"Ever 'eard of th' English Channel?" he asked a trifle mockingly. "Well, 'alf of it belongs to th' Frogs—or they thinks it do! Let's say Oi met 'em 'alf-way, so ter speak."

"Thank you," Lord Meridan said. "Good night!"

He flicked a golden coin towards the man, who caught it deftly.

"Thank 'e, sir. Ye be a lord, orl roight!" the man said, and moved off down the square.

Lord Meridan stepped back into the house, and, curious, Lucinda followed him.

He looked at the note and gave a soft ejaculation between his teeth.

"Good God!" Lucinda heard him say. "It can't be!"

"A *billet doux* from France?" Charles remarked, who had heard the whole conversation. "Only you, Sebastian, would have the nerve to keep up a correspondence with your French friends while we are at war. How do you reply—by the same method, or by pigeon post?"

Lord Meridan ignored him. He opened the letter and smoothed it out because it had been crumpled in the fisherman's pocket, and read it with a frown between his eyes. Once again he gave a little ejaculation.

He appeared to read the note through twice, then he folded it and put it in his pocket.

"Listen, Charles," he said. "This is urgent. We have got to get hold of Anthony Hawkesly and James Courtney."

"Whatever for?" Charles asked.

"You will hear in good time," Lord Meridan replied.

He turned to the major-domo.

"Go immediately in the carriage to Brooks's," he said. "Present my compliments to Sir Anthony Hawkesly and

Lord Courtney and ask them to meet me here as speedily as possible. Explain to them it is of the utmost urgency."

"Very good, my Lord," the major-domo answered, apparently unsurprised by such a request.

Lucinda did not say anything.

As if he suddenly remembered her presence, Lord Meridan said:

"I regret Lucinda, that I am unable to accompany you to the Opera tonight. If you wish to join our guests I will arrange for Greystone to escort you the moment the carriage returns. Unfortunately I personally cannot be present."

"I will remain here," Lucinda answered.

She waited, hoping that Lord Meridan would explain further, but he turned towards Charles.

"Come into the library," he said sharply.

"Dash it all, Sebastian," Charles said. "What about your guests—won't they think it is odd if you do not turn up?"

"Yes, of course," Lord Meridan replied. "I had forgotten."

He looked round. The major-domo had already left the hall, but the butler was standing there.

"Newman," he said, "ask Mr. Greystone to be so obliging as to leave at once for the Opera in a hired carriage and tell the guests in my box that her Ladyship is unfortunately indisposed and we are therefore prevented from joining them."

He paused, then asked:

"You are quite sure, Lucinda, you will not change your mind?"

"Yes, go, Lucinda," Charles urged her. "I cannot think what all this twitter is about! It is so like Sebastian to create a tangle at the last moment. But you go and enjoy yourself. I will take you—it won't involve us in above a quarter of an hour."

Lucinda shook her head.

"No, Charles," she said. "Thank you very much, but I think Sebastian wants you. And I really do not mind."

"It is a pity for no one to see that gown," Charles said.

"I will wear it another time," Lucinda answered.

She held out her hand to him and as she did so Lord Meridan walked impatiently into the library.

"Can't think what all the pother is about," Charles said in a low voice. "But, anyway, I gather you won your battle tonight."

"I hope so," Lucinda whispered.

"Sebastian always did hate a scene," Charles said reflectively. He looked at Lucinda out of the corner of his eyes. "Perhaps you knew that? Or did you guess it?"

"I guessed it," Lucinda answered.

"I don't know whether you are a very clever woman or a child of the devil," Charles told her.

Lucinda merely laughed as she went up the stairs.

When she reached the landing she stood for a moment thinking. Then, moving past the drawing room, she went to the far end where there was a small door, which was almost unnoticeable, set between two pillars.

When Lord Meridan was away, and she had been alone in the house, she had spent quite a considerable time exploring the whole place.

She found this door and it was locked. She had asked the housekeeper for the key and was given it, with the explanation that the housemaids were not supposed to use the small staircase that lay beyond it.

Lucinda had opened the door and gone down what appeared to be almost a secret staircase, wending its way to the ground floor.

Here she found herself in an elegant little room which she thought at first must be a powder closet. Then she discovered that it led through a door concealed by books into the library.

It took her some time to puzzle out that when the house was built it had been convenient for whoever was then Lord Meridan to be able to reach the bedroom floor from his sitting room without having to go up the main staircase.

Perhaps the present owner, Lucinda thought, also found it convenient—she did not know. But what she had learned, quiet inadvertently, was that everything that was said in the library could be overheard.

Moving now very softly across the room, which was lit only by the last flickering rays of the sun coming through a small window, Lucinda reached the concealed door which led into the library and heard Charles say quite clearly:

"For God's sake, Sebastian, come to the point! Why all the Cheltenham theatricals? Are the Duns after you? Has someone called you out? I cannot conceive otherwise why you should spoil Lucinda's party and leave the poor child alone upstairs while we two hold a board meeting . . ."

"I will explain everything when the others arrive," Lord Meridan said testily.

"Well, tell me one thing," Charles asked, "who the hell is that letter from? Who has caused all this commotion?"

Lord Meridan seemed to hesitate a moment, then he said:

"Do you remember Yvonne de Beausole?"

"The play-actress?" Charles asked. "Is it likely that I should forget her? I had to kick my heels around Paris for two months while you were dancing attention in that direction! Don't tell me she has written to you after all this time?"

"She has not only written," Lord Meridan answered, "she is in trouble, Charles."

"What sort of trouble?" Charles enquired.

"She is a prisoner of Bonaparte's," Lord Meridan told him, "and we—you and I, Charles—are going to rescue her!"

Lucinda, listening the other side of the door, gave a little groan.

This meant danger, she was sure of it. Danger to Sebastian. Her heart contracted at the thought, and the words seemed to dance before her eyes—Danger! Danger!

10

Kingsclere picked up the reins: The black horses reared once or twice, and then, with a thunder of hoofs, started away at a pace which set the curricle rocking and swaying.

Lucinda felt the light wind on her cheeks, but it was not cold and she had no need to draw her fur-trimmed driving cape closer around her.

She glanced up at Kingsclere sitting straight and erect beside her, his eyes on the road ahead, and she knew that although he had said nothing he was almost as exhilarated as she was.

This was a race against time and both of them knew that the challenge in itself was irresistible.

It had taken nearly an hour and a half since Lucinda had first learned what was being contemplated for her to send for Kingsclere, get her portmanteaux packed and creep down the back way to the stables.

She had only waited to hear exactly what her husband was planning before she moved away from the false door in the secret ante-room and ran to the library.

"My yacht is at Brighthelmstone," she heard Lord Meridan say. "We can get there soon after dawn and set sail before the sea mist has lifted."

"My dear Sebastian, you cannot go sailing straight into Boney's invasion barges," Charles expostulated.

"I am not such a nitwit as that," Lord Meridan replied coldly. "We will sail west and move down the Normandy coast under the lee of the land."

"It sounds reasonable," Charles said, "but what happens when we arrive at our destination?"

"We will make our plans when we get aboard. Between the four of us we should be able to think of some plan of attack."

"And how do you intend to reach Brighthelmstone by dawn?" Charles enquired. Lucinda imagined him glancing at the clock on the mantelshelf as he spoke.

"We will change horses at Meridan," she heard her husband reply. "Prinny holds the record so far—Brighthelmstone in four and a half hours! We might contrive to best him. I believe there is a wager of a thousand guineas against it in the betting book at White's!"

"How do we go?" Charles asked.

"You and I will travel on horseback," Lord Meridan replied "and the other two can come in my curricle. That will give us time to get the sails hoisted and be ready to start as soon as they arrive. . . ."

It was then that Lucinda had crept upstairs.

Sir Anthony Hawkesley and Lord Courtney had still not arrived. That at least gave her a little time in hand.

She rang for her abigail and sent a chambermaid, who was tidying the room, in search of Kingsclere.

She prayed that he would not be off-duty and it was with a feeling of intense relief that about ten minutes later her maid announced that he was waiting to speak to her in the boudoir.

By this time Lucinda had changed from her beautiful embroidered gown into a dress of emerald green with a driving coat of rich velvet in the same colour frogged with silver braid.

Her hat trimmed with feathers to match, made her look as though she was just about to take a short constitutional in the Park rather than embark on a wild rush to the coast.

There was something reassuring in Kingsclere's steady blue eyes as he listened to her.

"We must reach Brighthelmstone before his Lordship," Lucinda said in a low voice. "He and Colonel Holstead will be riding. did you know that?"

"The order came before I left the stables, milady," Kingsclere said slowly.

"Two other gentlemen will be following in his Lordship's curricle," Lucinda said, "but we must be ahead of them all. Do you know where his Lordship's yacht is anchored?"

"Yes, I know that, milady," Kingsclere said stolidly.

"Then get me there before anyone else arrives," Lucinda commanded, and asked apprehensively: "Is it possible?"

To her relief Kingsclere smiled.

"We'll do it, milady."

It seemed to Lucinda that centuries passed before two footmen came for her luggage and informed her that the curricle was ready.

Her abigail had already commanded them to take the luggage down the back stairs, and Lucinda followed down the narrow stone stairway, which was very different from the broad carpeted staircase she normally used.

Long flagged passages brought her eventually to the covered way down which she and Charles had come on her wedding day and which led to the stables.

There Kingsclere was waiting, the horses champing restlessly and tossing their heads as though they knew what was expected of them.

Lucinda's luggage was stowed away at the back. There was no groom, so there was plenty of room for her two heavy portmanteaux and the square leather box which held her bonnets.

She caught the expression on Kingsclere's face and guessed that he was impatient with such feminine fripperies, but her realization of the importance of clothes was too new for her to be prepared to sacrifice her appearance, whatever the dangers which lay ahead.

At last they were off, speeding down the empty streets, across the Thames and into the open countryside.

The moon was rising in the sky—a full moon without clouds—which turned the road to a ribbon of silver and made the flickering candles in the curricle lights quite unnecessary.

"No one in the stable will tell his Lordship that we have left, will they?" Lucinda asked anxiously.

"If they do, milady, they knows that I'll skin 'em alive when I return!" Kingsclere answered, and there was a grimness about his tone which told Lucinda that no one would dare thwart him, however pressed they might be.

She was, moreover, certain that Lord Meridan would

not ask questions or even remember her existence. Just in case he should do so, she had left instructions with her abigail to say that she was asleep.

"Where will we change horses?" she asked, after they had travelled several miles.

"Meridan, milady."

"Meridan?" Lucinda echoed. "Surely that would be indiscreet?" His Lordship would be certain to hear of it.

"Not at Meridan Hall, milady," Kingsclere corrected, "but in the village. The landlord of the posting inn is a cousin of mine and he keeps good horseflesh. He'll also be able to relate whether we are ahead! However much his Lordship travels across country, he has to pass the Dog and Duck to turn into the drive of Meridan Hall."

Lucinda gave a little sigh and settled herself comfortably in the seat.

If she had not been anxious about what lay ahead, this drive would have been one of unsurpassed enjoyment. She had never believed that horses could go so fast or that anything could give her as much satisfaction as knowing that she owned them.

She remembered that Sir Galahad, the horse she had bought on her wedding day, was at Meridan and wondered if on her way back she would be able to call and find out how he was getting on.

"On the way back . . . ?" the words echoed in her ears. It was a question—a big question, to which for the moment there was no answer.

Despite her preoccupations with her clothes and her new position in Society these last weeks, Lucinda had heard all around her of Napoleon Bonaparte's plans to invade England.

Some people said there were thousand upon thousand of barges waiting at Calais and Boulogne for the right wind to carry them to Dover.

Others had said pettishly that the whole thing was a hum and Bonaparte had invented the story just to frighten the English and keep some of their fleet away from the Mediterranean.

It was difficult to know what was the truth.

Lucinda had heard that bonfires had been built along

the coast and that soldiers were continually on the alert, ready to signal the first sign of the hated French.

It was a crazy idea of Lord Meridan's to attempt at a time like this to rescue a woman from France, especially when she was apparently a prisoner in the very heart of the battle-front.

But Lucinda knew it would be useless to argue. She had not known her husband long, but she was certain of one thing—he was man enough to make up his mind and to refuse to change it, whoever might oppose him. And who was likely to do that?

She had already met Sir Anthony Hawkesly and knew him to be a charming good-natured young man who had a love of adventure which would make this seem one of the best invitations he had received for a long time.

The same applied to Lord Courtney, who was, if anything, even more irresponsible than his friend Sir Anthony.

They were dandies, but of the type who were not content with sitting about at their tailors or taking their exercise at the faro tables.

They hunted, shot, rode their own horses at race meetings and were on occasion quite prepared to challenge someone they disliked, not with duelling pistols but with their fists.

In fact, Lucinda thought with a little sigh, they were the type of young men she would expect Lord Meridan to have as friends—men who in a crisis would behave like men and not like the Tulips of Fashion who only hung about St. James's.

Yet however much she might like and admire the four men who were about to cross the Channel, and love one so much that her heart beat quicker at the thought of him, she was neither stupid nor blind. What they were doing was an act of complete and absolute lunacy!

Courage would not overthrow the armed soldiers who would be patrolling the coast; and bravado could be soon exposed when it came to stepping ashore on French soil.

"It is mad . . ." the horses' hoofs seemed to be beating out as they sped along the country lanes. . . .

"But I love him . . ." the wheels seemed to answer as a shower of dust and gravel followed in their wake. . . .

Presently Lucinda looked over her shoulder at the road

winding behind her and wondered if she would see two riders on horseback or a curricle following them.

"What horse will his Lordship ride?" she asked Kingsclere.

"He has a favourite stallion, milady. They call him Black Boy, but he's not as dark as these beauties, having two white fetlocks. He's a wonderful horse, but his Lordship will be slowed up a little by Colonel Holstead. The only match for Boy is Vulcan—the bay. I expect your Ladyship remembers Vulcan?"

"I know them both," Lucinda said, thinking of how many hours she had spent in the stables during her first days in London when, alone in Berkeley Square, she had sought the companionship of the horses.

"We must go faster!" she cried in a sudden terror.

"We'll do it, milady—don't worry," Kingsclere replied soothingly.

"How much start do you think we have got?" Lucinda asked.

"Quite a lot, milady," Kingsclere answered. "After the grooms had Black Boy ready I told 'em there was something wrong with the girths, so they had to change the saddle."

"And was there something wrong?" Lucinda enquired.

If Kingsclere had not been looking ahead, Lucinda would have thought that he winked one eye.

"Well, milady, perhaps the knife I had in me hand slipped a trifle," he said a little hesitantly.

Lucinda laughed.

"Kingsclere, you are unscrupulous! You are giving his Lordship a handicap!"

" 'Tis us that's got the handicap, milady," Kingsclere replied, "with those two great portmanteaux of your Ladyship's up behind. I can feel them a-weighing us down. Suppose now, we leave them with my cousin at the Dog and Duck?"

"No, no, Kingsclere," Lucinda answered. "I must have my gowns with me. You would not want me to arrive in France and have the French ladies putting me to shame?"

"France? Is that where ye be a-goin', milady?" Kingsclere asked, and there was both awe and astonishment in his voice.

"Yes, that's right," Lucinda said. "His Lordship is going to France to rescue a . . . a friend of his."

She hesitated again and added:

"If anything should happen to us, Kingsclere—if, by any chance, we do not return—will you take my horses home to Nat and tell him to look after them?"

"Ay, I'll do that, milady," Kingsclere said. "But you'll be a-comin' back. His Lordship isn't one to fail at anything he undertakes."

Lucinda felt her heart lighten at the words. Of course Sebastian would not fail. As Kingsclere said, he was successful in everything he undertook—gambling, racing, hunting—there was nothing in which he did not excel.

Her pride turned to a deep depression. How could she ever be of interest to him? How indeed, could she ever aspire to gain the love of such a man? And then Beau Brummel's words came back to her: "Do not be humble."

"I will win him," she thought, and looking up at Kingsclere, cried:

"Faster, Kingsclere, faster! We have to be there before them!"

It took them only two and a half hours to reach Meridan. It was a small sleepy village three miles off the main road and set among undulating green pasture land with verdant woods stretching away into the horizon.

The horses, sweating, with the foam from their mouths splashing on to the silver of their harness, drew up with a flourish in the cobbled yard of the Dog and Duck.

"Ostler! Ostler!"

Kingsclere's deep voice was loud enough to wake the dead.

In a few seconds two men came running from the stables, rubbing the sleep from their eyes.

"Change these horses! And sharp about it!" Kingsclere commanded. "I'll come and see what you have in the stable—I don't want any of your rubbish."

"And who says that I am likely to have rubbish in my stables?" asked an angry voice from the door of the inn.

Then the man's angry tone changed.

"So 'tis ye, cousin!" he exclaimed. "Well, I might 'ave known no one else would've made such an 'ullabaloo at this hour o' the mornin'!"

"I've got to have your best, Bart!" Kingsclere said, and dismounting went round to the other side of the curricle to help Lucinda alight.

She ran into the inn where the innkeeper's wife, wearing a red flannel dressing gown, was just coming down the stairs with a candle in her hand.

It took only a few minutes for Lucinda to wash her hands and face, sweeping away some of the dust from the journey, and by the time she had finished the innkeeper's wife had a cup of hot chocolate waiting for her in the parlour.

She gulped it down.

Outside she could hear the grooms, with their broad country voices, saying "Whoa! Steady, boy!" "Back 'im now!" as they got the new horses into the shafts.

Then, almost before she had set the cup down, Kingsclere was hollering:

"We're a-ready, milady!"

She ran outside and sprang into the curricle before anyone could put out a hand to help her.

The new horses were not to be compared with her own, but they were strong and fresh and set off at a good pace.

They did not leave the Dog and Duck by the side road by which they had come, but followed a narrow country lane farther south, and Lucinda guessed that they would join the main road a little farther on.

They had travelled less than half a mile when Kingsclere pointed to his left.

"There's Meridan Hall, milady," he said.

Lucinda turned her head.

Over a brick wall she could see parkland stretching away to where, silhouetted against the dark woodland, stood the most exquisite house she had ever seen. The grey stones seemed almost silver in the moonlight and the windows gleamed like jewels. There was a huge lake in front of it and terraces winding like necklaces down to the water.

She had only a glimpse of it and then they passed two large wrought-iron gates and the house was out of sight.

"It is lovely!" she thought to herself.

She had a sudden feeling that she had seen the house before. Then she realized it was only because it was so beau-

176

tiful and so perfect that it was like a dream house which one had known in one's sleep, and which on waking became familiar.

"I could be happy here," she thought, ". . . happy with Sebastian . . . and his children."

The idea made her quiver a little. And before the impossibility of such a thought thrust her into despondency she told herself that one day that, too, should come true.

They were back on the main road and making what speed they could before Lucinda remembered to ask an all-important question.

"They are not ahead of us?"

"No, his Lordship has not passed the Dog and Duck," Kingsclere answered. "My cousin said he could swear to it."

"But would he have heard him?"

"Trust Bart to keep his eyes and ears open," Kingsclere reassured her. "Your Ladyship saw how quickly he appeared in the yard when we arrived. Well, he was in bed and asleep a few seconds earlier, but he heard our horses in the distance and he had his shirt and his trousers on before we could reach the inn."

"Then he is certain to hear his Lordship," Lucinda said, reassured.

"He would have heard him, and I don't believe, milady, that even Black Boy could have come quicker than we have done," Kingsclere said with satisfaction. "We've beaten His Royal Highness's record for the first part of the journey, at any rate."

"Four and a half hours to Brighthelmstone, wasn't it?" Lucinda asked.

"Ay, that's right," Kingsclere answered. "But they weren't carrying any surplus weight. They say His Royal Highness even left his fob behind in case the extra ounce or so would slow the phaeton."

"I am sorry, Kingsclere," Lucinda said with a little smile. "One day we will come to Meridan and I will bring nothing with me—not even a reticule!"

"Then, milady, we'll have the chance to show them what we can do," Kingsclere answered stolidly.

Dawn had still not broken although there was lightening

in the sky when they reached the outskirts of Brighthelm-stone.

The little fishing village which the Prince of Wales and Mrs. Fitzherbert had made so fashionable was quiet and undisturbed in the waning light of the moon.

There was, Lucinda noticed, a mist coming up over the sea and she thought with a sense of relief that Sebastian had been right and at least they could slip away unnoticed.

The harbour where the yacht was anchored was a few miles out of Brighthelmstone, but Kingsclere knew his way and they did not pause but hurried along the coast to where an inlet of the river made a natural harbour with cliffs rising on either side of it.

It was hard to see clearly. There were a number of boats anchored in the calm water and amongst them Lucinda thought there was one of a much larger size which would undoubtedly be Lord Meridan's.

"You cannot stay here, Kingsclere," she said nervously. "If the others arrive they will see the horses."

"I'll go back by another road, milady," Kingsclere promised. "as soon as I have seen you aboard."

He pulled the horses to a standstill and shouted at the top of his voice:

"*Lapwing* ahoy! *Lapwing* ahoy!"

It was the first time that Lucinda had heard the name of Lord Meridan's yacht, and seeing the long, graceful lines of the boat with her elegant masts pointing towards the sky she thought the name was somehow appropriate.

"*Lapwing* ahoy!" Kingsclere yelled again.

"They will be asleep," Lucinda said in a suddeny agony. "They will not hear us! His Lordship will arrive before they can reach the shore!"

"I'll wake 'em!" Kingsclere said grimly.

But even as he cupped his hands around his mouth a voice beside them said:

"Can Oi help 'e, sir?"

It was a fisherman.

"Have you a boat?" Lucinda asked quickly.

"Ay, lady. 'Tis down there. Oi be a-takin' me nets aboard," the man answered.

"Will you row me out to the *Lapwing*?" Lucinda enquired. "I will give you a guinea to do so."

178

"Ay, Oi'll do that," the man answered. "An' if ye be in a hurry Oi'll take ye afore Oi gets me nets."

"Yes, please do that," Lucinda answered. "My coachman will give you a hand with my portmanteaux."

She reached out to take the reins from Kingsclere. He got down and the two men carried her luggage to a rowboat.

The moonlight was fading and now the mist seemed to be coming in from the sea, so that for a moment it blotted out almost everything except the horses and the lobster pots on the quay.

It was very quiet and Lucinda found herself straining her ears for the sound of horses' hoofs in the distance.

Would she be in time? Would she get there before Sebastian? She was quite certain that if he arrived now, even at this late hour, he would refuse to take her aboard.

"Hurry! Hurry!" she longed to shout, and then to her relief she saw Kingsclere coming back through the mist. She almost threw the reins at him and scrambled down from the curricle.

"Thank you, Kingsclere—thank you more than I can ever say," she said breathlessly.

"It's been an honour to help you, milady," Kingsclere answered.

"Do not let his Lordship see you, will you?" Lucinda asked, giving a last glance over her shoulder towards Brighthelmstone.

"His Lordship won't see me, milady," Kingsclere promised. "An' good fortune accompany you!"

His words came back to her through the mist as Lucinda was running towards the water's edge. She found the fisherman and he helped her into his boat. He pushed off carefully from the side of the rough wooden pier and at last they were on the water with the tiny wavelets lapping gently against the side of the boat.

They drifted for a moment until he got his oars ready; then as he started to row she saw that he was not wasting much time. In a very short while the side of the *Lapwing* loomed up above them and the fisherman's "Ahoy there!" got a sleepy response from the watch.

"Oi've a passenger for ye," the fisherman yelled.

A surprised face looked down at Lucinda.

179

"Fetch the Captain immediately," Lucinda commanded. "I am Lady Meridan."

There was a round of running footsteps over wooden boards, subdued voices, more footsteps, and at last a man whom she guessed to be a Petty Officer said in a breathless voice:

"The Captain's compliments, my Lady, and he will be with you in a few minutes."

A rope ladder was let down, and if Lucinda had not been used to what her mother had often described as her "tom-boy" trick of climbing trees, she might have found it difficult.

As it was, she scrambled up it quite easily and was helped respectfully aboard by the Petty Officer, hat in hand.

A moment later, still buckling his coat, the Captain marched from his cabin.

"My humble apologies, my Lady," he said, "for not being on deck to welcome you. His Lordship expects us always to be ready for visitors, but I was not anticipating anyone so early in the morning."

"Can we talk, Captain?" Lucinda asked. "I have something of import to impart to you."

"Of course, my Lady," the Captain answered. "Will you allow me to show your Ladyship the way to the cabin?"

"Please order my luggage to be brought aboard immediately," Lucinda said. "And will someone give this piece of gold to the man who brought me here?"

She drew a sovereign from her reticule and handed it to the Captain who passed it to the Petty Officer who gave it to the fisherman.

Lucinda turned to follow the Captain towards the cabin when a thought struck her.

"Please inform the man," she said, "that if anyone asks questions he is to say that he has not seen me nor brought me here."

The Captain seemed slightly surprised as he passed the order to the Petty Officer who passed it to a seaman who apparently passed the information on.

As she reached the companionway Lucinda heard the fisherman guffaw and say in his loud, rough voice:

"Aha! It be loike that, be it? Well, Oi thought her were a fancy piece myself!"

The captain tut-tutted beneath his breath.

Lucinda smiled. What did it matter what anyone thought, so long as Sebastian did not learn of her whereabouts before they sailed?

Lord Meridan and Charles Holstead were in fact congratulating themselves on having had a successful journey even if they had not beaten the Prince's record.

"We would have done it if you had not insisted we drink wine at Meridan," Charles complained.

"I am really not particularly concerned as to whether we beat Prinny or not," Lord Meridan said. "At the moment we have other more important things to think about."

"Well, it would have been pleasant to have been able to tell him of our triumph," Charles said. Then with his eyes twinkling he added: "If you were man enough to do so—I can imagine nothing which would upset him more!"

"Let him enjoy his childish record," Lord Meridan said. "We are engaged on a dangerous mission, Charles, and we must treat the matter seriously if we do not want to spend the rest of the war languishing in a French prison—I am told they are monstrously uncomfortable."

"This is your crazy idea, not mine," Charles retorted. "Personally, Yvonne de Beausole can be the prisoner of the Emperior of China for all I care. Besides, if you ask me, she's not suffering. She'll twist the gaolers round her little finger."

"She appealed to me for help," Lord Meridan answered. "I cannot very well chuck her letter on the fire and ignore her distress!"

"My dear Sebastian," Charles said, "it is not Yvonne's appeal which has brought us posting here—it is the challenge which excites you. In your heart you believe that except yourself no one could rescue a piece of muslin from Boney's clutches! So you are damn' well going to have a crack at it!"

They reached the harbour as he finished speaking and they drew in their reins, trying to peer through the mist.

"I hope to God the yacht is there!" Charles said. "I can

do with a rest and a drink. If you want the truth, Sebastian, I found the last part of the journey cursed exhausting."

"You are out of condition, that's what is wrong with you," Lord Meridan answered.

He was looking as immaculate and unperturbed as if he had just stepped out of the door of his house in Berkeley Square. His cravat was unwrinkled and the only things to proclaim that he had travelled hard and fast were that his highly polished boots were dusty and his horse was sweating beneath him.

"Would you condescend to give the yacht a holler?" he asked his companion.

"Do you think they will hear me?" Charles enquired doubtfully.

"If the watch is asleep he will get the push," Lord Meridan answered. "My instructions are that they are to be ready to set sail day or night with the least possible delay."

It gave him a sense of satisfaction when, within a few minutes of Charles's shout across the water, a boat with three men in it came swiftly towards the pier.

The Petty Officer sprang ashore.

"Good morning, my Lord!" he said, saluting.

"Good morning, Petty Officer!" Lord Meridan answered. "I see you have two men with you. Will you arrange for one to stay here with the horses until a curricle arrives with the grooms?"

"Very good, my Lord," the Petty Officer said.

Lord Meridan embarked in silence. The seaman who was left to hold the bridles hoped that the grooms would not be too long in relieving him.

The Captain was waiting aboard to greet his master.

"I thought I might surprise you, Captain Jenkins," Lord Meridan said.

"Not at all, my Lord," the Captain answered. "We try always to be ready for your Lordship's arrival."

Lord Meridan glanced at Charles Holstead.

"Good service, eh, Charles?"

"Excellent!" Charles answered.

"Set the sails immediately, Captain Jenkins," Lord Meridan went on. "I have two further guests arriving shortly; then we leave for France."

182

"For France, my Lord?"

The Captain raised his eyebrows slightly. But his voice was too respectful for the words to sound as if they were a query.

"For France," Lord Meridan said, "and for Boulogne to be exact. We sail west at first. Captain Jenkins, cross the Channel as unobtrusively as possible and try to creep in along the lee of the Normandy coast."

"Very good, my Lord."

Lord Meridan walked towards the companionway and was soon sitting comfortably below decks in the big for'ard cabin. The steward was commanded to bring wine and breakfast.

The noise of rushing feet overhead, the creak of the rising sails and the rocking of the boat at anchor as the wind lifted them made Lord Meridan lie back in his chair with a smile of satisfaction on his face.

"Like old times, Charles, isn't it?" he said. "And I cannot help thinking that no one else would have got off to a quicker start."

"Let me collect," Charles said. "We must have left Berkeley Square soon after eleven . . ."

"Eleven o'clock and thirty-five minutes to be exact," Lord Meridan said. "If Anthony and James bestir themselves we will get away before the dawn has broken and while there is no one about."

"Does it matter if we are seen?" Charles asked.

"Too many damn' spies along the coast for my liking," Lord Meridan replied. "I never did trust half those Frenchie fellows who say they came over with the Revolution. If you ask me, quite a number of them are in the pay of Napoleon."

"I have often thought that myself," Charles said.

There were sounds on the deck above which brought Lord Meridan to his feet.

"The others are here!" he exclaimed.

A few seconds later the door opened and Sir Anthony Hawkesly and Lord Courtney came into the cabin.

"Well, you have taken a hellish long time getting here!" Lord Meridan said.

"Curse you, Sebastian," Sir Anthony replied, "we beat the record!"

"I do not believe it!" Charles cried.

"Or very nearly," Lord Courtney admitted. "If Anthony had not stopped to pick up his clothes we should have reached Brighthelmstone five minutes before Prinny's memorable achievement!"

"I like that!" Sir Anthony exclaimed. "It was James who kept complaining he did not want to go to France in his best evening breeches!"

"Anyway, you are here," Lord Meridan said. "That is all that matters. Yes, Captain Jenkins?"

"We are ready to sail, my Lord. They are raising the anchor."

"Very good, Captain."

The Captain saluted and the door closed behind him.

"Well, we are off!" Charles exclaimed. "My God, Yvonne is a fortunate young woman, if she did but know it!"

"What about rescuing a few other charmers while we are about it?" Sir Anthony asked. "I don't see why Sebastian should have all the fun on this trip?"

"Now, listen!" Lord Meridan expostulated. "We must plan our campaign."

"We will make plans when you have given us something to eat," Lord Courtney said. "Damme! I am peckish after that long drive."

"And so am I," Sir Anthony agreed. "You are being a dashed poor host, if I may say so, Sebastian."

"Breakfast is ordered," Lord Meridan answered. "In the meantime, a glass of wine?"

He filled four glasses just as the steward came in with breakfast.

They heard the rattle overhead as the anchor came up on the winch and the smack of the wind in the sails. Then there was a sudden list and a surge forward as though, like a horse, the yacht was straining at the leash and eager to be off.

Lord Meridan raised his glass.

"To us," he said, "and the rescue of a damsel in distress!"

"To us!" Charles Holstead repeated gravely. "And let us hope to God that we get home again."

"I wonder if anybody would mind if we didn't?" Lord

Courtney said as he set down his glass. "I have the uncomfortable feeling we would not be missed!"

"Oh, really, James!" Sir Anthony exclaimed. "You always throw a damper on anything. Think of the tears that would be shed if we were not around! The gloom in Brooks's would be noticeable even by Prinny when he is in his cups!"

"I hope you are right," Lord Courtney said gloomily. "Anyway, I shall make my will and leave it with the Captain. That is, if we are to go ashore—and I am quite certain that Sebastian intends that we should."

"You are much more likely to be sunk before we ever reach the coast," Charles said seriously. "I think, James, you should wear a lifebelt of some sort, if you can get one round your stomach!"

"My stomach!" Lord Courtney exclaimed. "I am a jolly sight thinner than you, Charles, as well you know. I will bet you a monkey that I can give you inches!"

"Done!" Charles Holstead said.

"Now wait a minute,'" Lord Meridan intervened. "Before you two start chipping at each other, let us get a few things settled. We cannot just walk ashore in an idiotic manner without making proper plans."

"Well, you are the Commander-in-Chief," Sir Anthony said. "What do you suggest?"

"There are four of us, to start with," Lord Meridan said, sitting himself comfortably in a chair and pouring himself a glass of brandy. "Now who speaks French?—and I do not mean the sort of *"j'aime, tu aimes"* you try out on the love-birds."

"I was once top of my form at Eton," Lord Courtney said, "but that was when the French master was ill!"

"Personally, I never soil my mouth with the Froggie tongue," Sir Anthony announced. "I've got along very well without it, even though it is the fashion at Clarence House to say in French what you can say far better in English."

"The trouble with you, Anthony," Charles said, "is that you were born with the Union Jack over your head."

"If by that you mean I am English," Sir Anthony said aggressively, "I do not mind telling you, my dear fellow, that I am damned proud of it!"

"And you, Charles?" Lord Meridan said, as though Sir Anthony had not spoken.

"Well, I can say a few words here and there," Charles said. "And I used to be able to understand a bit when I was younger. I had a French mistress for several months three years ago. You will remember her, James—a rather pretty little dove. Can't remember what her name was now, but she was so damned avaricious—always asking for more money—that I couldn't stand the pace."

"My head is to let!" Lord Meridan exclaimed loudly.

"Why?" Lord Courtney asked before Charles could think of some witty repartee.

"Because, having chosen you to accompany me, I thought only of your loyalty and the fact that you are all handy with your fists. I forgot that what we need is an interpreter, or at least someone who could ask the way to the château."

"You, Sebastian—surely you have all the graces?" Charles asked.

Lord Meridan looked slightly shamefaced.

"As a matter of fact, French never was my subject," he confessed. "Oh, I can get along all right, but nobody is going to take me for a Frenchman. Greek and Latin were my subjects at Oxford, but they are not going to help us. They tell me when I'm making love I come up to scratch, but that does not mean that I have what you call a large vocabulary."

"Devil take it, we're sunk!" Charles ejaculated. "Better send for the Captain and ask if there is anyone on board who can speak the jargon."

"There is no need to do that," a voice said from the door. "For I am persuaded that I can be of assistance to you all."

The four men turned swiftly at the sound of a woman's voice, and gazed spellbound as Lord Meridan jumped to his feet and said angrily:

"Lucinda! What the devil are you doing here?"

11

Lucinda did not answer, and from the other occupants of the cabin there was for a moment the silence of stupefaction. Then Charles found his voice.

"Dash it all, Lucinda!" he exclaimed, rising to his feet, "you are as unpredictable as Bonaparte himself!"

Lord Courtney and Sir Anthony also rose. There was no doubt from the admiration in their eyes and the smile on their lips that Lucinda's appearance, if a surprise, was a welcome one.

She had changed from her dust-covered riding dress into a most elegant gown of sea-blue batiste trimmed with green ribbons. As she moved across the cabin towards the chair that Charles held out to her she looked not unlike a nymph which might have sprung from the waves.

She smiled, then glanced a little nervously at Lord Meridan. She saw by the expression on his face that he was angry.

"I am very sorry, Sebastian," she said, "if my arrival should . . . inconvenience you; but I . . . I felt that I might be useful to you."

"How did you get here?" Lord Meridan enquired. "It is impossible that you could have been ahead of us at the rate we were travelling."

"Then I achieved the impossible," Lucinda said gaily. "We changed horses at Meridan before you and Charles arrived."

"You were in your curricle?" Lord Meridan asked.

Lucinda nodded.

"But it is beyond the bounds of credulity!" Charles ejaculated. "Sebastian and I came across country. We let the horses have their heads. If you went by the road . . ."

His voice trailed away as if he could not put his astonishment into words.

Lucinda laughed.

"I will admit to starting before you did," she said.

"How did you know we were coming . . . ?" Charles began, only to be silenced by Lord Meridan.

"If you will excuse us, gentlemen," he said with an imperious wave of his hand, "I would like to speak to my wife alone."

"We will go on deck and see if there is any sign of the French Fleet," Sir Anthony said tactfully. "If there is, I only hope, Sebastian, that this vessel of yours will be able to show them a clean pair of heels! I have no fancy for being blown out of the water by a twenty-pounder."

"I told Sebastian that the whole idea was devilish dangerous," Lord Courtney was saying a trifle plaintively as they filed into the companionway, followed by Charles, who only turned at the last moment to say:

"Deal gently with Lucinda, Sebastian. I am sure that she has beaten Prinny's record—and I am in a fever to return to London and tell him so! A woman! It'll give him a heart attack!"

He shut the cabin door with a little bang.

Lucinda, conscious of the ominous silence between herself and her husband, started to speak quickly.

"I did not tool the horses," she said. "Kingsclere held the reins. I knew, Sebastian, that if I did not arrive aboard the yacht before you did you would refuse to let me embark."

"Naturally," Lord Meridan said, and added: "How, may I ask, did you learn of this project?"

Lucinda looked embarrassed, then with an obvious effort she raised her eyes to his.

"I . . . I listened," she faltered.

"At the keyhole—like a servant?" Lord Meridan asked scornfully.

"No," Lucinda replied, "in the little room which leads off the library. It has a staircase which runs up to the bedroom floor. Did you know about it? I cannot conceive why it was ever built or why anyone should want to use it."

Lord Meridan appeared for the moment to be flicking an imaginary fleck of dust from the lapel of his coat.

Then he said almost harshly:

"Wherever it was, you were listening, and that was not particularly lady-like or an action I should have expected from my wife."

"I am . . . sorry," Lucinda replied, "but if I had not learned about it that way you would have just sailed away to France without telling me . . . without even saying good-bye!"

"That is not the point," Lord Meridan said even more vehemently because he saw the justice of her remark. "You promised me . . ."

"Yes, I know," Lucinda interrupted. "I promised when you were so kind about the Comte that I would behave more . . . circumspectly and in a manner that was becoming to the Countess of Meridan. But this was different, Sebastian—you must see that! It was not I who was getting into a scrape, but you."

Lord Meridan glared at her for a moment, then despite himself the corners of his mouth twitched.

"Really, Lucinda," he exclaimed, "you are incorrigible! You have an answer for everything! But you know as well as I do that you should not be here on this yacht—to help me rescue a lady who, to put it bluntly, is not accepted in Society."

"She is an actress, is she not?" Lucinda asked. "And I believe she is also what they call 'a bit of muslin'?"

"Lucinda!" Lord Meridan thundered. "How have you ever heard of such an expression?"

"As a matter of fact that is what Charles said in the libarary," Lucinda anwered. "He said, 'She was an amusing bit of muslin, Sebastian, but is she really worth rescuing?' "

"You cannot take into account all that Charles says," Lord Meridan said briefly. "I am not certain that he is at all the right company for someone as young as you."

"Of course, he did not know I was listening," Lucinda interposed.

"Of course not!" Lord Meridan said. "And I hope that he will never find out."

"He is bound to guess, though," Lucinda said, "unless he thinks that I am a witch or a fortune-teller."

"Will you not make difficulties!" Lord Meridan said in an exasperated voice. "You have got us into a pretty coil, if you ask me. Here am I, setting off on what I admit is a somewhat wild adventure with three bachelor friends—and what would everyone say if they knew that I had carried my wife into danger?"

"Why should anyone know?" Lucinda enquired. "Surely you can trust Charles and Sir Anthony and Lord Courtney not to chatter? Besides, until now I have always been told that you never cared a fig what Society said about you."

"That was before I met you," Lord Meridan retorted almost sulkily. "The devil takes it! But when a man is married he has to think about the honour of his name and the behaviour of his wife!"

Lucinda crossed the cabin and put her hand on his arm.

"Forgive me, Sebastian," she said and added beseechingly: "And pray do not be angry with me. I know full well that I should not have come. But I could not have borne to be left behind, wondering what was happening to you . . ."

She paused and quickly added the word ". . . all" to her sentence.

"Well, I cannot turn round now," Lord Meridan said. "It would serve you right if I ran ashore farther along the coast and left you to walk home!"

"You would not do anything so cruel!" Lucinda cried. "Besides, think what a scandal that would cause—the Countess of Meridan with bleeding feet trudging unaccompanied down the country lanes. . . ."

"Curse you, Lucinda!" Lord Meridan said in despairing tones. "You need a good spanking, that's what you need. I cannot think what your father was doing all those years not to give you one!"

"I got lots when I was small," Lucinda said happily, "but they never did any good."

"You have been one long headache ever since I have known you," Lord Meridan said, working himself into a passion. "First there was your madcap behaviour after your wedding! Then making everyone talk about you with your horses, Kingsclere and the black phaeton! After

190

which you nearly killed Jacques de Falaise. And now this! I swear I cannot think why I got married at all."

"To get back into Almack's—don't you remember?" Lucinda answered.

Her words seemed to throw Lord Meridan into an even greater fury. Angrily he poured himself a glass of brandy from the decanter which stood at his side.

Then before he could drink it Lucinda's hand was once again on his arm:

"Please . . . please do not be vexed with me," she said pleadingly. "I shall be useful, I know it. How can any of you get anywhere without knowing the language?"

"Why can you speak it so well?" Lord Meridan asked suspiciously.

She saw the expression in his eyes and laughed in a manner which was almost irresistible.

"It was not Comte Jacques," she said, "nor Madame Bertin, although I do talk French with her because it makes her so happy. No, my grandmother was French, and Mama used to boast about it until the war and now she does not like to mention it."

"I suppose that accounts for the darkness of your hair?" Lord Meridan said, as if he had noticed its colour for the first time.

"Yes, I am like her," Lucinda agreed. "Hester takes after Papa's side of the family. I have a close resemblance to the painting which used to hang in the salon but which now has been put away on the top corridor."

Lord Meridan did not say anything and Lucinda went on:

"We had a French governess when we were small, but Hester never seemed to get the hang of what she was saying. It all seemed to come naturally to me. When she left I tried to continue conversing. Fortunately there were French prisoners not ten miles away from our home. I would ride over with the Catholic priest and translate to him what the poor men wanted to say."

"So that is the explanation," Lord Meridan remarked, and Lucinda noticed that either the brandy or the explanation had appeared to mollify him. He no longer seemed incensed.

Encouraged, she sat down again on a chair, and putting her elbows on the table said earnestly:

"Do you not think it would be a good idea if we obtained a map and had a council of war? You cannot just walk into France demanding Mademoiselle Yvonne de Beausole."

"I know exactly where she is," Lord Meridan replied. "She had drawn a little plan on the back of her letter. The château is outside Boulogne, not far from the beach, and is, I imagine, not inconspicuous."

"In which case it should be easy for the French to keep a watch on it," Lucinda said drily.

"Why the devil should they want to do that?" Lord Meridan enquired.

Lucinda did not speak for a moment, and then she said:

"You are quite convinced, Sebastian, that this is not a trap?"

"A trap?" he asked incredulously. "Who would want to trap me? That's a nonsensical idea, if ever there was one!"

"Yes, yes, of course," Lucinda agreed. "It was foolish of me. But I thought there was talk of Napoleon having invasion barges at both Calais and Boulogne, in which case there is likely to be quite a number of soldiers about."

"There is always that possibility," Lord Meridan said. "But I see no reason for you to concern yourself over the details, Lucinda. Whatever happens you will remain on board."

"Oh no, Sebastian!" she protested.

Lord Meridan rose to his feet.

"That is one thing I am not going to argue about," he said. "It is an order and you will obey it. You have no right to be here, Lucinda, and I am certainly not having you running into danger. If anyone could be assured of getting themselves into a tangle, or cause a battle to break out, it would be you!"

He put his glass firmly down on the table with a bang. As he did so, and before he could say more, the cabin door opened.

Charles looked in.

"There is a sail to starboard, Sebastian," he said. "I do not think it is likely to cause us any anxiety, but I thought you would wish to know."

"Yes, indeed," Lord Meridan said. "Give me a telescope, Charles. Does it look like one of ours?"

"It is impossible to tell," Charles answered.

"Whichever it is, let us hope it does not see us," Lord Meridan said.

He picked up his hat from where he had thrown it on a chair and placed it on his head, and taking the telescope from his friend's hands went from the cabin.

Charles did not follow him.

"So you have not been knocked out for the count?" he said to Lucinda with a hint of laughter in his voice.

"No, I am still on my feet," she answered, "though slightly winded! At first Sebastian was as mad as fire!"

"Who could blame him?" Charles said, sitting down on the edge of the table and looking down at her. "You must have known there would be the devil to pay when you set off from London."

"I was determined not to be left behind," Lucinda said simply.

"Poor Sebastian!" Charles said, his eyes twinkling.

"Why do you say that?" Lucinda asked.

"Because he thought he was marrying a nice meek and mild little woman who would make no difference to his life," Charles answered. "She was supposed to sit at home sewing—or whatever women do with their hands—and have babies! He did not bargain for a firebrand like you."

Lucinda's eyelashes swept her cheeks. Then suddenly she looked up at Charles and asked in a very small voice:

"Do you think that he has a dislike of me?"

Charles looked back at her with a quizzical expression in his eyes, and he asked softly:

"You love him, don't you?"

Lucinda's hands flew to her cheeks.

"No . . . yes . . . oh, how did you guess? Is it so obvious?"

"Only to me," Charles told her. "You see, Lucinda, if I had had the luck to meet you before your wedding day I would not have let you marry Sebastian."

"You wouldn't?" Lucinda asked, wide-eyed.

Charles shook his head.

"No, I would have had a thundering good try at marrying you myself. You are the sort of person with whom a fellow could never get bored. And it is not only that, Lucinda. I can't help it, but I am falling in love with you."

"Oh no, Charles . . ."

Lucinda held out her hands.

He took them and pulled her to her feet. She was standing beside him, and because he was sitting on the table, and she was so small, their faces were on a level with each other.

"I am sure of it now," Charles said quietly. "I love you—it is something that I never expected to say in all sincerity to any woman. Will you run away with me?"

"You do not really mean that!" Lucinda answered. "Think of the scandal!"

"Pooh! A fat lot I care for scandal!" Charles said. "No, that's not true. I haven't a title, like Sebastian, and I am not as warm in the pocket either—but the Holsteads fought for King Charles and managed to keep the house out of the hands of those cursed Roundheads. You wouldn't be ashamed of me, Lucinda. And I know that we would deal well together. Also I believe I could make you a sight happier than Sebastian will ever make you."

Charles, who had spoken quickly, paused for breath.

"That was a hellish long speech, Lucinda," he said. "Never thought I would find myself spouting like a poet to any woman in those terms."

Lucinda's fingers tightened on his.

"Thank you, Charles," she said; "dear, kind Charles, you have been a friend to me since the very beginning, haven't you? One day you will really fall in love with somebody who will love you in return."

"But I love you," Charles persisted. "Come away with me, Lucinda."

"I wish I could say yes," Lucinda answered. "It would be exciting, wouldn't it? Tearing away in a post-chaise with Sebastian chasing after us brandishing his pistols. . . ."

She paused a moment, her eyes alight with the idea. Then she said a little dolefully:

"There is only one thing—he might not care . . . he might be glad to be rid of me."

"If you ask me, he would miss you more than he knows himself," Charles said. "But do not let us talk about Sebastian. Will you let me take you away? Not in some rotten post-chaise—that would be the outside of enough. I have my own horses, and good ones."

"But not as good as Sebastian's," Lucinda said.

"To hell with Sebastian!" Charles raged. "Here I am, offering for you, and all you do is talk about your husband!"

"Not only because he is my husband . . . but because I love him," Lucinda said. "Oh, Charles, swear to me by all that you hold sacred that you will never let him know! Perhaps one day he may really be interested in me. I would be just like all his other women—running after him like hungry dogs while he throws them a bone occasionally when he thinks about it."

"Good God, Lucinda, that's Sebastian right and tight!" Charles exclaimed. "You have thought it all out, haven't you?"

"Of course," Lucinda answered. "Will you keep my secret?"

"You know I would do anything you asked of me," Charles said. "I only wish you would listen, Lucinda—I am telling the truth when I say I love you,"

"I know you are," Lucinda answered, "and I am grateful, Charles . . . inexpressively grateful. Because you have asked me to run away with you it means . . . oh, much more than I can tell you! But I do thank you!"

Her eyes were misty for a moment. Then at the expression on Charles's face she bent forward and kissed him gently on his cheek.

"You will always be one of the kindest men I have ever met in my whole life," she said softly.

"Damme, Lucinda, if you talk like that you are going to make me cry . . ." Charles began and then before he could complete the sentence he saw that the door was open and that Lord Meridan was watching them.

They sprang apart guiltily.

Lucinda felt the colour flooding into her cheeks as she realized that Lord Meridan must have seen her kiss Charles and would undoubtedly put quite the wrong construction on it.

"Your pardon if I am an intruder in my own cabin," Lord Meridan said heavily. Then throwing the telescope down on the table he said sharply:

"I was foolish enough to believe, Charles, that you were a friend of mine and realized Lucinda was my wife, I see I was mistaken."

"Now, Sebastian, do not take on that tone with me!" Charles answered. "It is not as you think—or anything like it."

"I still have the use of my eyes," Lord Meridan said thunderously

"Oh, please, Sebastian," Lucinda interposed, "do not misunderstand us! Charles had said something very kind to me . . . I kissed him without thinking. There was nothing wrong or even indiscreet in it."

"That," Lord Meridan said unpleasantly, "is a matter for conjecture."

"I give you my word," Lucinda replied, "and Charles will give you his—there was nothing wrong in that kiss, I promise you. It was the sort of kiss I might give to anyone."

"And doubtless do," Lord Meridan interrupted. "The Comte probably enjoyed such favours before you did your best to beat his brains out."

"That is unjust and unkind," Lucinda retorted. She had been miserable and apologetic, but now she felt her temper rising.

"I am afraid you must think me old-fashioned and a prude," Lord Meridan said pompously, "but as I have already said to you so often, Lucinda, I expect the woman who bears my name to keep up some appearance of gentility, to follow some of the conventions. But it appears that, where you are concerned, you have not the slightest idea of how a lady of quality should behave."

There was so much vehemence in Lord Meridan's voice that Lucinda went pale.

"Hell take it, but you are going too far, Sebastian!" Charles ejaculated. "If you want to call me out, do so, and I will accept your challenge without hesitation. What do you want to make it—ten paces? Or shall we shoot each other across the table and make sure we both die?"

"You will do neither!" Lucinda cried, recovering almost instantaneously from the attack Lord Meridan had made on her. "If you think either of you is going to be so bird-witted as to fight over me I tell you here and now I will not have it."

She turned towards Lord Meridan.

"How dare you attack me, Sebastian, or say that I do not know how to behave like a lady, when you certainly do not behave like a gentleman! I suppose if I were the sort of wife you thought you were marrying I would now retire to my bed and weep bitter tears into my pillow because you have insulted me. Well, all I can say is that I am used to insults!"

Lucinda paused for a moment and drew a deep breath. Then, her words falling over each other, she continued:

"What about the gowns you have been buying for Lady Devereux—the one for which you were prepared to spend a hundred guineas? And what about the way you went off with Charles to play around with a lot of ladybirds, the very day after we were married?"

Lord Meridan made a sound of anger or protest, but Lucinda would not be checked.

" . . . Oh, it's no use looking shocked and pretending I should not know about such things," she stormed. "You have just said I am not a lady. But I am not going to have you making a cake of yourself with Charles just because I kissed him for being kind to me . . . and I am very much in . . . need of . . . kindness."

Lucinda's words were spilling out of her mouth in a low and furious voice. Her eyes were brilliant with anger and her breasts were heaving tumultuously. She looked more attractive and more exciting than she had ever looked before.

It seemed as though Lord Meridan and Charles Holstead were spellbound.

Now as she finished speaking there was a pause, and neither of them said anything.

Lucinda crossed the cabin and pulled at the bell-rope which hung on a panelled wall.

"We are not going to go on talking this type of fustian," she said, "when there are so much more important matters to consider. It will not be long, I imagine, before we are in enemy waters and within sight of France itself."

Still Lord Meridan said nothing, only watching her with a strange expression on his face. And Charles, who opened his lips to speak, after a glance at his friend, closed them again.

The steward knocked at the door and came in.

"Ask Lord Courtney and Sir Anthony Hawkesly if they would be so obliging as to step down into the cabin," Lucinda said decisively.

"Very good, milady."

The steward vanished, and Lucinda, a defiant expression in her eyes, looked towards Lord Meridan.

Then, as if the sight of him softened her, she ran towards him and dropped down on her knees beside his chair.

"Oh dear, I know I am behaving outrageously!" she cried. "My wretched tongue! I should not have said all those things. It is my tiresome temper . . . and when I lose it there is no knowing what I will say."

She looked up at him, her eyes wide and apprehensive, her lips quivering a little.

"I am sorry," she faltered. "I will try to be a lady . . . I will, really."

Just for a moment Lord Meridan's expression did not change, but the irresistible little twitch at the corner of his mouth brought a twinkle to his eyes.

"I would lay almost any bet against you succeeding in that aspiration," he said softly.

"But I will . . . try . . ." Lucinda said a little piteously.

He put his hand on her shoulder and his fingers almost half encircled the white column of her throat.

"Perhaps it would be a pity if you tried too hard," he said, and now there was no mistaking the chuckle that seemed to be wrenched out of him.

"Oh, Sebastian . . . you are not angry," Lucinda said.

"You aren't, are you? I . . . could not bear it if you went on being incensed with me."

"You are a naughty brat—and I am furious!" Lord Meridan said.

Just for a second she dropped her cheek against his hand.

"I am . . . very . . . very contrite," she murmured.

"That's a lie!" Lord Meridan chuckled. "But I suppose one more does not matter."

Charles moved to a port-hole and looked out to sea, as

198

if he could not bear to watch what was happening in the cabin.

"You . . . forgive me?" Lucinda asked softly, quite unaware that there was anyone else present except herself and her husband.

"You are an incorrigible nuisance—an imp sent specially to torment me," Lord Meridan replied. "But I forgive you."

"I . . . I am so glad," she whispered.

Her face was very close to his. He looked into her eyes and it seemed for a moment as if the world stood still and they were alone, completely and utterly alone—and nothing else mattered.

Then, as something stirred and quivered within Lucinda, the door opened and Lord Courtney and Sir Anthony came hurrying into the cabin.

"We have a good breeze behind us," Lord Courtney said. "If it keeps up, the Captain says we shall see the French coast well before dusk."

"That is exactly what I want!" Lord Meridan exclaimed.

"If I can get ashore under cover of darkness I can reconnoitre and find out all I want to know."

"You—go ashore?" Sir Anthony asked. "What about us?"

"That is what I want to discuss," Lord Meridan said, as though it had been his idea to send for them. "I have a plan—now where is that map?"

"It is here," Sir Anthony said, setting it down on the table. "The Captain says he can vouch for its accuracy because it was only taken a few weeks ago from a French warship which was captured by one of ours."

"That is useful," Lord Meridan said. "Now this is what I intend to do . . ."

He spread out the map and taking a quill from a nearby writing-table he started to trace the course of the yacht across the Channel and under the lee of the French coast.

"We will creep up inshore. I imagine the château is about here"—Lord Meridan made a cross—"on the outskirts of Boulogne. You see this cove? Unless it is occupied by French vessels we might anchor the yacht there, and then I will get some sort of vehicle to convey me along the road to the château."

"If Yvonne is a prisoner—she might be locked up," Charles suggested. "How do you propose releasing her in that case?"

Lord Meridan drew from his pocket the note which the fisherman had brought him.

"This is what she says and she writes good English," he said, opening the mauve writing paper.

"*. . . I am a Prisoner of the Emperor, kept here in this Château, unable to get Away, to visit Paris or revoir més amis.*

"*The Château is West of the Town, near the sea. It is Easy to Find and I have Dreamed that you—so Strong, so Resolute and so Galant—will come and rescue me.*

"*I long to Escape to England, to be Away from all the Miseries of War and all the Privations my poor Country has had to Suffer from the Tyrant.*

"*Viens à moi, Sebastian—tout de suite, tout de suite! for you are the only Person who can Save me now, and I cry for You because, mon Brave, I am Desperate.*"

"Poor woman!" Lord Courtney ejaculated sentimentally. "She must be suffering to write in such a way."

"Remember she is an actress," Charles said cynically. "From what I recall of Yvonne she would manage to dramatize a walk with her pug down the *place*."

Lucinda was watching Lord Meridan's face.

"I expect she has offended Bonaparte in one of her plays," he said, as if he had been reflecting on the matter. "I have been told that, like all commoners, he is extremely touchy about anything which concerns himself and his importance—Yvonne always had a nice turn of comedy."

"From what I know of her," Charles said, "the only thing that is making her despair is the fact that she cannot get to Paris and spend money. If any woman knew how to empty a man's pocket in record time it is Yvonne de Beausole!"

Lucinda found herself wondering how much Sebastian had spent on her; but now the argument for and against Lord Meridan's idea of going ashore alone made her conscious of the danger he wished to undertake.

"What I shall do," he was saying, "is get a horse of

some sort—there is certain to be a farm nearby—and ride up to the outskirts of the château and scale the wall. As I understand this letter, Yvonne is quite free to move about so long as she does not leave the premises. I will find her and, if I cannot bring her with me right away, make plans for her escape! Come back and tell you exactly what the situation is."

Amongst the murmur which followed these words it was Lucinda who asked the only relevant question.

"And if you do not . . . come back," she asked, her heart heavy within her, "what do we do then?"

"Yes—that is a good question," Lord Courtney agreed. "What do we do, Sebastian?"

"If I am not back by daylight," Lord Meridan answered, "you must heave up the anchor and set sail for England."

Charles Holstead threw back his head and laughed.

"You are doing the 'Cheltenham Tragedies' a bit strong, Sebastian!" he challenged. "You know full well we would do nothing of the sort! No, I have a better idea. One of us will go with you, and when you climb the wall—if that is what you are determined to do—whoever is your escort will remain behind. He will keep his eyes skinned and if you run into any trouble he will hurry back to the yacht and relate to us what has happened. In that way we shall all know what has transpired."

"That is more sensible!" Sir Anthony exclaimed. "Besides, why should you have all the fun, Sebastian? We have not come all this way to rock about on the waves. I never could stomach the sea at any time."

"Very well," Lord Meridan said. "I concede that it might be sensible for someone to come with me. But the rest of you are to stay on board, remember, and take care of Lucinda. Whatever happens she is not to be involved in any danger—is that clear?"

"But of course," Charles said. "She should be safe enough here. The only thing which might mess up your plans is if a French coastguard vessel—or, for that matter, a man-o'-war—is passing the cove and thinks to enquire what the devil we are doing there!"

"I thought of that," Lord Meridan said. "We will fly the French flag."

"Fly the French flag . . . !"

For a moment the three other gentlemen around the table were shocked.

"Deuce take it! Unpatriotic!" Sir Anthony exclaimed.

"No—Sebastian is right," Charles interposed, before Sir Anthony could say more. "You know whom we have to deal with! When one is at war it is fair and square to deceive the enemy."

"You are convinced it is not a trap?" Lucinda asked.

"You asked me that before," Lord Meridan said, frowning. "I have known Yvonne de Beausole for many years. She is a clever actress and much feted in Paris—and I do not think I am being conceited when I say that she had a tenderness for me. I do not credit that she could write me a letter which would involve me in any obvious danger." He paused and then asked: "What do you think, Charles?"

"Oh, I agree," Charles answered. "Yvonne would not be two-faced enough to lay a snare for you, Sebastian. After all, what would be the point? You are not a General, an Admiral, or even in the Cabinet—political prisoners of any import are usually in one of those categories."

"No, no—it is genuine enough!" Lord Meridan agreed testily. "I would trust Yvonne with my life."

"That is exactly what you are doing," Lucinda said, and for a moment there was a strange silence.

Lord Meridan pushed the map away from him.

"It is all settled," he said; "but supposing anything goes awry and you do have to come to my rescue, then you had best put Lucinda in irons and lock her up in her cabin! Otherwise she will be up to mischief for a certainty!"

He spoke jestingly, but Lucinda felt there was a hint of seriousness in his voice.

"I promise I will not do anything to make things more difficult," she said. "I only wish I felt happy about the efficacy of your plan. Supposing someone asks you questions? How will you answer them?"

"My French is passable enough for that," Lord Meridan replied. "My difficulty is in understanding what the Froggies say."

"Exactly," Lucinda answered; "so you see the person who accompanies you should be me. I could talk to the peasants or perhaps the gardeners and find out far more than you will."

"Now, Lucinda," Lord Meridan said warningly, "I am making it quite clear—I am not having any of that nonsense!"

"You were asking when you first came aboard if anyone spoke French," Lucinda said. "You must have thought it might be necessary."

"It might be necessary later," Lord Meridan said loftily, "If I cannot reach Yvonne—but we must make plans of that sort as we go along. To begin with, only one thing is necessary—to discover if she is free to escape. They will certainly not be guarding her from the sea; they are much more likely to picket the roads to Paris."

"Why do you think she came to Boulogne in the first place?" Lucinda asked. "If she loved Paris so much, why did she ever leave?"

Lord Meridan shrugged his shoulders.

"Perhaps she came for a holiday," he said. "These play-actors get very tired and overwrought."

"From what you have told me of her, it sounds strange," Lucinda said.

"Stop imagining things are worse than they are!" Lord Meridan commanded. "Now, who is going to accompany me? I suggest we cut the cards—the highest being the winner, or the loser, however you like to put it."

There were cards in the drawer of the table. They spread them out and everyone drew solemnly.

"May I draw, too?" Lucinda asked, only to be given an emphatic "No!"

Lord Courtney took the first card. It was the ten of hearts. Sir Anthony drew the knave of diamonds. Finally, Charles turned one over and they all saw it was the king of spades.

"Good!" Lord Meridan said with satisfaction. "Charles and I are used to voyaging together—it will be nothing new."

"Both of them . . ." Lucinda thought with a little catch of her breath.

And she knew that although she had believed that Lord Meridan held the whole of her heart, one small but very vital part of it belonged to Charles.

12

Lucinda sat in her cabin and pressed her fingers over her eyes. Even if she had not done so it was impossible to see much, for the yacht was shrouded in mist and the lanterns in the cabins were heavily shaded.

It seemed to Lucinda that a whole lifetime had passed since Sebastian and Charles had rowed away from the yacht in a small boat and waved their hands gaily as if in salute.

She had felt then as if her heart went with Sebastian, and as the little boat disappeared into the mist it was with an effort that she did not scream out to them to return. She knew that nothing she said, not any argument that she put forward, would be of any avail, and her helplessness brought the tears to her eyes.

Plans had been changed not once but a thousand times. Always they came up against the insurmountable snag of not being able to speak the language fluently, and however much Lucinda begged to be of use, they would not take her with them.

Finally it was agreed that a row-boat would carry Sebastian and Charles along the coast as near as was possible to the château outside Boulogne. There they would disembark and walk the rest of the way, hoping that they would not be noticed or have to converse with anyone.

Sebastian's original idea of hiring two horses was impossible owing to the fact that not only would any farmer or horse-dealer suspect his accent but he was very unlikely to understand what was said to him in return. So it was decided they must walk, and only Charles was gloomy about it.

"If I had known I was going to have to tramp about like a blasted peasant," he grumbled, "I would not have worn my best hessians. Damn it all, Sebastian, you ask too much of your friends!"

"Pay no attention to him," Sir Anthony said. "I will come with you."

"You obey your orders and stay on the yacht with Lucinda," Lord Meridan said sourly. "If anything untoward occurs, then you and James and the strongest of the crew will have to come to our rescue."

Lucinda had felt, even as he said it, that it was all too likely a contingency. She raised her head and listened to the soft lap of the water against the sides of the yacht and thought, as she had thought a thousand times before, that Sebastian and Charles should have been back by now.

She was not looking forward to their being accompanied by the French actress. She knew, although she tried to hide it even from herself, that she was desperately jealous of this woman who could summon Lord Meridan across the Channel and into enemy territory by a few lines scribbled on a scented sheet of writing paper.

Was she as beautiful as Lady Devereux? she wondered, or as passionate and exciting as Juanita da Riva?

Whatever she was like, Sebastian had responded to her cry for help and Lucinda tried not to visualize all the terrors that might result from his impulsive chivalry.

Suddenly she started to her feet. There was the sound of an oar—she was sure of it!

Sir Anthony and Lord Courtney must have heard it, too. She heard the table on which they had been playing cards thrust aside and the tread of their feet hurrying up the companionway and on to the deck.

She followed them, snatching up a velvet wrap trimmed with sable from the bed where she had thrown it after her last fruitless visit to the upper deck. This time she was not mistaken.

As they stood straining their eyes in the direction from which the sound had come, the boat suddenly materialized almost like a wraith and a second later it was alongside the rope ladder.

It was then that Lucinda saw with a sudden stab of her heart that while there were three seamen in charge of the boat, Charles was the only passenger.

She knew before she saw his face that he was the carrier of bad tidings and he clambered up the rope ladder and on to the deck.

He saw Lucinda standing with Sir Anthony and Lord Courtney and his cold hand went out and clasped hers as if to comfort her, before he said:

"It was a blasted snare—and Sebastian walked right into it! Come into the cabin!"

Lucinda's other hand fluttered to her breast as if to quell the tumult that his words had evoked. She knew that whatever Charles had to tell her she must not show her fear. If she lacked courage, or became in any way hysterical, she was sure they would obey Lord Meridan and carry her off to England and safety.

Breathlessly she followed Charles into the cabin where the shaded lanterns cast yellow pools of light on the table.

"Get me a drink," Charles said briefly. He sat down at the table and put his head in his hands.

"What . . . has happened?" Lucinda asked, a catch in her breath. "I . . . do not think . . . I can bear it, Charles, unless you tell me immediately."

Her words, the intensity of her voice, brought his eyes up to her face. He saw what she feared and said quickly:

"No—no—he is not dead. But he is a prisoner—a prisoner of Bonaparte."

"What?" Lord Courtney exclaimed. "Is Boney involved in this?"

Sir Anthony set a glass of brandy down in front of Charles, saying as he did so:

"Let's hear it from the beginning."

Charles took a gulp at the brandy and then in almost colourless tones he said:

"We reached the place where Sebastian had decided to disembark, without difficulty. There appeared to be no one on the shore—and the sea was deserted. It was still misty—but we could see quite clearly the lights of Boulogne a little farther along the coast. As we stepped off the beach Sebastian spied the château. It was perhaps a quarter of a mile ahead of us, every window ablaze with light and we could see it quite clearly."

Charles paused a moment and took another drink.

"Go on," Lucinda whispered almost beneath her breath.

"We thought at first there might be some sort of party there—but then there was no sign of any carriages. The drive when we reached it was empty. We moved a trifle up a side road. There was a low brick wall apparently surrounding the château.

"'What are we going to do?' I asked Sebastian.

"'I might as well drop in while the lady is still awake,' he replied. 'I would hate to surprise her in her curling rags.'"

Charles took another gulp of the brandy.

"I suppose we should have realized then it was suspicious that the place seemed so deserted," he said. "But Sebastian was delighted with himself at having reached his destination without any difficulty....

"'You know what we have arranged, Charles,' he said to me. 'If everything is up to scratch I will give you a signal and you can come and help Yvonne down to the boat. She is certain to have a pesky amount of luggage with her—what woman will travel without a collection of fals-de-lals!'

"He paused and added: 'If I do not come back, reconnoitre a bit. It will mean there is something wrong. If I am taken prisoner—which appears on the face of it very unlikely—post back to the yacht and take Lucinda home to England,'"

"That I will not have," Lucinda interrupted. "I told him so before he left."

"I know," Charles said gently, "but somehow I do not collect that Sebastian was listening."

"Well, what happened?" Lord Courtney asked. "The deuce take it, Charles, you spin a tale out interminably!"

"I want you to know the details," Charles answered. "Sebastian climbed over the wall, crossed a rough bit of pastureland and then came to a lawn. As he reached it a woman came out from the château, stood on the terrace looking out to sea.

"I pulled out a small telescope which I had taken with me and put it to my eye—and, sure enough, even in the dusk, I could see it was Yvonne. She was wearing an evening gown and looked extraordinarily attractive."

"You couldn't possibly see that—it was too dark!" Sir Anthony remarked impatiently.

"It was just an impression, of course," Charles said apologetically. "Anyway, she stood there alone and Sebastian walked up to her. She turned and held out both her hands to him and he kissed them. I could see them very clearly in the light from the windows. I thought to myself, 'This is where I come in,' and I put my legs over the wall."

Charles paused for another sip at his glass, and Lucinda, putting out her hand, laid it on his arm and said urgently:

"I cannot bear it, Charles—you must relate what happened!"

"I saw Yvonne point to the right down the coast, as if she was showing Sebastian something in Boulogne. He put his hand up to shade his eyes, as if he could see better that way. Then suddenly—so quickly that I could hardly comprehend what was happening—two men appeared out of nowhere. They crept up behind Sebastian. One of them had a club in his hand and he brought it down with a hell of a crack on Sebastian's head. He tried to struggle—tried to give them a leveller—but he collapsed—I saw him with my own eyes! Then they half carried him, half dragged him, into the house."

Lucinda put her fingers in horror over her mouth.

"By Jove! They must have been waiting for him!" Sir Anthony ejaculated.

"It was obvious," Charles said. "As I hesitated—not knowing whether to go to his rescue—trying to decide whether it would be better to go for them or try and creep up later—Yvonne went to the edge of the terrace where she had been standing before and waved her handkerchief...."

Charles paused for a moment.

"... She waved it up and down for several seconds, and I waited, feeling it was a signal of some sort, and not wanting to get myself clubbed, as poor Sebastian had done."

"What happened?" Lord Courtney enquired.

"About a minute or so later," Charles replied, "I heard

the sound of marching feet. Men came from the other side of the garden marching along a path which ran below the terrace. There were five of them—four men and a sergeant."

"Soldiers!" Lucinda hardly breathed the word.

"The whole damned thing was a trap!" Sir Anthony said bitterly.

"And Sebastian was caught like a rat!" Charles said. "The sergeant put two sentries on the gate and two on the terrace outside the door through which they had taken Sebastian. Then the sergeant and Yvonne went inside the house."

"Hell! But wasn't there anything you could do?" Lord Courtney asked.

"What?" Charles questioned. "One pistol against five fully armed men and the two others who had clubbed Sebastian?"

He paused and made an expressive gesture with his hands.

"I did what Sebastian ordered me to do—I came back here."

"Not to take me back to England!" Lucinda flashed.

"That is what we should do," Charles said doubtfully.

"And leave Sebastian to those murderers?" Lucinda enquired. "I am not chicken-hearted, if you are!"

"Now, Lady Meridan, do not be unkind," Sir Anthony pleaded. "There was nothing Charles could do at the time. But we have got to rescue Sebastian—of course we have."

"I have not told you the end of the story," Charles said unhappily. "While I was still waiting—another man, obviously a servant, came round to the entrance on a horse. He sat there waiting a few minutes and then Yvonne appeared again. She had a note in her hand and she held it out to him. She appeared to be giving him instructions and he listened intently.

"Of course I could not hear what they were saying—but he whipped up his horse, hurried down the drive and, turning right, took the coast road towards the town. He was travelling at a gallop and I had the feeling—although I might be wrong—that he was going for further reinforcements."

"All to keep prisoner one unconscious man?" Lord Courtney asked scornfully.

"Perhaps they suspect that he is not alone," Charles suggested.

"Hades! Was there ever such a coil?" Lord Courtney ejaculated. "What are we to do?"

"I have another piece of bad news for you," Sir Anthony said. "When you were away, Charles, I had a talk with the Captain. He tells me that we have few arms on board—a cutlass or two, a musket which I do not believe has been fired for half a century, and our own pistols."

"Curse Sebastian! Didn't he think that we might need decent weapons?" Charles said in exasperated tones.

"We do not need a yacht—we need a warship," Lord Courtney retorted. "What do you say that we sail back to England and ask the help of the Navy?"

"To rescue one Englishman?" Charles challenged. "Even if he is Sebastian. I cannot see my Lords at the Admiralty agreeing to that! Besides, Boulogne is a regular hornets' nest. They would merely think he was deranged in his head to venture into it!"

Lucinda, who had been standing, drew a chair up to the table.

"I have an idea," she said. "Now please listen to me. . . ."

At about nine-thirty the following morning a carriage drawn by a quite sprightly piece of horseflesh rolled along the coast road to Boulogne.

Seated in the driver's seat the cabman was hunched in a moth-eaten coat, its cape as frayed and weather-beaten as the ancient hat he wore pulled low over his forehead.

Only the fact that he pulled the reins with an elegance and skill which was somehow out of keeping with his appearance might have attracted a second glance in his direction.

The occupant of the carriage was a very different story. Seated on the back seat, accompanied by a huge bonnet box and a smart leather portmanteau, was a figure wearing a green travelling coat surmounted by a bonnet trimmed with a furore of brightly coloured feathers.

Only a woman would have realized that the young female so gorgeously dressed proclaimed her lack of breeding and sensibility by the fact that her cheeks were highly rouged and her lips plenteously reddened with salve.

Her hair beneath her bonnet was frizzed and curled into innumerable little ringlets, and although the effect was bizarre, it was none the less deliberately and archly pleasing.

The sentry at the gate of the château which stood back from the sea-shore was suitably impressed.

"I am Madame Jeanette from Paris," the young female declared in fluent French, "and I have brought Mademoiselle de Beausole all the latest fashions for which she has been pining in this unpleasant windswept edge of the world."

The sentry, a corporal who, like many of Napoleon's new intake of recruits, was pitiably young, giggled.

"*Tiens,* it's not as bad as all that," he answered. "I could show you a bit of life in the town if you have a mind to it."

"I might indeed accept your invitation," Madame Jeanette said, with a glance which made his heart beat faster. "But first there is business to be done. *Allons!* There's a lot of money in this baggage!" She patted the portmanteau as she spoke.

"I bet whatever Mademoiselle buys she won't look more chic as you, *Chérie,*" the sentry said with a wink. "Pass on!"

Madame Jeanette thanked him with a smile and the carriage rolled up the hill to the door.

Here she was challenged again by two other sentries.

"No one can enter without a permit," one said sourly, in a patois which proclaimed that he came from Provence.

"Well you had better hurry and get one from Mademoiselle," the modish visitor told him sharply. "I had her explicit instructions to call here before she left for Paris. I have other ladies waiting for me in the town, and I can assure you that I would not be in your shoes if they get a look at my goods before Mademoiselle sees them!"

The sentry appeared to understand the force of the argument. He went inside, consulted a servant and a few minutes later the message came that Mademoiselle de Beausole's visitor was to go upstairs.

"Bring that portmanteau with you," the servant was told sharply, and slipping the hat-box over her arm Lucinda, with her heart beating almost suffocatingly, went tripping up the stairs into a bedroom on the first floor.

Her first glance took in a large bed draped with muslin, and then sitting at a dressing table she saw the mistress of it, wearing a transparent négligé.

Yvonne de Beausole was attractive, with a Frenchwoman's expressive face and a mouth which seemed made for comedy.

She had enormous violet eyes fringed with dark lashes and a tip-tilted nose which gave her the fascinating expression of a rather mischievous gamine.

"*Mon Dieu!* What brings a Parisian *couturière* to this outlandish spot?" she asked.

"I heard that you had need of me, Mademoiselle," Madame Jeanette answered, curtsying in the doorway and then advancing to allow the portmanteau which followed her to be carried in by the sweating servant.

He set it down with a bang on the carpet.

"Next time I will get Jacques to help me," he said in surly tones. "It is too heavy for one pair of hands."

Mademoiselle de Beausole ignored him.

"*Vraiment?* You have come from Paris?" she asked excitedly.

Lucinda nodded.

"I have brought you, Mademoiselle, the very latest gowns and the *dernier cri* in bonnets," she said. "Even the Empress herself has not seen them."

"*Mère de Dieu!* You are an answer to my prayers!" Yvonne de Beausole exclaimed. "I have been hibernating here thinking that I should go to the asylum with nothing to occupy my mind—and now, like a fairy godmother, you appear to help me! *Enfin*, I need a dozen new dresses at least!"

"I have brought only three with me, Mademoiselle," Lucinda told her, "and one or two bonnets. But I have many more at the place where I am staying and I can easily fetch them for you later."

"Let me see them—let me see them at once!" Yvonne de Beausole commanded.

Lucinda opened the box and drew out a bonnet that

212

Madame Bertin had designed for her only the previous week.

She had not yet worn it, and she felt quite a little pang of disappointment when she saw how becoming it was and how artfully it framed Yvonne de Beausole's piquant little face.

"*C'est ravissant!*" the actress cried. "Never, never have I seen anything so enchanting! Just wait until the Emperor sees it."

"The . . . Emperor?" Lucinda faltered.

She had no time to say more. The door was flung open and a short, squat little man walked into the room in a quick, imperious manner. There was no mistaking—indeed there was no ignoring—the authority and the suspicion in those dark eyes which seemed to take in everything at a glance.

The actress in her flowing négligé with the feather bonnet perched upon her dark hair swung round, and Lucinda, holding the hat box, stood very still, her mouth open at the surprise of seeing him.

"Sire, I was not expecting you so early."

Yvonne de Beausole rose from the dressing table and swept a deep curtsy, which was followed a little belatedly by one from Lucinda.

"I got your message last night, but I could not come until this morning," Napoleon said. "You have him? He actually arrived?"

"But, Sire—did I not tell you that he would find such a challenge irresistible?" she replied. "These English—when it comes to gallantry—they are foolhardy to the point of idiocy."

"So it seems," the Emperor said drily. "I did not believe, however, that he would put his head into a noose."

"I told you that I had but to raise my little finger," Yvonne de Beausole said, preening herself a little.

"Where is he now?" Napoleon asked sharply.

"That was the difficulty, Sire," the actress dimpled at him. "I felt Your Majesty would not fancy his sampling those very delicious wines that you had delivered here only last week. And if he was not to be put in the cellar—then where?"

Napoleon smiled indulgently.

213

"I will not play the guessing game," he said. "Where have you put him?"

"In the store cupboard below the stairs," Yvonne de Beausole said with a little chuckle. "Where there is nothing more intoxicating than home-made jam and a few pickled onions!"

Napoleon Bonaparte laughed.

"You are very inhospitable, *ma chère* Yvonne. We must see if we can repair that omission. I would not like such a distinguished visitor from across the Channel to be uncomfortable."

"Will you see him now?" Yvonne de Beausole asked, her eyes sparkling. "The key is on my dressing table. We can send for him."

Lucinda looked down, lest the actress should see the hatred in her eyes.

She knew that this woman was enjoying the idea of torturing a man who had once been her lover, and there was no doubt who it was who at the present enjoyed her favours.

In her excitement Yvonne de Beausole had leaned forward eagerly to point where the key lay, and her filmy négligé of muslin and lace parted to reveal the generous curves of her naked body.

Napoleon's hard eyes softened.

"There is no hurry," he said. "You look very attractive, my dear—in that bonnet."

There was a thickening in his tones which did not escape his mistress.

She glanced at Lucinda, who quickly packed up the hat box and closed it.

"Shall I return later, Mademoiselle?" she asked.

"Yes, do that," the actress agreed. "Or, if you prefer, you can wait downstairs."

"I might go and fetch the other gowns which I told you were at my lodgings," Lucinda suggested.

The actress's eyes lit up greedily.

"*Oui, oui,* fetch them," she agreed.

Napoleon, bored with the conversation, walked across to the bed. Already he was unbuttoning his tunic and there was no doubt that he was impatient.

"Shall I get a servant to remove the portmanteau?" Lucinda asked.

"No—no—leave it," the actress replied.

"Then I will only take the bonnet box away," Lucinda said. "It looks untidy."

She stooped to fasten the strap, and as she did so she inserted herself between the dressing table and Yvonne de Beausole.

It was a matter of a second to reach out and take the key which lay there beside the toilet accessories and then to hold it under the bonnet box and carry it from the room.

She heard Yvonne de Beausole give a little cry of love and delight as she left the room and Napoleon's voice answering her, deep and amorous.

Lucinda flew down the stairs.

The servant who had brought the portmanteau up to the bedroom was standing in the hall. She thrust the bonnet box into his hand.

"Call my carriage," she said in authoritative tones. "And immediately you have done so Mademoiselle requires an omelette for the Emperor. Also the special wine His Majesty likes most is to be brought up from the cellar."

"*Diable!* It is beyond endurance," the man grumbled. "I'm on my feet day and night. It would be easier to join the Army—at least I wouldn't have a woman ordering me about!"

"You had best be quick or you will get into trouble," Lucinda advised him. "Order my carriage—I cannot wait here all day."

Still grumbling, the man walked through the hall to obey her, and in a second she had whisked behind the staircase.

There was a door there and quickly she put the key in the lock and turned it.

"Sebastian!"

She hardly whispered his name and yet almost before she had finished speaking he was at the door.

She could see the darkness of the cupboard behind him and that he was blinking his eyes in an effort to accustom himself to the light.

"Lucinda! What . . ."

Her fingers went up to his lips.

"Stay still—do not move!" she said.

She went back into the hall, leaving him concealed.

The man was coming back towards her and from the open doorway behind him she could see the carriage pulling round in front of the sentries.

She went to a mirror and fumbling in her reticule brought out a little pot of rouge.

"Don't wait," she said over her shoulder to the servant. "I have to attend to my complexion! These sea-winds—they are the invention of Satan!"

"I wasn't thinking of waiting," he replied sourly. "An omelette, indeed—and wine—when there's so much else to do!"

He went clumping down the stairs to the kitchen.

Lucinda turned round.

On the sofa in the hall she had seen two things had been thrown down—a cloak and a hat. She was well aware that they were the Emperor's, but they were exactly the same as those worn by his officers—plain, unadorned. It fed Napoleon's vanity that he looked the same as those who served him but was in fact their absolute master.

Lucinda snatched them up. Under cover of the staircase she handed them to Sebastian.

"Move quickly," she whispered. "The carriage is at the door—and it is our only chance to get away before they realize what is happening."

He pulled the hat low on his forehead, and putting on the cape flung one side of it over his shoulder to hide his clothes.

Then tripping ahead of him, almost running, and prattling away gaily, Lucinda hurried towards the carriage.

"Voyons! We must bestir ourselves," she cried in a high-pitched voice which not only the sentries but Napoleon's escort, which was waiting outside the front door, could not help but hear. "If the Emperor wants something he wants it immediately, and we have such a short time before we must return. How long do you think it will take us to get the other gowns? And where did the Emperor say that place was? Tiens, what a scatterbrain I am! I find it so difficult to remember addresses."

She was in the carriage and Sebastian swept in after her.

"Vite! Vite!" she cried, and the urgency of her tone made Lord Courtney on the box bring his whip down hard on the horse.

The horse leapt forward and now they were rolling down the drive.

The sentries looked up apathetically. They knew the carriage was there and saw no reason to check it a second time.

Lucinda bent forward and blew a kiss to them.

"I am coming back in an hour or so!" she cried.

They grinned and she waved her hand.

Now the horse was gathering speed.

"My God! Lucinda—how did you do it?" Sebastian asked. "And why the hell are you here when I told you not to come ashore?"

"It is a good thing she did," Lord Courtney said from the box. He glanced back over his shoulder.

"Are we out of sight?" Lucinda asked.

"Yes," Lord Courtney replied.

"Pull up here—they will be at the corner of the wood," Lucinda said.

"Who will be?" Lord Meridan asked, and knew the answer as Charles and Sir Anthony came running out from behind the thicket and clambered into the carriage.

"Thank the Lord you are here, Sebastian!" Charles said, and added anxiously: "Are we likely to be followed?"

"I do not know," Lucinda answered, and then gave a little cry. "Fool that I am! I should have locked the door of the store room! Now they will see it open and realize that Sebastian has gone!"

"Where is the boat?" Lord Meridan asked.

"Gone back to the yacht," Charles replied. "We thought it was dangerous for it to hang about and as we have a carriage it should not take us more than twenty minutes to reach the cove where the yacht is anchored. Make that lazy nag go faster, James!"

"I will drive," Lord Meridan said briefly. "Do not stop."

He clambered across the carriage and climbed on to the box seat. There he changed places with Lord Courtney.

As if the horse recognized the touch of a master hand it

contrived to move a great deal quicker than it had done previously.

"Lucinda, you are a wonder!" Charles cried, taking her hand in his. "I do not think I have ever been so frightened in my life as I have been this last half-hour wondering what had happened to you, praying you would pull it off."

"You realize who was there . . . ," Lucinda answered,

". . . Napoleon?"

"Napoleon!"

Both Charles and Sir Anthony ejaculated the name incredulously.

"Yes, Boney," Lord Meridan echoed from the box seat.

"This is his cape and his hat I am wearing."

"The devil take it, but what a souvenir!" Sir Anthony exclaimed.

They were hurrying along the coast road. There were carts drawn by white bullocks and women in their red camlet jackets, high aprons and wooden sabots, who turned in astonishment to look at the carriage travelling in a cloud of dust and filled with rather spectacular-looking young people.

"People are staring at us . . . if the soldiers wish to find us there will be plenty to direct them," Lucinda said in a low voice.

"We shall not be long now," Lord Meridan answered.

"If I remember rightly there is this long straight stretch, then the road curves down to the cove."

"That's right," Lord Courtney replied, and then glancing over his shoulder he said in a very different tone: "Does that look like horsemen to you, Charles?"

Charles, who was sitting beside Lucinda, got up on the back seat.

"It is horsemen," he said, "and they are coming pretty fast."

The crack of Lord Meridan's whip made it unnecessary for them to tell the driver what they feared.

"Will they catch us?" Lucinda almost whispered.

"I think we are far enough ahead," Charles answered, "but be ready to run."

Sir Anthony was standing up in the carriage, his eyes fixed on the road behind them.

"There are eight—no, twelve—of them," he said. "And

they are soldiers—I can see the sun gleaming on their buttons."

Lucinda also stood up to look back, but the carriage was rocking and shaking from side to side with the speed at which it was travelling and she fell back on to her seat with a bang.

"Do not worry," Charles said soothingly. "We will make it—I am sure we shall."

At the same time he drew his pistol from his pocket and made sure that it was primed and ready to fire.

Lucinda saw that Sir Anthony and Lord Courtney were doing the same.

"They took mine," Lord Meridan shouted above the roar of the horse's hoofs.

He urged the animal faster and yet faster and now it seemed as though the carriage might easily turn over.

Then the road turned and they saw beneath them a little way out to sea the yacht with her sails full and tugging at her anchor. On the shore the boat was waiting, the seamen's faces raised towards them.

Lord Meridan drew the horse to a standstill, then while the wheels were still moving sprang to the ground.

The three men followed him, but when Charles went to help Lucinda Lord Meridan was there before him.

They began to run, but Lucinda was encumbered by her skirts. Lord Meridan bent and picked her up in his arms and they all ran, their boots squelching in the wet sand until they reached the row-boat.

Lord Meridan deposited Lucinda in the bottom of it, dropping her on the hard boards.

"Shove off!" he cried, and the others scrambled in with the waves lapping at their boots.

There was a roar of hoofs on the road behind them and now the soldiers were dismounting and hurrying down the shingle.

"They are going to fire," Lord Meridan said sharply. "Pull at your oars! Keep your heads down!"

As he spoke he thrust Lucinda down so roughly that she gave a little cry.

Two bullets went whistling in the air a few inches above their heads.

219

"Pull, damn you!" Lord Meridan cried. "Pull for your lives, boys! We'll be out of range in a minute."

The seamen bent to their oars. One splintered an oar and another buried itself in the boat.

"They've got me, by George!"

He put his hand up to his arm, and Lucinda, raising herself from the bottom of the boat, saw the expression of his face.

"He's hit! Oh, Charles—you are hit!" she cried.

"Row, blast your eyes, row!" Lord Meridan command-ed, and the boat seemed almost to heave itself out of the waves.

"They are falling short!" Lord Courtney exclaimed, raising his head a little. "Are you all right, Charles?"

"It is only my arm," Charles answered with white lips.

They could hear the shots behind them, then they were out of range.

Lucinda sat up in the bottom of the boat and gently drew Charles down beside her.

She saw his coat was torn where the bullet had passed through it, and now a red patch of blood was seeping over the grey whipcord.

She knew by the pallor of his face and the tightness of his lips that he was in pain and she saw with relief that the yacht was only a few lengths away from her.

Somehow they got him on deck and down the compan-ionway. But before they could get him into the cabin the anchor was up and the ship was under way.

"Cut his coat off him," Lord Meridan ordered Sir Anthony and Lord Courtney. "The Captain will extract the bullet. But we must get away from this fox-hole first. Boney will be sending a man-of-war after us—you can be certain of that."

"Oh no!" Lucinda protested. "We cannot be hunted any more!"

"They won't catch us," Lord Meridan answered reas-suringly. "Do not be afraid. This yacht is built for speed—which is more than Boney's ships ever were."

Lucinda ran to her cabin to tear up some of her linen to make bandages.

When she came back Charles was being plied with brandy and the Captain had extracted the bullet.

"Strap me if I ever laugh at a soldier again!" Charles said weakly with an effort at humour. "I had no idea that a cursed bullet could hurt so much."

"Drink and forget it," Lord Meridan said sharply, and then in a gentler tone added: "You did not deserve that, Charles—it was meant for me, and I was the one who should have stopped it."

"Glad to be of service," Charles said, and his lips twisted a little as if even to speak was an effort. .

Lucinda put a pad on the wound and bound it neatly.

"Try and go to sleep," she said.

"I will do nothing of the sort," Charles protested. "I want to hear what happened."

"We will tell you the details later," Lord Meridan said. "Now I only want to express my gratitude. If it were not for all of you I would have spent the rest of the war in some stinking prison."

"Why, in heaven's name, was Boney so eager for your company?" Lord Courtney asked.

"Yvonne made that very obvious," Lord Meridan answered. "Although I did not tumble to it at first. The moment I arrived she asked me what was being said in England about the invasion. She pointed out the ships and barques which were anchored all along the coast right into Boulogne and, I imagine, beyond Calais."

"The invasion fleet!" Sir Anthony exclaimed.

"Exactly," Lord Meridan answered. "When I thought it out during the night shut in that airless cupboard I realized that the reason she had sent for me was because Napoleon was curious—he wanted to know if we, as a country, were frightened. He thought that I should be able to tell him not only what England was saying and thinking, but if the Court was perturbed. Yvonne would have told him that I was in the Prince's confidence—they have quite a respect for our Prinny on the Continent."

"The impertinence of it—that is what astounds me!" Lord Courtney ejaculated.

"It was a trap," Lord Meridan said bitterly, "and I was fool enough to walk into it like any village yokel with his brain to let. I could kick myself now. And if it were not for all of you . . ."

"No—Lucinda,"

"—only Lucinda. We none of us had an idea between us.'"

His voice trailed away and his eyes closed wearily.

"He will sleep," Lucinda said in a whisper.

She pulled a blanket over him and they all moved quietly from the room.

"Come up on deck," Sir Anthony said tactfully to Lord Courtney. "We can help keep watch for any man-of-war which may have the impertinence to be curious!"

They clattered up the companionway and Lucinda turned towards the cabin.

She felt suddenly weary and deflated. The excitement had ebbed away, leaving her curiously empty. She found she could think only of Yvonne de Beausole's fascinating face.

She walked across the cabin to a port-hole and stood looking out.

The yacht was leaving a heavy wake but was skimming over the water like a bird. The sea was calm, but there was sufficient wind to fill the sails and she was light to handle.

"Do you want me to express them?" a voice asked behind her.

She turned to find Lord Meridian was closer than she had anticipated. He was looking down at her and something in his eyes made her drop her own and turn a little away from him.

"Express what?" she asked a little uncertainly.

"My thanks," he answered. "It is usual—when a lady saves one's life—to say thank you."

"We . . . were fortunate," Lucinda said gravely. "If the Emperor had not arrived at that precise moment . . . it might have been much more difficult."'

"Did you know the risk you were taking?"' Lord Meridan enquired.

She shrugged her shoulders, still not looking at him.

"You did not really expect us to sail away and leave you a prisoner?"

"I am not concerned with the others," he answered, "but with you. Why did you come ashore when I told you not to?"

"Because it was the only possible way to enter the château and find out what had occurred," she answered.

"How could anyone else, without knowing the language, have the least expectation of success?"

"The whole idea from start to finish was hare-brained," Lord Meridan said almost humbly. "But you still have not let me thank you . . ."

"I do not want your thanks," Lucinda interrupted.

" . . . And you still have not told me why you came to rescue me," he finished.

She turned to look at him almost in surprise.

"You could have gone back to England with Charles," Lord Meridan continued. "Wasn't that what you would have preferred? It is doubtful if I should have survived the war—prisoners have a convenient way of dying."

"Do you think I would wish that?" Lucinda asked.

"Wouldn't it have made things much simpler?" Lord Meridan enquired. "You love Charles, don't you?"

"You know full well that I do not," Lucinda said. "I like him . . . he is a kind friend and I am flattered that he thinks he loves me . . . but that is all—what I feel for Charles is not love."

"How do you know it isn't?" Lord Meridan enquired.

"Because it isn't," Lucinda insisted. "Love is different . . . very, very different."

"But how do you know?" Lord Meridan asked her. "I think you told me once that you have never been in love. If that is so, how are you so sure that what you feel for Charles is not love?"

Lucinda looked out of the port-hole.

"I . . . I just know," she answered.

She felt the colour rising in her cheeks. Then her heart gave a sudden leap, for Lord Meridan had put his fingers under her chin and she turned her face up to his.

"What are you feeling, Lucinda?" he asked. "Are you frightened of this emotion that you have never known before? Why are you trembling? And why is your heart beating so quickly?"

She could not answer him, but could only stand there, quivering beneath his hands and knowing that her breath was coming quicker between her parted lips.

"You have driven me mad, Lucinda," she heard Lord Meridan say, and thought she must be dreaming. "—I think I knew I loved you before we came aboard this ship. But when I saw you kissing Charles I wanted to kill him— Charles, who is my best friend and for whom I have the

223

deepest affection. And then when you waved good-bye to me from the poop and I saw your eyes—wide and frightened—I knew that nothing mattered save that I could come back to you, and that I should lose you in such a crazed and foolish manner."

Lucinda could not answer, she could only tremble. Suddenly she was free and Lord Meridan had moved away from her and across the cabin.

"Perhaps I am besotted," he said, "it was only in the loneliness of that dark cupboard last night that I started to imagine that you could love me in return. How could I expect such a miracle after the way I have treated you—marrying you as I did; leaving you alone in London; snarling at you because I thought you interfered with my freedom! My God! Who wants freedom to land oneself in this sort of tangle!"

His voice was suddenly bitter and without turning round he said:

"I am sorry, Lucinda. You would be well advised to have nothing to do with me. I have flaunted my mistresses in front of you as though they were jewels—and now I see how tawdry they are, and everything else I have done by way of amusement."

For a moment there was silence.

Then a small, rather tremulous voice from behind him said:—

"You . . . you are not being humble, are you, Sebastian?"

"Humble? Why not?"

"Because . . . Mr. Brummel says one should never be humble . . . and when you are strong and . . . masterful . . . and very . . . overbearing . . . I . . . I like you best."

Lord Meridan did not turn.

"Like . . . ?" he questioned.

There was a sudden excitement in his voice which made the word sound like a pistol-shot. He waited, every muscle tense, a fire glowing in his eyes.

Then softly, so very softly that he could hardly hear it, Lucinda whispered:

"That is how I . . . I love you . . . Sebastian . . ."